KICKING THE SKY

ALSO BY ANTHONY DE SA

Barnacle Love

Anthony De Sa

A Novel

Kicking the sky

ALGONQUIN BOOKS OF CHAPEL HILL   2014

Published by
Algonquin Books of Chapel Hill
Post Office Box 2225
Chapel Hill, North Carolina 27515-2225

a division of
Workman Publishing
225 Varick Street
New York, New York 10014

Excerpts from *The Little Prince* by Antoine de Saint-Exupéry.
Copyright 1943 by Houghton Mifflin Harcourt Publishing Company.
Copyright © renewed 1971 by Consuelo de Saint-Exupéry. English translation
copyright © 2000 by Richard Howard. Used by permission of Houghton
Mifflin Harcourt Publishing Company. All rights reserved.

This is a work of fiction. While, as in all fiction, the literary perceptions and
insights are based on experience, all names, characters, places, and incidents
either are products of the author's imagination or are used fictitiously.

LIBRARY OF CONGRESS CATALOGING-IN-PUBLICATION DATA
De Sa, Anthony.
Kicking the sky : a novel / by Anthony De Sa.—First edition.
pages cm
ISBN 978-1-56512-927-6
1. Boys—Fiction.   2. Portuguese—Canada—Fiction.
3. Toronto (Ont.)—Fiction.   4. Domestic fiction.   I. Title.
PR9199.4.D486K53 2014
813'.6—dc23   2013038534

10 9 8 7 6 5 4 3 2 1
First Edition

For my wife, Stephanie, and for our wonderful boys—
Julian, Oliver, and Simon

KICKING THE SKY

— *Prologue* —

I T WAS THE SUMMER that no one slept. During the last sticky week in July, the air abandoned us, failing to stir and stream through our streets and between our crooked alleys. The grass in our lanes stood tall and still, barely rooted to an urban soil of gravel and discarded candy wrappers. The narrow brick row houses that lined Palmerston Avenue and Markham Street—painted electric blue or yellow or lime green—became buffers to the city noise. A persistent hum was all we heard.

I can pinpoint the very moment it all started to change, when the calm broke: when news that twelve-year-old Emanuel Jaques had disappeared spread through our neighborhood in the whispered prayers of women returning from Mass. They gathered along their fences and on their verandas speaking in hushed tones that went silent whenever children drew near. We ignored their anxious looks and their occasional shouts to get home and lock the doors.

Manny, Ricky, and I had agreed to meet in the Patch, a square of unpaved lane covered in rocks and waist-high weeds that grew amidst the dumped garbage the city wouldn't take. We'd piled old tires and torn at cardboard boxes to construct a fort in the Patch's corner. With our fortress built, we huddled inside, Ricky scooching close to me, his shoulder touching mine. I was eleven, almost twelve, and everything I said or did was an attempt to show everyone around me that I wasn't a kid anymore. We could start our own search for Emanuel, be the ones to bring him home. Manny stabbed at the cardboard ceiling with a screwdriver, puncturing holes of blue sky. Ricky imagined how we'd look in the newspaper, HEROES splashed above our photo. His enthusiasm for my idea began to chip away at Manny, whose interest was heightened by the mention of a possible reward.

We weren't exactly sure where to begin, but we figured we'd have a better chance of finding a missing boy than a bunch of clueless adults who worked all day, and most nights. We'd ride our bikes into the heart of the city, comb the Yonge Street strip until we found him.

Worry about what had happened to Emanuel, the Shoeshine Boy, was closing in on us. Our parents had told us to be afraid, warned us of the dangers lurking on the city's main drag. But we wouldn't let their fears stop us. They didn't understand, but Manny, Ricky, and I did. As long as we stuck together we were untouchable.

Little Boy^s

One night he forgot to put her under glass, or else the sheep got out without making any noise, during the night . . . Then the bells are all changed into tears!

ANTOINE DE SAINT-EXUPÉRY

THE OLD SCHOOL BUS screeched to a stop. It always arrived at the same time, just after I'd gone to bed. It parked in front of Senhora Gloria's bungalow across the street. Senhora Gloria was the neighborhood gossip who saw and heard everything. She knew the details of all our lives, and what she didn't know, she made up. She'd gossip with anyone who had big ears and was willing to listen. Senhora Rosa, who owned the neighborhood variety store, had the biggest ears and an even bigger mouth. My mother would say those who talk of others always have something to hide themselves. If my mother felt frisky she'd add, the devil makes grit. I didn't really care how awful Senhora Gloria was. It was Agnes, her fifteen-year-old daughter, who made my stomach churn hot and turned the spit in my mouth to dust.

From my bedroom window I could look onto Palmerston Avenue and stare at Senhora Gloria's bungalow. Every morning I'd wait to catch a glimpse of Agnes brushing her hair on their front porch. She'd pull it like a rope over one shoulder as she bent over the railing. When she finished brushing, she would hold her hand up and wiggle her fingers, as if playing an imaginary piano, allowing strands of hair to sift into the flowerbed. She always looked clean and fresh, like the girls in those Kotex commercials, her brown hair shimmering in the sun, her cheeks peppered in pink. She had delicate features—almond eyes and a tiny nose—like the statue of Our Lady of Fátima. But unlike the Holy Mother, Agnes's lips were plump and glossy. Her sides pinched in, her waist carved out, so that her hips swung side to side as she walked. She was perfection.

My mother's name, which she hated, was Georgina, spelled in Portuguese with a *J*. Part of me knew she hated her name for the same reasons she didn't want to mix with other Portuguese women like her, hunched over and picking worms all night. My mother closed our front door behind her. The lock clicked into place, a sound I had first heard the night Emanuel Jaques went missing. I pressed my forehead against the window screen, into the bulge that had formed over the years. I could feel my hair sticking up, electrically charged. It had rained all day. It was a hot rain, the kind that falls when the sun is out. Clinging to the night air was the smell of wet concrete.

I watched my mother walk down our front steps. Her thick hair was tucked underneath a kerchief, and she was dressed in a housedress, with a light sweater buttoned over it. It was too hot to wear a sweater, but it wasn't proper for my mother to go out of the house with her arms bare. The laced hem of her slip touched my father's rubber boots. She carried a plastic bag, no doubt stuffed with cornbread, a wedge of Queijo São Jorge, and some fruit, probably bruised or overripe. My mother never threw anything out. The food would have been wrapped tightly with napkins. The moon's glow that filtered through the chestnut trees above fell onto her kerchief and face.

She turned around to close the gate behind her. Poncho, the neighbors' golden Lab, had a habit of shitting on our grass, or worse, lifting his leg and peeing on the statue of Jesus that stood on our tiny lawn, inside an old upright bathtub. The tub was half buried on its end in the same spot it landed after it had been dropped from my window when we renovated the upstairs bathroom three years before. The ball-and-claw feet—spray-painted gold—pointed back toward the house. Inside the cavern stood Jesus holding his plump sacred heart. My father had glued down plastic flowers, so that it looked like Jesus was floating on a cloud of petals. At night Jesus looked like a rock star lit up by a row of Christmas lights clipped to the rim of the tub.

My eyes moved past my mother's silhouette, across the street to the porch lights that drew the moths and mosquitoes close in a swarm. Men and women filed out of their homes, locking their doors behind them. They headed down their front paths and when they met at the accordion doors of the bus, they nodded politely before they lowered their kerchiefs or adjusted their hats over their foreheads, and stepped onto the bus.

My sister came into my room and stood beside me. She leaned against the window, her hair in a towel, wound like a turban, another towel wrapped tightly under her armpits. "You better go to bed," she said, like she was in charge. She was sixteen and she had been acting like that a lot lately. Terri's fingers were slender, curled as they were around the sill. But she was tough. She had my mother's coloring: olive skin, chocolate eyes, brown hair, which was not as thick or as wavy as my mother's. I was fair and had pale blue eyes that turned gray on sunny days.

Terri had shiny pink splotches on her shoulders. One was the shape of Africa, and the other one I couldn't figure out.

"You got sunburned bad."

"You wanna peel my back?"

"No."

She reached up and peeled off some skin, rolled it into a ball, and flicked it at my face. "Tomorrow's gonna be a busy day, twerp. Piggy's coming home." She nudged me with her Africa shoulder and smiled. The clock on my nightstand glowed 10:55.

It was an annual event—*a matança do porco*—the slaughter of the pig. Usually my family killed a pig in the fall, while we pickled peppers, jarred tomato sauce, and made wine. But this year, my father had received word from his sister, Maria de Jesus, that she was close to clearing her paperwork with the government and was coming from Portugal to live with us.

"Do you know anything about the kid that's gone missing?" she said, her eyes searching the street below.

"He doesn't live in our neighborhood."

"I know that, stupid. I'm just wondering what you've heard."

"Not much. We're going to look for him tomorrow." Emanuel had last been seen by his brother and a friend on crowded Yonge Street, across from the new Eaton Center, our first *real* mall, which spread across two full city blocks and sparkled like an enormous glass cage. That's where we planned to start our search.

"The cops have been looking for two days and haven't found him, but you and your little friends think you will. Good luck with that."

My mother was on the bus now, sitting at the back in the same spot she always chose. She placed her temple against the window. I hoped she would look up to my bedroom window and smile. She was fond of telling me that the key to success was good teeth, white and straight. No matter if you were a man or a woman, a row of pretty teeth drew people in. When I would ask how she kept hers looking so bright, she'd say, "Drink and eat your food at room temperature," revealing her row of Chiclets, sometimes tapping them with her nail.

As the worm-picker pulled away, I wondered where the bus would take them this time. What deal had been struck with which Portuguese security guard at which park or golf course? They moved around, picking the juiciest worms for bait shops across the city. A penny a worm. In addition to this work, my mother had decided to postpone her holiday and had agreed to take more shifts at the hospital to cover other people's time off. Payments on my father's dump truck kept coming due and jobs to dig basements had slowed down. We all have to work together, make sacrifices, my mother would whisper.

My father had gone to a meeting at St. Mary's church hall only a couple of hours before to get an update on Emanuel's disappearance and to help form a community watch group to search for him. From there, he would head to his night job cleaning the TD Bank on the corner of Queen and Euclid. Once that was done, he'd make his way to a bar, the dark one without a sign on the corner of Queen and Palmerston. It was a block away from our house and we called it the cellar because of the metal hatch on the sidewalk just outside the side door.

Through the hatch they'd roll kegs down a ramp made of hundreds of little wheels. He'd have a beer, or maybe two. My mother would be home before him. He wouldn't even know she'd been gone.

2

Before the sun rose and my mother stepped out of the house to board the streetcar that took her to St. Michael's Hospital, she came into my room wearing her mustard-colored uniform: an angel emblazoned on her breast, and her quiet white hospital shoes covered in tiny holes that the German woman at Sasmart said were for *aeration*.

"How many worms did you get?"

"Shh. Sleep." My mother laid out a fresh T-shirt and pair of shorts on my bed and sat down beside me.

"Are you going already?" I wanted her to lie down, the way she used to when I was small and she'd hum Portuguese songs as I doodled in my sketchbook. She leaned over and kissed my forehead, then blew on the spot. The gold medallion of Mother Mary was tangled with a tiny swallow charm I had never seen before.

"Is this one new?" I asked, reaching up to pinch the charm between my fingers.

She pushed my hand away from her necklace. "Play safe. Stay close to home."

"Can't you stay home today? It's Sunday." My mother worked in the hospital's sterilization department, where they fired up all the test tubes and beakers that held diseases and body parts.

"They asked if I'd work another shift. I'll be home this afternoon, and we'll all go to five o'clock Mass. Your father's driving up to the farm with your uncles to get the pig. If you need anything, your aunt Edite is home." I felt her weight lift from the bed. She hovered over me and smiled, little gray pillows under her eyes.

"A benção, Pai," I said, returning from the kitchen with a glass of milk in hand.

"Deus te abençoe," my father replied. "Is early. Go back to bed."

The kids whose parents came from mainland Portugal, *the continent*, did not ask for blessings from their parents or uncles and aunts; this was an Azorean show of respect. We did it without giving much thought to the words tumbling out of our mouths, the same way we prayed the Our Father or Hail Mary.

My father stood at the front door, struggling to slip his construction boots onto his feet. "I going up to the farm today with your tio Clemente." The rule in our house was that, except for morning blessings, only English was to be spoken. *Let this country shape you*. My father would quote Mateus, the man who had helped him when he first came to Canada. "Words will make you strong," he'd say. My father didn't have a lot of words to express himself, and I think he felt not having them had held him back. It would be different with me. I learned about every word I could and used them in sentences to impress my teachers. I couldn't use them with my friends, though. With them I could only think the words, but knowing I could use them was enough.

My father looked up at me with bright eyes as he tucked his Thermos under his arm. He had lost most of his hair at an early age and all he had left was a salt-and-pepper rim of clown hair, cut short. He was almost fifty years old, much older than my friends' fathers, and quite small, five foot five or six. He blamed his height on not having enough food growing up and having too much weight slugged across his back.

"What you do today?" he asked.

"Nothing really. I could come with you," I said, telepathically urging the invite out of him. *Ask me to come, now. Come on, ask me.* I took a sip of milk, watching him over the rim of my glass. He walked over to me and wiped my milk moustache with his thumb.

"Maybe next year," he said, half grinning. He turned and left through the front door without another word. I swiped my wrist across my mouth.

When they first came to Canada, the women would go to the farm with the men. My mother said it wasn't really a pig hunt, just a bunch of men who went to a farm, jumped into a pigpen, and chased the fattest pig down. The pigs all cost fifty dollars, so the men went for the biggest one. "The poor things don't even know what's going on. They just squeal and grunt as the men run and slip in mud and shit before landing their prize pig," she had explained. "Maybe if they weren't already drunk they'd see how ridiculous they were."

After breakfast, I headed out the front door. I was about to hop on my bike when I saw Agnes. Her head hung low over the railing as she heaved. She tossed her hair back, then steadied herself by sitting in the lawn chair on the veranda. Her face was pale. She caught me staring at her. I looked to the ground. I found a branch I could brush against the fences—*Rap, rap, rap, ping. Rap, rap, rap, ping*—as I pedaled up the street.

I rode a Raleigh Chopper, red like the Ford Gran Torino they called Striped Tomato on *Starsky & Hutch*. My father had bought me the bike around Easter. He said it was a boy's bike, not like the other one I had been riding, which had been my sister's. I had spray-painted hers silver, but only small blotches of paint covered the purple frame because I hadn't held the can far enough away. My new bike's sloping main tube and curved back with its squared banana seat made it the best bike on the block. But it was the three-speed gearshift that gave me the kind of cool I wanted.

Our street felt like a ghost town. None of our neighbors were on their porches. They weren't watering their lawns or hosing down their walkways and windows. It was a bit early but I figured the women were probably in their basements cooking Sunday dinner. Maybe their husbands had already escaped to Crupi Bros. Bakery for an espresso or to some other café where they could gather round a radio to listen to the Portugal soccer game. I stopped in front of Senhora Barbosa's house. She sat dressed in black, behind her front window. Her lips caved in because she wasn't wearing her dentures. She scowled at me and drew the curtains. I thought of the missing boy, Emanuel, and imagined what it would be like if we found him safe somewhere. We'd make the front page of the newspaper and they'd interview us on television. Our neighbors would look at us differently. We'd be saviors who might see some reward money.

I headed over to Senhor Cardoso's garage, which had recently been hollowed out by a fire. We had agreed to meet there by nine o'clock, which would give us a few hours for the search before we had to be home to get ready for Mass. But Ricky and Manny were not where they were supposed to be.

I went past our meeting spot and on to Red's house. I leaned my bike against his garage. He lived alone in the big house. Sitting bare-chested at an open window, he'd call us over to climb up onto his garage to pick the sour apples before they ripened and fell to the ground making a mess. Afterwards, he would invite us in for a glass of water, but we never accepted, choosing to drink from his garden hose instead.

I climbed the antenna that hugged the clapboard siding, then scrambled onto the roof of his garage. From up there I could see everything. I bit into a small apple. Its sour juice ran down the corner of my puckered mouth. I saw Aunt Edite, arranging the lawn chair on her third-floor fire escape. She wore a big white hat, white sunglasses, and a bikini, carelessly covered by a kind of Indian sari dappled in little mirrors. Edite worked at the *Toronto Star* and people said she had taken the job in the hope of finding out where her son, Johnny, might be. She hadn't seen him in a couple of years. He never returned home from Vietnam, and Edite was convinced he was somewhere in Canada, hiding from the American government, eating raccoons and berries and sleeping in caves or under spruce trees, biding his time until it was safe to go home. I pictured Johnny like the Vietnam War vets I saw in a television special—his brain fried because of the things he had seen and done. Edite wasn't technically my aunt but we were told to call her that—a sign of respect, my father insisted—even though she preferred to go by her first name alone. She was my father's first cousin, the daughter of an uncle he barely knew who had left the Azores years ago to make his fortune in America.

I was just about to skip across the rooftops when I saw Peter. He was in his fifties and pencil thin. He lived in the garage at the top of the laneway and never spoke. A lot of the kids were mean to him, throwing rocks or yelling nasty things, in an effort to get him to chase. It never worked. He wore thick glasses like Buddy Holly. His clothes were always the same too: navy cigarette pants, a white shirt with a narrow collar, red Converse high-tops, and a pocket protector with an assortment of pens. The silver of his pens sparkled when they caught the sun, turning them into medals.

"Hey, Peter!"

Skittishly, he scanned around him before looking up and nodding. His squinty eyes looked to the ground and he walked faster, pulling his wire bundle buggy behind him. The hair on the top of his head was thinning and I saw a bump, the size of a golf ball, behind his ear.

I took off. It was a game Manny and I loved to play. We chose opposite rows of rooftops, picking sides over rocks, paper, and scissors. I knew the Markham side was harder, a total of eight pitched roofs, compared to the five on the Palmerston side, but I wanted the thrill of hopping from one to the next, some flat, others steep. Ricky would call out the start and then run between us through the lane, offering a play-by-play and adding to the excitement. I liked the jumps best, sailing over the dark crevices between buildings.

I took my time leaping across the shingled roofs, jumping in long and graceful strides over sheets of tin and Plexiglas swatches. I made note of Senhor Pacheco's freshly installed row of two-by-fours, lined with three-inch nails to shoo nesting pigeons, Senhor Cunha's jumble of dragons-tooth barbed wire tucked under some gutters. Senhora Rego had a new laundry line attached to a post centerd like a cross on the pitch of her sagging roof. I stopped above Mr. Serjeant's garage, the tallest pitched roof in the lane. From there I could see MISSING CHILD posters taped to garage doors and telephone poles. They featured a black-and-white photo of the boy with his straight-edged bangs, and a smaller picture of the kind of shoes he was wearing when he went missing, white sneakers with three stripes along the side.

I wasn't sure how long I was up on the roof when Manny and Ricky appeared from the heat's haze. They were crouched at the top of the laneway, in front of Peter's garage. I hand-dropped from Mr. Serjeant's garage, ran back up the alley, hopped on my bike, and with my ass in midair, pushed down hard on the teeth of the pedals until the bike no longer veered from side to side, the pace set. I skidded and kicked up some gravel.

When I reached them, Manny was trying to zap an empty cigarette pack by holding a magnifying glass in front of the sun. Manny was darker than the rest of us—*moreno*, my mother would say, which wasn't as bad as *mulato*—and he had darkened even more over the summer. His hair, which he styled with a pick he always kept tucked in his back pocket, was shaped in a sort of Afro, and it sparkled as if dusted with sugar.

"Hey, we were supposed to meet at Senhor Cardoso's. Aren't we going downtown to look for Emanuel?"

"Shh," he said, raising his finger in my direction.

Ricky shuffled his feet a bit but held his squat. He used his bruised arm as a visor. I couldn't remember a time when Ricky's arms or legs weren't bruised. He said he fell a lot but we all knew his dad beat him. Ricky squinted up at me and smiled before his thin fingers resumed tapping on the lid of a Bick's pickle jar held tightly under his arm. I could see bugs trying to climb up the side of the jar, only to slip down before they reached the top. Every once in a while I heard a ping: a grasshopper banged its head as it tried to hop out. Ricky placed the jar on a bed of gravel, made sure it was in the shade. Ricky's bangs lay flat across his forehead, cut like the teeth of a dog. He trimmed his hair himself but never washed it. He had a tiny face, and his eyes, nose, and mouth were all bunched up like the holes in a bowling ball. Ricky was much smaller than the rest of us, a runt, Manny teased, like Wilbur the pig in *Charlotte's Web*. But unlike Wilbur, Ricky actually did have a special gift. I once saw him pick up a robin that Manny had hit with his slingshot. He cupped the bird's limp body in his hands and brought it to his lips, whispered something into its head, then threw it in the air where it took flight.

"The fire's gonna start," Ricky said. "It's gonna burn to a crisp."

"Shut up!" Manny wasn't going to let Ricky break his concentration.

"Look, there's smoke! It's gonna go."

"Shut up, Ricky." Manny's hand trembled as he forced a stream of spit from the gap between his front teeth. He had remarkable aim and could hit a pop can from ten feet away with laser precision.

I rested my hand on Ricky's shoulder. He bobbed his head into my shadow and looked up. I saw the birth of the flame, a black dot creeping wider. On its edge the dot became rimmed with blue, then orange, and in an instant the pack of Peter Jackson cigarettes turned into a ball of fire. I loved that moment, when fire took over and gobbled everything, the invisible trigger. Flashpoint.

Manny fell back on his heels and banged the back of his head on the garage, laughing. He reached for Ricky's jar. "Let's try a grasshopper."

Ricky tucked the homemade terrarium into his belly, under his *Keep on Truckin'* T-shirt.

"Nah," I said. "We should start looking for Emanuel. Gotta get that reward money."

Manny twirled a cigarette that had magically appeared from his sponge of hair. At school, Manny could hold a double pack of Laurentian pencil crayons in his big Afro of tight curls. The crazy thing was, if you asked for peacock blue, he knew exactly where to reach.

"So are we still going downtown?" I said.

Manny dropped an eggy fart.

"Ah, Manny, that's rotten."

Ricky pinched his nose and giggled.

"We gotta go now," I said. "My dad's gonna be home soon."

"I don't feel like it," Manny said.

"Why not?"

Once Manny set his mind to something he wouldn't budge. And if Manny said no, Ricky wouldn't come either. Deep down, I knew we didn't have enough time to do a thorough job anyway, to gather all the clues that would lead us to Emanuel. I reached into my pocket and pulled out a roll of cap gun tape. I held one end in my mouth and unfurled the long strip, holding it taut for Manny to aim his beam once again. Manny licked his lips and with fierce concentration raised the magnifying glass. Curls of smoke wafted into the beam's path. He lowered the magnifying glass closer to the strip until his hand hovered about six inches above the first pocket of gunpowder.

"I really don't want to go either, but I have a feeling we'd find him, you know." I wasn't going to let Manny off that easy, but the truth was I was afraid to go. That's why I had wanted to go to the pig hunt with my father. I'd have an excuse.

"The kid's been gone for two days now," Manny said.

"Three. Since Thursday afternoon, but if we start looking now—"

"They say the guy he left with was a queer." Manny shook his head.

"So what?"

"They just disappeared?" Ricky asked.

"Yeah," Manny said.

"How do you know this?"

"My mom was on the phone last night, talking to Senhora Gloria. It's what Sean's mother said. He's the kid who was with the Jaques brothers on Thursday. Everyone's talking about it. The man asked Emanuel to move camera equipment." Manny swung his head from side to side in disbelief.

"Is that all they know?" I asked.

"That's all they'll tell us." Manny grinned.

A *pop*, followed by a succession of *pop*, *pop*, *pop*! Wisps of yellow smoke curled in the air, and the smell of sulphur traveled up our noses. Manny looked pleased with himself.

"Look," he said, digging into his pocket and bringing out the small Swiss Army knife his brother had given him when Emanuel went missing. "My brother said you need to be smart on the streets. We gotta stick together." He drew the blade across his thumb, and the blood came out in a straight line. "You in?" I wasn't quite sure what he meant, but Ricky understood. He gave Manny his hand, thumb poking out like he was hitch-hiking. Ricky squeezed his eyes tight and Manny pricked his thumb with the tip of the blade.

"You're next, Antonio," Ricky urged.

I couldn't take my eyes off Manny as I gave him my hand. He pricked my thumb, much deeper than I thought he had to. I fought hard not to show them how much it hurt.

"So now I think we need to press our thumbs together, seal our blood," Manny said.

"I think it only works if you use chicken blood, like a sacrifice," I said.

"You got a chicken handy?" Manny said.

"Would another animal's blood work?" Ricky said. "I saw a dead squirrel in the laneway and—"

"No, Ricky, we need the blood of a fuckin' unicorn. See any of those in the lane?"

"He's just trying to help," I said.

"Let's just get this over with."

"My grandmother told me you're supposed to tape a coin to your pricked thumb if you want something to come true," I said.

We all made a teepee with our thumbs. Pressing hard made the burning feeling go away.

"Do we say something?" I said.

"I don't know," Manny said. "What would your grandmother do?"

I ignored him.

"Go on, Antonio," Ricky said.

"To sticking together," I said.

"You're a fuckin' poet."

We squatted there, not saying anything. There was something about becoming blood brothers that made me feel stronger—a superhero transformation. I wanted to ask them if they felt the same way but I let the idea of what we had just done tingle my skin. I always dreamed of having brothers.

"I think Emanuel was shining shoes so he could buy a new bike," Ricky said. "Maybe he helped the guy with the cameras for some extra cash," he added, before shoving his bloody thumb into his mouth.

"What, and he never came back? You're nuts. They're saying he did things for money. And it wasn't shining shoes. My mother says he—"

"I don't believe what they say." I had caught the worried looks and whispers too. "My mom says his name means 'God be with you,' so God's with him."

"Your mother still thinks the world is flat," Manny said. "She probably crawls on her hands and knees, afraid she'll fall off the edge. And your father, he thinks that landing on the moon was a scam, trick photography or something. They think like that, like they're still living back on their farms in the Azores. Much as I'd like the reward money, if you ask me, this kid's a goner."

My throat tightened and my eyes burned as if tears were already in them.

"God can't be everywhere. If He were, He'd have guided Emanuel home by now." Ricky's calm voice caught me off guard. He scrambled to his feet, lifted his bike, and rode away down the laneway.

Ricky saw the world differently from Manny and me. I knew how he got all those crumpled bills stuffed in his pockets. There was a hole cut out in Senhor Jerome's fence at his pool hall. Men were known to stick their dicks through the hole: a two-dollar bill got you a handjob, and a blowjob cost a fin. I caught him once, Ricky, grabbing a five-dollar bill a man slipped through the hole. He ran away from the scene. I pretended I hadn't seen a thing.

Senhora Rosa's variety store was a square house she had converted to a storefront. It was halfway up Palmerston, exactly thirteen houses up from ours, and it was the corner house to the narrow laneway that led into the main lane. I pushed the door handle, which was shaped like a large Coke bottle, tripping the store's familiar chime. Everything inside twisted and twirled: colored balls and blinking dolls wrapped in cellophane dangled from invisible strings tacked to the yellowed ceiling. Senhora Rosa catered to her Portuguese customers, selling assorted cheeses, barrels of pickled fish, salted cod, and olives bobbing in brine. I looked up at the large clock at the back of the store as Manny beelined for the ice-cream fridge. It was 2:20 p.m. Upon hearing the bell, Senhora Rosa scurried out from behind a curtain made of colored strips of plastic, which hid her kitchen. She had her hair in curlers wound with a sheer kerchief.

"Ah, Antonio." She looked over and saw Manny reach so far down into the fridge that his feet lifted off the ground. "Manelinho!" When she spoke, the raised mole on her forehead moved; Manny called it her third eye.

"Bom dia," Manny said, sliding shut the glass door to the

fridge. Tossing a dash of Portuguese always increased our chances of getting a bubblegum thrown in.

"We're going to go look for Emanuel," I said.

"You're not going anywhere but home." Her eyes darted from me to Manny and back. She reached for a bug swatter and came at me from around the counter. Manny dropped a couple of quarters on the counter and we ran out, stumbling on the broom handle that held the returned jugs of milk, stringing them by their red handles. We jumped all three steps, hopped on our bikes, and began to pedal off into the laneway. She called after us, "The streets aren't safe. The boy's still missing! No one should let . . ." Her voice grew fainter, the clicking of straws covering my spokes drowning out her warnings.

Manny and I made our way to the Patch. The sun threw our shadows ahead of us. Manny tilted his head back to squeeze the bit of grape juice from the silver foil inside of his Lola container. As we neared my garage, I saw Manny look up to my rooftop. My sister was lying on her bath towel just outside our second-floor window. She was listening to CHUM FM on a small transistor radio—it was the only station she listened to; it had all the best rock and pop. She wore a yellow bikini. Her shoulders were covered with a towel but the rest of her glistened with Johnson's baby oil.

"If the neighbors see you, they'll tell Dad!" I shouted up to her.

"Fuck the neighbors! I pinned up some sheets," she called down.

I screened my eyes against the sun. A couple of sheets clipped to the clothesline hung like square clouds and blocked the neighbors' view from their backyards.

I recognized the thunder of my father's dump truck. The shiny red cab rumbled down the laneway. My father pulled at the chain and the truck let out a honk from deep in its gut. Up there in the driver's seat, he seemed so much taller than he really was. He always wore a straw hat, a Sam Snead, which covered the top of his shiny head. Manny and I pressed our backs to a garage door to let the truck go by, *Manuel Rebelo and Son Ltd.* painted on its side in gold letters. The truck puked out fumes that made the air taste like pencil shavings as its huge tires kicked up the grit and gravel.

When the cloud of dust settled, the truck had stopped in front of my uncle David's garage. My father and Uncle Clemente got out. Their boots were caked with dried mud. My eyes darted up to my sister. I heard the crack of a flicking towel and saw her slink back in through the window.

"We have a piggy for you," my uncle Clemente taunted.

My father grinned. "Climb up, boys," he said. "Take a look at this."

3

WHEN I WOKE UP EARLY the next day I ripped the bandage from my thumb, unsealing the penny I'd pressed against my knife cut all night.

I dressed quickly. They needed a whole day to slaughter the pig and I was afraid I'd miss the most important part. I grabbed a Pop-Tart and ran through the lane. I reached my father's truck just in time to hear the hydraulics hissing as the dumper lifted higher and the hinged door swung open. The animal rolled a bit, then slid along the bed of the dumper, before dropping through the tailgate onto the rough gravel. It was still alive.

It lay motionless for five seconds—I counted—before it kicked its trotters in tandem. I jumped back. Its hind and front legs were bound, its mouth held tight with twine. There was snot stringing from its twitching snout. They hauled the pig into the cool shade of Uncle David's garage. A few of the neighbors gathered round, nodding their approval. My father had chosen this day because everyone was home—the first Monday of August was always a holiday.

"A nice pig!" Senhor Batista wheezed as he prodded it with his boot. He was Senhora Gloria's second husband and Agnes's stepfather. He looked like Ichabod Crane. Only he had a hole just underneath his Adam's apple, the result of some kind of neck or throat cancer. He took a drag on his cigarette and blew the small puffs of smoke through the hole.

The men standing together formed a fence. I had always wanted to be part of a slaughter but I was beginning to feel queasy. Blood trickled from the pig's mouth, mixing with the sand and grit. My father wiped his neck with a handkerchief.

"Agora, lift him up. Make him go on top of the mesa."

My father, especially when tired or drunk, would mix Portuguese with English. I looked away. I could tell by its breathing the pig was exhausted.

My uncles were dressed in their rubber boots and plaid shirts. On a count of three—*um, dois, três*—four men lifted the pig off the floor and onto an old barn table. Later, the same table, scoured with hot water and bleach, would be properly set for the first meal. But the bleach and the hot water, and the way my aunt and mother would rub off the germs of shitted trotters and pig slobber and bloodstains, couldn't erase what it was that we raised to our mouths. I wiggled my fingers in my pocket and touched a stick of Juicy Fruit, warm and mushy. I peeled the silver wrapper off, put it in my mouth, and chewed. I breathed in the gum's smell with relief.

The pig continued to struggle, letting out high-pitched squeals. My uncles took up their positions along the pig's haunches and pressed their weight against its rough skin. An invisible force pulled me toward the pig, and before I knew it I had climbed onto the table and found myself sitting on top of the pig's hind leg. My father held the animal in a headlock. He looked at me and I straightened my back and made myself taller. I glanced around me, trying not to look at its snout, trying hard not to meet the pig's eye. Shoulders and torsos leaned in on me. I bit my lower lip so that the men wouldn't see it quiver. Stupid. The heels of my hands pushed down harder onto the pig's flesh.

My father pulled up his sleeve. Uncle Clemente placed the blade under the pig's throat. I stared at the men outside in the morning sun watching the slaughter.

Swish!

The pig's muscles tensed, its squeal stretched into a cry. Out in the laneway, the men were laughing among themselves. I was looking for Manny and Ricky when I saw a face I had never seen before. He stood in the laneway with the others, but he didn't belong. He was younger than all the rest, maybe twenty or so. His blue eyes looked at me sitting atop the pig. He smiled, and I thought he was the most beautiful man I had ever seen, more handsome than the Marlboro Man or any of the actors or singers my sister had cut out of *Tiger Beat* and plastered on her bedroom walls. I turned away, pretending I had to swipe my snot on my shoulder.

Blood dripped into the bottom of the bucket. The pig's breathing grew softer, and then it hissed and stopped. I dared to look again, but the blue-eyed man was gone.

I slid off the pig and slunk to the corner of the garage, wiping my hands on my shorts, trying to clean away the scratchy feeling of the pig's skin. My uncles looped the rope over the rafters and pulled the pig up off the table by its hind legs. The I-beam creaked with the pig's spinning weight. Uncle Clemente kicked the large pail under the carcass. His cigarette rested on the corner of his lip, the ash arched longer than the cigarette.

My mother and Aunt Edite came into the garage, carrying a bucket of steaming water between them. Aunt Edite wore a gypsy skirt and an almost see-through shirt. Her ankles were strapped with the ties of her espadrilles, the same kind my sister wanted but my mother forbade. Edite's arms were bare and tanned. Her streaked hair was tied up with a silk scarf.

"Come inside," my mother ordered.

I began to move in her direction. I was stopped by a splash. I turned to catch my father swinging back the empty bucket as the pig swayed in the air, encased in a swirl of steam.

"He's staying!" my father shouted. "Is a man's work!"

My mother stopped at the door to look back at me. I puffed up. "I'm okay," I said, loud enough for my father to hear. I walked back to the men, who had stopped what they were doing. I ripped the knife from my uncle Clemente's hand. I reached up and scraped the blade down the pig's haunches.

"Força! Mais força!" My uncle Clemente pressed my hand, instructing me to apply more pressure against the pig's skin. I saw my mother go inside.

Aunt Edite remained at the garage doorway. She pulled out a cigarette pack from her skirt's pocket. She tapped the bottom of the pack two times, then drew a cigarette out with her lips. It was a dare. Uncle Clemente took the knife from my hand and wiped it on his jeans. The smoke from Edite's cigarette made everything hazy like in a dream sequence on TV. All eyes were fixed on Edite. When it was clear she wasn't going to leave, Uncle Clemente reached out and cut an even wider slash into the pig's throat. Now the blood streamed like a faucet into the plastic pail. Edite did not flinch. She took a long drag of her cigarette.

My uncle David drew the full bucket to the side, blood sloshing out, staining the concrete, while Clemente placed a large plastic drum under the pig. I could feel my father's hands on my shoulders. His hands were large and sun dark, and their backs were covered with golden hair. A gentle squeeze was my cue to look up. Uncle Clemente raised the knife over his head before plunging it into the pig's belly, exposing the inches of white fatty layers that opened like flowers as the intestines tumbled into the pail, blue and purple and milky. The stench of pig shit and gases wafted across the garage and dug into my hair and clothes and throat. I started to breathe through my mouth.

Edite stood at the door and let the smoke curl out of her nostrils. She tossed her cigarette butt on the ground and pressed the toe of her shoe into it before disappearing through the door.

My father picked up a cup filled to the brim with wine. He took a drink and passed it around. The men all drank and mumbled prayers of thanks as they made the sign of the cross. My father offered me what remained in the cup. I took a sip, but I couldn't throw it down the back of my throat the way the men did. They waited for me to finish it off, one big gulp was all it would take.

"Filho, bring this stuff to the hole I dig outside." My father pointed to the jumble of guts. They'd bury the guts in the big hole beside Uncle David's fig tree and between the rows of peppers. It was good fertilizer, my father would say. He watched me stumble toward the open door then spew the Pop-Tart I had that morning onto the garage floor. I could imagine my uncles rolling their eyes, another thing to hose down on what was already a busy day. I could hear the men laughing in the laneway. Another hit of nausea pushed up my throat. I tried hard to hold it down, but the vomit poured onto the floor. I took a few steps, held on to the jamb, and bent over into the laneway, the sour gush pushing at my throat. I tipped my face up to the sun and my knees went soft. Blue eyes grew large as they swooped down on me. I felt hands grab hold of me under my arms, my face smothered in a chest, as everything turned black.

4

THE SOFA, CHAIRS, coffee table, and the console TV in my uncle's basement had once been the fancy furniture on the main floor, but his living room had been converted to a bedroom when my grandmother and Aunt Luisa arrived from Portugal. A large floral bedspread hung from a line and was held up by wooden clothes pegs with rusted hinges. It divided the basement kitchen from the family room. When we had large family gatherings the bedspread came down and was used as the tablecloth.

I lay still and watched my chest rise and fall, felt my heart beat inside it. I could taste traces of puke in my mouth. My mother stroked my forehead with the back of her hand.

"Did he hit his head?" Aunt Edite asked from behind the curtain.

"No, the neighbor catch him before he fall down." I could hear my father's voice, but I couldn't see where it was coming from.

"Who?" my mother asked.

"I don't know that boy," my father said.

"You don't ask the man his name? Did you thank him?"

As my father was walking out the door, Edite called out, "His name is James."

"You saw him?" my mother said.

"I saw him leaving. He moved into Paul Serjeant's garage only last week." Edite said *garage* in her New England accent, dragging out the *r* until it just floated in her mouth. How did she know James? I rode past Mr. Serjeant's garage all the time and had never seen him there. "He's looking for work. I don't know much more than that," said Edite.

My mother blew her cool breath on my forehead. I was getting too old for her to do this. Behind the curtain, I could hear my aunts whispering in English for Edite's benefit, their knives banging on wooden boards as they chopped onions and garlic and parsley.

"It's been a few days now. Still not a word. The boy is only twelve."

"They took his name away, you know. They gave him a new name, *shoeshine boy*. That's not a Portuguese name."

"That poor boy's mother must be crying like a Magdalena, cursing the day she came here."

"She knows. She must know," Edite said. "A mother does." The room went silent.

My mother didn't know half the things that went on in our world. She didn't know about what Ricky did at the pool hall or that Manny stole bikes. Or that I sometimes stood watch when Manny and Ricky robbed the houses of families on holiday in Portugal. They only took small stuff, but it was still stealing. She didn't know that Mr. Serjeant had shared a few beers with us in his garage a couple of weeks back. He called it his bon voyage party. That same night he made Ricky stand by the television and hold on to the two-foot-long rabbit ears so we could get a better picture. Ricky stood there for nearly two hours and never complained. A few days later, Mr. Serjeant left to live in the Algarve for a year with his Portuguese wife, Senhora Ana. She was homesick and he was going to try his hand at running a pub along the beach. He hadn't said he was going to rent out his garage.

"The ladies at the church are saying this," Aunt Zelia, who was married to my uncle David, said. "Emanuel was trying to save money to buy a ticket for his mother to go visit family back home."

"That's gossip. People say what they want to hear," Aunt Luisa said. "How about the story where he wanted money to feed a new puppy? There are other stories too, you know, about what boys shining shoes do for . . . extra money."

"Antonio," my mother said, "go home and lie down in the basement where it's cool. I'll bring over a bowl of sopa de estrelinha soon."

She blew hard into a tissue before she returned to the smoky kitchen.

I made my way to my uncle's front door and onto my bike, which someone had pulled onto the veranda. I took hungry gulps of air to clear my nose of the smell of pig.

Across the street, I could see Manny's sponge-like hair above the railing as he carried lawn chairs from his porch into the house.

"Hey!" I shouted.

He ran up to meet me at the gate.

"Let's go!" I said.

"Can't."

His mother stood at the front door. "Manelinho, bring the last chair inside!" She sounded anxious.

"Why are you clearing off the porch?"

"They found Emanuel. On the roof of Charlie's Angels sex parlour. He was under some boards, drowned." Then he whispered, "He's dead."

"Manelinho!" his mother wailed.

Manny jumped up all five steps of his veranda. He grabbed a lawn chair and pulled it inside, the screen door slamming behind him.

I walked my bike home quickly. My throat had tightened, and the tightness drilled painfully right down into my chest. I wanted to cry but I couldn't. My fingers found the front-door handle. Making my way down the stairs into the basement, I breathed in the familiar smell of old paper and worms. The floor was painted concrete—battleship gray—and some of the walls were covered halfway up with wood paneling. At the far end of the open space was a bathroom with a large shower, which my father used when he got home from a dirty day of digging, and where Terri and I showered after we came home from the beach and needed to rinse off the sand. It was next to the laundry area and across from the stove—every self-respecting Portuguese family had a second kitchen in the basement they used daily. The kitchen upstairs was just for show and it was rarely used. There was an old back seat of a Chevy my father had brought home one day with a console television, which stood next to the doorway to our *adega*, where fat-bellied oak barrels rested on large wooden blocks. An old hospital sheet, *St. Michael's Hospital* branded on its side, hid the wine. I was relieved to see that everything looked the same.

I sat down and flicked on the TV. The backs of my legs stuck to the vinyl car seat. My tube socks had been held up all day long by elastic bands taken from a Baggie that my mother kept in a drawer. Now I rolled down the socks and scratched the itchy red rings that had been carved around my calves.

We didn't have cable, so we could only watch one station on the main dial and, depending on the weather, tuned the channel with the second dial. *And remember, breakfast without orange juice is like a day without sunshine.* Anita Bryant, the former Miss America, strolled through an orange grove in her shiny white dress, her hair perfect. She looked so different from the woman who had been in the newspapers for leading the Save Our Children campaign.

"She should have stuck to selling oranges," Terri said. I could feel her presence behind the seat, the smell of soap moving with her. I hadn't heard her come downstairs.

"He's dead," I said.

My sister plopped down next to me. She sat closer to me than she normally would. Tucking her legs under her bum, she leaned against me, her arm pressing against my side. I didn't shift over. We listened carefully to the TV reporter.

"This is the street corner where Emanuel Jaques was last seen. Four days ago he was shining shoes, like so many other boys here, and then disappeared into what many consider the cesspool of the city, Yonge Street." The reporter spoke slowly, and his voice was level. "Reports suggest that he and his brother and friend were approached by a man . . ."

Terri nibbled on some strands of her hair. I poked my chin into my T-shirt and lifted the ribbed collar into my mouth. I sucked on the cotton.

"Emanuel's older brother said a man had approached the boys for some help. He allegedly offered the boys thirty-five dollars to move camera equipment. Emanuel's older brother and a friend ran to the nearest pay phone to call home to ask their mother's permission. Upon their return, Emanuel was gone. He had vanished." A picture of the large-eyed boy appeared on the screen. "Again, the search is over. The body of a twelve-year-old boy police have identified as Emanuel Jaques has been found on a Toronto rooftop."

"Ouch!"

My sister pinched my thigh—the teeny kind of pinch that hurt. "Don't ever go with anyone. Got it?" She got up to turn off the television, but stopped when she heard the cries of family from behind the interviewer's questions. There were TV cameras in the Jaques' living room, doilies on the tables and a big wooden cross in the corner of the room. Mrs. Jaques spoke in Portuguese between her sobs. She sat in an armchair with her eyes barely open, covering her mouth with a handkerchief. Her four other children stood frozen around their mother. Emanuel's father was in the bedroom, too stricken with grief to come out and be interviewed.

The reporter asked Emanuel's mother, "If you were speaking to the members of city council, what would she tell them to do about the Yonge Street strip?"

The oldest daughter bent down to translate into her mother's ear.

"Give me my son back" was the reply.

I skidded on my bike into my uncle's garage. I didn't want to come off as some stupid kid, I wanted to handle the news like a man.

It was clear from the way they were carrying on that the men didn't know yet, which meant my mother and aunts in the basement were just as ignorant. There was no TV or radio in the garage, and the women were too busy chopping up pig parts.

There wasn't much left of the pig by now, just the hind legs dangling from the wooden rafters. *Presunto* or bacon, I thought. My uncle Clemente caught me around the waist and shoved the pig's tail in my mouth. The men cheered him on as I squirmed in his hold. Part of the tail curled around my tongue and the rest lodged against the roof of my mouth. They all laughed as I gagged and tried to spit it out. I had to hook my finger to pull it out. I hunched over, and saliva filled my mouth to coat the taste. They patted me on the back while I looked to my father.

"You is a man now," he whispered, his stubble scraping against my cheek.

I reached for my father's warm wine and threw it hard against the back of my throat. This led to another wave of "Força!" and further bouts of approval with "Um homem. A man now."

I licked my hand clean.

They truly had no idea Emanuel had been murdered, and I wouldn't tell them.

I jumped on my bike and sped away, riding east along Queen Street, past the vacant storefronts, past all the drunks, past the broad thoroughfare known as Spadina Avenue, past City Hall that looked like a building out of *The Jetsons*. I kept going, racing with the fluffy clouds that ran along above the trees. The breeze dried my tears, rushed up my nose and filled my lungs.

I turned up Yonge Street and stopped in the shadow of the Eaton Center, across the street from Charlie's Angels. Above the door some products were being advertised in plastic letters: *Movies*, *Sex Toys*, *Magazines*, *Books*. The store's window promised SEXY GIRLS. Some men were boarding up the door and windows with plywood, but they hadn't covered everything:

the painted figure of a half-naked woman and the words *Your happiness may depend on it* were still exposed. It was a tall building, five stories high, and it looked like all the others that lined Yonge Street. The building had been blocked off with yellow tape. I stood there straddling my bike, leaning over my handlebars. My head felt fuzzy, but I hoped I'd see Emanuel's body. If I got close to him, I could pray in Portuguese, the way my grandmother taught me. *Prayers are heard faster if you pray in Portuguese*, she'd say. The news teams, reporters, and everyone else who gathered were all waiting for something to happen.

It was getting dark. I was pedaling up Palmerston Avenue so slowly I was barely moving, just fighting to keep my balance. *Where was everyone?* I passed one empty porch after another. I had never seen our street so dark. Curtains were drawn. Porch lights were switched off.

I turned across Robinson Street to go through the laneway. My uncle's garage door was closed. I made my way up toward the patch of light that beamed into the laneway from Mr. Serjeant's garage. I stopped. The man was painting the inside of the garage, whitewashing everything. His back was to me. I could see his blond curly hair poking out under his cycling cap. His tank top was drenched, glued to his skin.

"Terrible, isn't it?" He continued to paint, to my relief. He stood on a stool. I saw his ankles and thought his feet must be tanned too. It was the last thing I thought of before I realized he could see my reflection in a window.

"I'm James," he said. He twisted around to face me.

"I know," I managed, before I felt my tongue getting fat. My chest ached. James was in the middle of saying something when I turned away from him and pressed down hard on the pedals. I didn't let up until I came out onto Palmerston Avenue, where I saw my mother leaning over our front gate. Across the road, the worm-picker bus revved its engine and slowly rolled away toward Queen Street.

"Where did you go? Get in that house now!" She smelled of blood sausages, onions, and paprika. She had been crying.

I walked my bike through our gate and dropped it on the front lawn. The back wheel spun in the air.

It wasn't cold, but she drew her sweater tightly across her chest, tucked her hands under her armpits. I caught her looking out through the storm door before sliding the latch to Lock. Then she shut the front door and secured the deadbolt.

The sound of my mother's slippers slapping against her heels chased me up to the bathroom. I stood beside the tub and wiggled my fingers in the water. It was cold now. My mother stood in the doorway. With my back to her, I quickly undressed, wrapped a towel around my waist. I just stood there.

"What are you waiting for?" she said. "Get in the water before it gets any colder."

"I need privacy."

"You got to be careful, Antonio. It's not safe anymore," she said before leaving.

I dunked myself quickly, scrubbed my skin raw with the washcloth until a layer of gray scum covered the entire surface of the cold bathwater.

I wasn't sure how long I had been lying in my bed before John F. Kennedy's voice made its way up to my room and I knew my father was home. The recording of JFK was displayed on a bracket that once held a plate. My father played it over and over whenever he was sad or when he sensed things had changed, or were about to change. I heard my father's boots, the rhythm of his step climbing the stairs. *Ask not what your country can do for you—ask what you can do for your country.* There was his smell: Old Spice, Craven "A," the sweetness of homemade wine.

When he walked in I saw his forehead was covered in tiny beads of sweat.

He looked away for one moment and rocked forward as if he'd thought better of it and would leave. He cracked his knuckles.

He sat down and looked like he was about to say something. I could see the patches of silver stubble on his chin and upper lip. The veins in his neck pumped. He drew the heel of his palm across his forehead, then reached over and rubbed my earlobe with his thick fingers. His bottom lip trembled.

I didn't want him to cry.

"You not hurt?" He took another deep breath. I thought he was going to say something else, but he just got up. "Close you light," he said. Then he quietly shut the door behind him.

5

M Y NIGHTMARES BEGAN the night Emanuel's body was found. I was being chased, running barefoot through the laneway. The laneway looked different, like what it would have looked like a hundred years back, with barns in place of garages. There were open fields instead of fences. Small stones and shards of glass cut into my dirty feet. As I ran, my hands chopped the wind in front of me. I could hear pursuers puffing and blowing behind me, mocking *you boy with the pretty hair. I got something I'd like to share. Little boy with the pretty hair.*

I was still perspiring when I made my way down to the kitchen. I opened the window and cooled my head in the morning breeze. It was as if the discovery of Emanuel's body had cracked the heat wave.

I was shocked to see my mother sitting in the backyard, alone. She never missed work. A week after I was born, she was back on the job at the hospital. She told me she couldn't afford to stay at home. I felt shitty whenever she told me that story.

"Not going to work today, Mãe?"

"No, I need to stay home today." She took a sip from her tea cup and placed it down. She spun the cup a little in its saucer.

"Mãe?"

She didn't look my way.

"You know the swallow makes a sound," she began, so quietly I could barely hear her. "Not really a sound, a kind of whisper.

{ 42 }

Back home in São Miguel swallows were the first sign that the cold days were over." She lifted the teacup to her lips.

"I thought it never got cold in São Miguel."

"Damp like worms."

"I don't think I've ever seen a real swallow," I said.

"I didn't want to come here. Canada seemed so far away. I wanted to move to Lisbon."

I'd never heard that before. "Why did you come, then?"

"Your father came to Canada a few years before me. He needed to get away, and he was happy here. He said Portugal was too sad."

Manny and Ricky should have been somewhere in the laneway. I walked up and down the lane before deciding I'd just wait for them in the Patch. Every little sound made me nervous. I had been there fifteen minutes and I thought I'd give my friends ten more minutes to show up before making my way over to Edite's. My mother only let me leave the house because I promised I'd head straight to Edite's to take her some homemade jam.

A monarch butterfly landed on the ground, clapping its wings in the sun. I walked up to it. The trick was pinching its wings together, trying to not rub off any of the rusty powder so it could still fly. I reached down, my fingers ready to pinch. The air was jabbed by a muffler backing up. The butterfly took flight just as the jar under my arm smashed on the gravel.

The stairs leading up to Edite's apartment were narrow and dark. All her windows were open, and fans scanned the kitchen like giant periscopes. She had been living there for more than a year now and the place smelled of stale cigarettes. I passed by her bedroom: a mattress on the floor with a ruffled bedspread, a big Chinese fan on her wall in place of a headboard, and a silk scarf draped over her lamp. Clothes, blankets, beaded jewelry, and newspapers were scattered over the floor and bed. It wasn't like any other Portuguese house I had ever been to. Edite said she liked to keep it that way; she could scoop all her belongings into a garbage bag at a moment's notice and drive away in her convertible.

I walked down the hall and stopped to make the sign of the cross at Johnny's picture. It was perched on top one of the towers of old newspapers she kept piled along the hall. Johnny had large dark eyes, and his face was framed with black curls, nothing like his mother's. Edite sat at her kitchen table, reading the newspaper. Her cigarette smoldered in the ashtray.

SHOESHINE BOY, 12, FOUND SLAIN. Underneath the headline was a grimy photo of the Charlie's Angels storefront.

"You're here. What took you so long? Hold on, before you answer that let me call your mother." Edite picked up the phone and dialed. "You want some coffee?" she whispered, just as my mother's panicked voice came through. "Georgina, he's here. He's okay," Edite said, looping then unlooping the phone cord around her pointing finger. "No, it's okay. It's my fault. I forgot to call you when he arrived." I caught my mother's voice directing threats at me in Portuguese. Edite returned the receiver to its base. "In hot climates they drink hot drinks, you know. Supposed to cool you off." Before I could say no she was at the counter pouring me a cup from her percolator. I chipped away at the sugar until I got about four teaspoon-sized nuggets. I was used to having a milked-down version of coffee that my mother prepared for me, filled with crushed digestive biscuits to sop up all the liquid. "We're just a bit worried, Antonio." Edite poured herself a refill. She reached up to the cabinet and brought down a small bottle of something golden. I thought it was honey or maple syrup until she stirred her coffee and I smelled the booze.

The first time I met Edite, at Kensington Market, my eyes landed on her before my mother had even introduced us. She stood beside a barrel filled with pickled herring and plastic bins packed with dried beans, grains, and powdery spices. She was thin and beautiful. Her head was slightly tilted, and a cigarette was wedged in the corner of her mouth. She caught me staring and her coral lips stretched wide. I turned away to look at the rows of stacked cages filled with chickens, ducks, rabbits, and pigeons.

My mother's hand tightened around my wrist. She kissed the woman on both cheeks. "Antonio, meet your aunt Edite."

Aunt Edite wore makeup and painted her nails. She kept herself thin by cutting meat from her diet, drinking Tab whenever she wanted, and smoking Camels. She had also joined the Vic Tanny's fitness club on Richmond Street, something no Portuguese woman I knew ever did. There wasn't a hint of Portuguese in the way she spoke. She had moved to the States when she was fourteen, got married at sixteen, and was widowed at twenty. An industrial accident, my father told me. My mother had agreed to meet her in Kensington Market, amidst all the fruit stands and fishmongers, but then she practically had to drag her home with us. It was clear from the conversation on the way home that my father had no idea my mother knew Edite was in Toronto. Edite settled into her own apartment on Markham Street, a few houses up from where Ricky lived with his father. She said she needed to get away from America for a little while. She told my mother she had been offered a job here working for a newspaper, and she took it. She had worked at the *Boston Herald* before starting at the *Toronto Star*. Her hands were soft. Her fingers only knew typewriter keys, not harsh detergents and the chemicals used to disinfect toilets and strip floors.

A few nights later, I had overheard my father fighting with my mother. Edite was *louca* and *uma tola*, he said, which I knew meant she was nuts. A single woman living on her own would get people gossiping. He had an obligation to protect our family's reputation.

Sitting at the table, our coffees in hand, Edite began to read Tuesday's paper out loud: "'Behind the sleazy facade of this body-rub parlour at 245 Yonge Street police found the body of twelve-year-old shoeshine boy Emanuel Jaques. They smashed glass panes in the front door at 6:30 a.m. to search, and found a body on the roof at the back. The boy had been missing four days. Four men are being held for questioning.'"

Edite lowered the paper and slid it over to me on the kitchen table. Emanuel's sister, through her sobs, told the reporter that he "very much liked to make money but he wasn't greedy. He didn't rush out and spend it; he knew it had to go into the bank."

The sound of a baby crying pealed across the asphalt. I wondered why Emanuel's cry hadn't sped between the dirty buildings with their neon signs.

"I'm not sure what's going to happen next, Antonio. But things are about to get a lot worse."

"But they caught the men, didn't they? It's over."

"It's just beginning. Now it turns into a blame game. The Portuguese blame the politicians and the police for not protecting the boy. They'll take matters into their own hands and they'll target the homosexuals simply because they hate and fear them. The police will crack down on all the illegal stuff they've been turning a blind eye to downtown, especially among the homosexuals, because they think it will deflect blame and responsibility from them. And the politicians just see votes—they'll make promises they don't even believe, only to keep their butts in office."

We build their houses. We clean their houses. We mind their children. For what? For this? For them to do this to one of our children? This is not why we came. I had heard these words coming out of Edite's radio.

"You know what it is to be afraid, right?"

I nodded.

"Your mother didn't go to work today because she's frightened." Edite stared at me through the cigarette smoke.

"She freaked me out this morning. The way she was just sitting in the backyard not doing anything. I thought she was going to cry."

"She's frightened for you. She's thinking it could have been you instead of Emanuel."

"That could never happen to me."

"Why?"

I couldn't tell her that I was safe because me, Ricky, and Manny were blood brothers and would protect each other.

"Your mom and dad have to work. There's no one at home to look after you guys. I know you're a good kid, and you're lucky to have your friends, but things are going to change."

"How?"

"I can't say for sure. We'll have to wait and see. In the meantime I'll show you where I keep an extra key so that you can always come here."

I was thrilled Edite trusted me, but I could tell she was holding back. It was the way her words came out of her mouth—between little burps of breath.

"Aunt Edite, are you afraid?"

"Not really."

"How come?"

She smacked her lips. "Oh, I'm not Portuguese with all that sadness, the *saudade* they're drowning in. No, I stopped being Portuguese long ago."

"You can't just stop being Portuguese," I said. "Can you?"

Edite brushed past me and tousled my hair. "I know I don't let anyone tell me how to act or feel."

From her back landing, Edite was one of the few people who had a clear view of our laneway. She knew more about what went on there than any of the other adults in our lives. She never said anything about what she must have seen, though once she told me how much she enjoyed watching us race across the rooftops.

"What do you know about that new guy living in Mr. Serjeant's garage?" I said.

"His name is James. Spoke to him a bit. He reminds me of my Johnny." She put her cigarette down in the ashtray and raked her fingers through her hair. "He's just looking for a fresh start."

"From what?"

Edite ignored my question. "Your cousin Johnny was always getting himself into trouble. But deep down he was a good kid, you know. We should never have gone to war. We were fighting and we didn't even know who the enemy was." That was the thing about Edite; she spoke to me with words she would have used with adults. And when she asked me something, like *How's it going?* she actually waited around long enough to hear the answer.

"Do you think you'll ever find Johnny?" I asked.

She picked up her pack of Camels. I lifted the smoldering one in the ashtray and offered it to her, my fingers sticking to the lipstick ring around the filter.

Edite pinched the cigarette with her nails and took a long drag from it. She closed her eyes. "I have to keep hoping." The cigarette trembled between her fingers, and her foot tapped faster.

6

N OT LIKE THAT, Terezinha, the forks go on the right side of the plate," my mother said. Terri rolled her eyes. "My feet are killing me," my mother continued. "I waited in line for over an hour at the rectory. There were hardly any medallions left."

"Medallions for what?" Terri asked.

"Which saint did you get?" I asked.

"The ones Padre Costa blessed were a dollar more. By the time I got up, St. Benedict was sold and so was St. Jude."

"What does St. Benedict represent?" Terri asked, placing the last fork on the right side of the plate.

I told her, "He's the most powerful saint against evil spirits or magic spells."

"But what do you want them for?" Terri tried again.

"So who did you choose?" I asked, enjoying my sister's frustration.

"I was lucky enough to get a whole bunch of St. Anthony medallions." My mother set the last soup bowl on a plate and reached for my cheek, but I moved away.

"Why him? Isn't he kind of useless?" Terri smiled.

"Filha, he's the saint of lost things."

"But we haven't lost anything, Mãe," I said.

My mother stayed up that night sewing the medallions onto my undershirts and inside the pockets of my pants. The next morning, Terri charged into my room, flicking her bra strap at me. "Mom's losing it! She sewed those damn things on everything I own."

"Maybe she thought it would keep the creeps from going at your boobs."

Terri jumped over my bed and lunged at me. I deked her out and ran down to the basement.

My mother wouldn't let me go out with my friends. She said my friends weren't allowed out either. I knew Ricky's dad didn't really have rules for him, so he didn't count, but my mother was wrong. Manny's parents hadn't cranked up the rules in their house. Manny and Ricky had been hanging around without me. But I saw the worry on her face and stopped pushing. She had to go back to work, so she left long lists of chores for us to do, things to keep us at home and out of trouble—polishing the brass doorknobs, dusting the gumwood baseboards on the main floor, and vacuuming the living-room broadloom so that the stripes the vacuum cleaner left wouldn't get messed up. I noticed that one of the jobs on my sister's list was to take over to Senhora Gloria some mail that had been accidentally delivered to our mailbox.

"I'll drop off the letter if you Windex the windows," I said.

"Here's what you can do," Terri said. "Drop off the letter *and* lug the hampers down to the basement."

"What'll you do off my list?"

"Nothing." She looked smug, like she knew perfectly well the reason I had offered the trade.

———

I had planned on ringing the doorbell and delivering the letter to Agnes by hand but at the last minute lost my nerve. As I lifted Senhora Gloria's mail slot, the door swung open. Senhora Gloria looked like a nun in her brown habit—the costume she wore whenever she went out to collect money for the church. After examining the letter, she reached into her small patent leather purse, never taking her eyes off me. "Come with me. I have something for you," she said as she walked into the darkened hallway.

I thought of politely turning round and running off the porch. Instead, I followed her into the hall and then down the narrow stairs into the basement. Running my hand along the railing, I thought about Agnes's hands and fingers touching each spot a few times throughout the day.

Agnes was lying on the couch in the basement, belly down. She wore striped socks, each toe a different color. She clicked her feet in the air, watching *Gilligan's Island* and ignoring me.

"Agnes, go get some money from my room." Senhora Gloria cupped my chin and rubbed her thumb across my cheek.

Agnes sat up but took her time getting off the couch.

"Go! What are you waiting for?"

"That's okay, Senhora Gloria." I forced a smile, tried not to notice Agnes's embarrassment.

Alone in the basement with Senhora Gloria, I could hear the steady hum of the large box freezer. I looked at the starched white band that cut across her forehead. "It's so tight. Doesn't it hurt, Senhora Gloria?" I said, pointing to the band. It sounded like something a little kid would ask, and I couldn't believe the question had come out of my mouth. A couple of the older nuns at St. Mary's elementary school still wore habits, but I could never ask them—they were mean and didn't hesitate to use the strap. Senhora Gloria smoothed her hands over her breasts and patted down the front of her long dress.

"Not so much. But this one—" She looked over her shoulder, then lifted her skirt to reveal the brown woollen socks held up by metal clasps. Lumps of bluish fat covered her thighs, and veins that looked like purple spiders stretched across her bumpy white skin. With eyes widened she lifted the silver clasp of her garter to reveal the dimple that had cut into her inner thigh, above the knee. "This one hurts! Just like Jesus on the cross." She smiled before whispering, "You can touch it. Go ahead. It's like Jesus's cut." She caressed my hand, bunched my fingers for me so that only my index finger pointed, and drew it over her knee toward her thigh. The ball of my fingertip felt the warmth from the small dent in her skin. The heat traveled up my finger, to my wrist and arm. She made a sound like she was sinking into a hot bath, and threw her head back, her face lit up by the fluorescent bulbs, and I could see shiny bits of metal in her teeth.

I almost knocked Agnes over as I ran up the basement steps, and I didn't stop until I heard slapping flesh. I paused to listen, to see if Agnes would cry, but I heard nothing. I bit my lower lip so hard that I knew I had made teeth marks. The storm door slammed behind me.

Although the rest of my mother's to-do list was waiting for me, I couldn't go home. Not yet. I roamed the laneway until I found myself at Mr. Serjeant's garage. Ricky was sitting on a bench with a rag pressed to his right cheek and eye.

"Ricky," I said.

His eyes opened. He lowered the rag.

"Whoa, what happened to you."

"It's okay," he said. "James has gone to get ice." The ice factory was just a couple of blocks away, and we sometimes hung around to grab the frozen chunks left behind after the trucks pulled out.

The pieces of Ricky's shattered clacker—Ricky could get the two glass balls to clack together so fast they looked like hummingbird wings—remained on the bench beside him, his middle finger still curled like a comma in its plastic tab.

"Keep pressing," I said as I lifted the rag back to his face. Mr. Serjeant's garage faced the laneway, like all our garages did, but his had a second-floor loft at the top of a ladder. The boards creaked above me.

"You should see the tits on this one!" Manny cried. "Her nipples are the size of Frisbees."

"Are you crazy?" I yelled back.

"Yeah, crazy in love. You gotta see this."

"What the hell are you doing up there? Get down!"

Manny's face popped into view from the opening up to the loft. "What's your problem? James saw the clacker smash in Ricky's face. He told us to make ourselves comfortable. He's nice, he wants to help."

I looked up and down the alley, checking for the stranger Manny and Ricky now called a friend, and instead saw Agnes coming our way. I cupped my hand in front of my mouth, blew and smelled. The mouthwash I had swooshed before delivering the mail was still working. The wheels of her bundle buggy squeaked. It was filled to the brim with what looked like laundry. She stopped, but she did not look at me. The left side of her face was red and swollen. I should have stayed at Senhora Gloria's. I should have known she would blame Agnes for stopping whatever it was she stopped. I should have protected Agnes, but instead I ran like a frightened little boy.

"Is your washing machine broken?" I asked.

Agnes swept past me as if I was invisible. She bent over Ricky so that her lips were right beside his cheek. I imagined her breath tickling his skin. "You'll be okay," she said. "Keep pressing."

I stood a few feet away from Agnes. "He'll be fine," she said, to no one, then resumed her trek up the laneway, her thick braid tapered at the end, swinging from side to side.

"You guys gotta see this place!" Manny yelled down.

I climbed up the ladder and peered over the edge of the floor. The place had been cleared out except for a mattress. Manny was on his knees tracing the figure of a centerfold that had been stapled to the joists. One slanted wall of the pitched roof was covered with nude pictures, like a giant quilt. A gooseneck nightlight had been placed on top of a thick book.

"I don't think we should be up here," I said, lowering myself back down the ladder.

Manny climbed down after me. "This guy's cool. He's got more pin-ups than Corrado's barbershop. He said when he's not around we can use his place, like a clubhouse."

On one side of the garage a long workbench ran the length of the wall. Hoops of rope and wire hung on nails. The one window had been covered with a garbage bag and sealed tight with duct tape. A shiny blue chest with gold hinges and lock was directly under the window. In the corner of the garage James had placed a shower curtain that ran on a track like those in a hospital room. Rubber ducks swam around the hem of the curtain. I couldn't see what was behind until Manny swept the curtain aside to reveal two full-length mirrors on the walls and a bike frame that twirled from a meat hook. Beside the curtained area was a hot plate, some propane tanks, and a wooden table with two mismatched chairs. The far wall was empty of any decoration, except for a red Videosphere. The TV, looking like a space helmet with its smoky visor, was Mr. Serjeant's. It was the exact one I dreamed of having in my bedroom. A box with a mirrored disco ball sat on the shag rug, which practically covered the entire concrete floor. Large pillows littered the space. Manny pulled one to the center of the room and sat, cross-legged. "Look up!" he said.

A piece of heavy cloth had been stretched across the aluminum garage door. A border of duct tape held it down. Splashes of color and dribbles of paint covered the canvas. Very little white space remained. Instead, the strokes moved from thick, bold stripes to thin lines that swerved and curled like my sister's hair when the tub was drained.

"He's an artist," Manny said.

"He's twenty-one," Ricky mumbled through the rag.

Manny lay back on the rug with his fingers laced behind his head. "Magic carpet, take me on a ride!" he said as he grabbed one side of the rug and curled it over his legs.

Ricky giggled.

Suddenly, Amilcar came into the garage. He lived on Palmerston, but his laneway was shared with Euclid, one block over. Amilcar was nine when he came to Canada. His family had come from mainland Portugal, as he never failed to remind us dirty Azoreans. My mother told us that he was only a boy and that he didn't really know what he was saying, that he was only repeating what he heard from his parents. I knew he said it because he was an asshole. Even though he was fourteen now, he was in our class. He had been held back a year when he first arrived and then he failed the following year. He was much taller than the rest of us. In the changing room after gym class he liked to gyrate his hips until his dick, much larger than any of ours, twirled like a helicopter blade in front of his bush.

"What's up, Ricky? One of your customers poke you in the eye?"

"Shut up," I said, sitting up.

"Who's gonna make me, you little shit?" Amilcar said.

Manny stood and took two steps toward Amilcar, but the older boy pushed by him and came into the garage.

"Where's the English man?" Amilcar asked, looking around. He brushed aside the shower curtain to reveal the suspended bike frame. "You better not be cutting into my business." Amilcar made money by stealing bikes and selling them off to Big John, who lived in the Project, a public housing complex. Manny knew Big John too; just a couple of weeks back he had flaunted the two twenty-dollar bills he got through his dealings with him. But even Manny would agree that his operation was small-scale compared to Amilcar's take.

Manny stepped in Amilcar's way, arms crossed in front of his chest, just before Amilcar turned to climb the ladder.

"Get out of my way." Amilcar stared Manny down but Manny stood firm.

"Hey, you guys." My sister rode by the garage opening on my bike.

Terri's ten-speed had been stolen earlier in the summer, forcing her to lace up her roller skates whenever she went out.

Manny had denied stealing it, even offered to find her another, more expensive one. He said he wasn't kidding; he'd do it if I gave him a pair of her panties. I told him he was a pig. Amilcar was the more likely thief anyway. We stepped out into the laneway to see her reach the end of the alley. She turned around and pedaled back toward us. As she got closer, Amilcar cupped his dick and balls with one hand and made sucking noises with his tongue. "Hey, baby, come and get it."

Just as Terri sped by, Amilcar's arm darted out. He grabbed her boob but couldn't get her tube top down.

"You're a prick" was all I could muster.

Terri skidded. The bike swung around.

"Is that why she's back for more?" Amilcar said.

I recognized the look on my sister's face—the flashing of teeth, the concentration that caused ripples right between her eyes. She pumped my pedals until her fine hair whipped in the wind. She expected Amilcar's hand to reach for her, and just as it did, her arm struck out in the air to grab his face.

The bike continued on its path. I ran to it before it wobbled and crashed to the ground. When I turned back, Terri had pinned Amilcar to the ground with her body, pushing hard on his face with her hand, banging the back of his head into the concrete. Amilcar flopped around like a fish out of water.

James appeared out of nowhere and popped Terri off of Amilcar like a cork. Amilcar held both hands against his blood-smeared face. Manny and Ricky stood, open-mouthed. Everything had gone silent, except for Amilcar's whimpers and my sister's heaves.

"Go home, you little shit," Terri said, catching her breath. "Tell your parents what the Açoreana did to their rude son."

"Puta!" He dropped his hands, and we could see the five little half moons that formed on his face, one on one side from her thumbnail, the other four on his left cheek. "Puta!" he repeated. Blood oozed from all the cuts except one.

James's shadow touched Amilcar. He offered his hand to help Amilcar up. Once Amilcar was on his feet, James grabbed his collarbone and pinched hard. Amilcar's body contorted. James put his lips close to his ear. "That wasn't nice," he said, and he wagged his finger like a scolding mother.

"Who the hell are you?" Amilcar said.

"I'm the guy who lives here, and these are my friends. Now get your ugly ass outta here, before I do something I ain't gonna regret."

Amilcar gave James a hard look, then ambled up the laneway.

I saw James up close now: his eyes were an unnatural blue, his nose was crooked like a hockey player's, and his teeth were slightly crowded. He had a cleft in his stubbly chin, and his Adam's apple stuck out like a Ping-Pong ball. A smooth pink scar ran along his jawline. It made him look dangerous.

Ricky offered his rag to Terri, and she wrapped it around her hand like a prizefighter.

"You okay?" James asked.

"I'm fine."

"Must hurt."

"It'll hurt later, but that's okay." She looked up the laneway to where Amilcar had disappeared. "It was worth it."

James smiled, scanned my sister's face and body. It wasn't like he was being a pig or anything, more like he was photocopying her into his brain.

"I don't need a knight to ride up on a horse and save me," she said. "Especially one that carries a bag of ice, not a sword."

James looked around. "I don't see a horse." When he failed to get a laugh he added, "You got a bit of a bite."

Terri bent down and picked up a few chunks of ice from the burst bag that lay on the ground. She buried one piece into her bandaged hand and put the smaller piece into her mouth, crunched it between her teeth. Her eyes never left his. "Come home!" she said to me. "Mom will be back soon."

Later that evening, my mother took another shift at the hospital, and my father went to clean the bank downtown. Edite came over with some Avon catalogues. According to my sister, they were going to do *girl things*. I snuck into the hallway and held my breath outside the living-room door.

"Looks like you lost a big chunk of your nail."

"It'll grow back."

"No boy is worth it, Terri."

"What do you think of James?"

"He's a bit too old for you."

"He's got gorgeous eyes."

"I'll give you that."

They both giggled.

"Antonio. You can come in, you know," Edite said. I could hear Terri slapping the roof of her mouth with her tongue. "I can see your reflection on the TV screen."

I stepped inside.

"How long have you been standing there?" Terri asked.

"I just got here," I said.

Edite laughed. "Do you want to join us?"

Terri's eyebrows told me what my answer should be.

"I was just wondering if I could . . . if I could maybe . . . go play with my friends in the laneway. The street lights aren't on yet . . ."

"You'll stay close? You'll stay together? And you promise to come home the minute the street lights come on?"

I nodded three times to make sure I covered all her terms. "Okay."

The second I walked from my garage into the laneway I saw James's garage door open. It's what I'd hoped I'd find. My next hope was to see Manny and Ricky in there with him. I heard their voices as I got closer and quickened my pace.

Set atop a wooden crate, Ricky sat in a chair. His head was the only thing that poked through the cut-out in a garbage bag. A shiner was beginning to take shape around his eye. He smiled when he saw me. Above his head, the hungry moths that had been drawn into James's garage spiralled around the bare light bulb like kamikazes. Manny was lying on the shag rug, a pile of *Playboy* and *Hustler* magazines next to him. I closed the garage door, in case anyone passed by and decided to snitch to our parents, and sat cross-legged on the rug. Manny threw a couple of magazines into my lap.

"Where's James?" I asked. And as if on cue, he appeared from behind Ricky. He had been crouched behind him, mixing some soap and water in a bowl.

"Let's get this started," he said, winking at me. Then he turned to Ricky. "If you're going to hang around here, you need to be presentable. And I'm sorry but that sad-ass haircut you got yourself isn't good enough."

We all laughed, even Ricky.

James tilted the bowl over Ricky's head. The sudsy water ran right off his bangs and across his nose. Ricky squeezed his eyes shut and blew some air out of his mouth like a wet fart.

James began to work Ricky's hair with his fingers, while humming "The Barber of Seville" from *Bugs Bunny*. We all joined in, our voices growing louder in unison.

James rinsed Ricky's hair, then dried it with a towel, finishing off by wiping inside Ricky's ears with his towel-covered finger. Then he circled Ricky, assessing. As James passed by me, I was aware of myself smelling him.

"How long's it been, Ricky?" Manny said. James combed Ricky's hair and flicked the comb against the wall.

"Too long," James joked. He flipped the bowl and placed it over Ricky's head. He pressed the bowl against his forehead and cut straight across, evened out all the jagged points. Hair fell onto Ricky's nose and cheeks. He sneezed. "Ta-da!" Then James made his way around the rest of Ricky's head, trimming to the edge of the bowl. Finally, he lifted away the bowl, cracked the damp towel in the air, and took a long bow.

"Okay, look," Manny said. "If you take this one's titties and Miss January's face, throw in the centerfold's ass and the beaver on this one, you've got the perfect woman."

James laughed, lowering Ricky back to the floor. "It's not that easy, Dr. Frankenstein."

"A guy can dream," Manny said.

Ricky slipped the garbage bag over his head, grabbed the towel off the floor, and rubbed his damp hair. "How do I look?" He tilted his face upward to show us both profiles.

"Like Moe from the Three Stooges," Manny said.

"Change the 'i' in Ricky to an 'o' and you look like Rocky," I said. "All we need is a dead animal strung up in the garage for you to practise your left hook." Ricky puffed up like a boxer.

"Okay, now that the crate and chair are here, who's going to help me get this thing up?" James said, nudging with his foot the box that held the disco ball.

Ricky's hand shot up as if he were desperate to answer a question in class, and I went to the box and picked up the ball. With almost no effort, James lifted Ricky onto the chair, then held the chair still as I handed Ricky the ball.

"See that eyehook there, Ricky, screwed into the rafter? Just attach it to that," James told him. Ricky stretched up, then let go, and the ball wobbled a bit. James looped the cord through the space between the rafters, before letting the last length drop along the wall. "You guys ready? Countdown! Five, four, three, two, one." He plugged it into the outlet and the ball began to spin.

"Pretty cool," I said.

"Couldn't have done it without you," James said. "Now, I got a surprise. Close your eyes." Ricky covered his eyes with his hands. Manny didn't close his, he just buried his face into a centerfold as if there was some scratch-and-sniff part to it. I half closed mine, but I could still see through my eyelashes. The moths in the garage were confused, chasing the specks of mirrored light that swept around the room.

"Open up!" he shouted. He carried a slab of supermarket cake, a few lit candles arranged on top.

"Whose birthday is it?" Ricky said.

"No one's. I just thought it could be like a garage-warming cake."

"How much are you paying for this place?" Manny said.

"Forty bucks a month," James said, setting the cake in the middle of the rug. "A neighbor up the street, Red, is handling everything for Mr. Serjeant."

"How'd you know we'd be here?" I asked.

"I just had a feeling," James said, pulling on the lobe of his left ear and smiling.

"You have forks and plates?" Manny asked.

"Who needs them. It's best to eat cake with your hands."

Manny took the first chunk, digging his hand into the corner of the cake. Then we all tore into it, grabbing at big pieces without caring what fell on the floor or how much icing smeared across our mouths.

"Why don't you guys finish that off and work on your moves a bit. The chicks dig cool dancers. I gotta take a leak." James cranked up the dial on the radio, then lit a cigarette and headed out to the backyard. Peter Frampton's guitar blared.

Manny was licking his fingers and shouting the lyrics that didn't exist, just as Frampton's guitar soared in a wild riff and the theme from *S.W.A.T.* began. Ricky twisted his body to the sound. Neither of them could stop laughing. "Do the hustle with us, Antonio," Ricky said, just as the laser beats of a Disco Dynamite hit came on. They knew the first steps, and before long we were dancing in unison, laughing, jabbing at what was left of the cake and getting dizzy in the circling lights.

James returned from the backyard, smiling. "I'm glad you boys came by tonight," he shouted over the music. As he said it, the street lights came on. I swallowed the bit of cake in my mouth and hurried home.

7

YOU'LL BE TWELVE in a few weeks and you still don't know how to tie a proper knot," my mother said. We were about to leave the house when she knelt in front of me in the hallway and tied my shoelaces so tightly I couldn't feel my toes. "That's better."

Terri walked about twenty feet ahead of us, irritated that she had to be there at all. But my mother had insisted that today was a day for family. No one was exempt except for my father, who had left earlier to get an espresso and to avoid the crowds. We hadn't walked more than halfway up our street when my mother stopped to stare at a man pounding a For Sale sign into the Machados' front lawn. Senhora Machado was watching from her porch.

"Bom dia, Georgina," Senhora Machado said.

"Angelina, I had no idea you were moving. Why didn't you say anything?"

Senhora Machado began to sweep. She would not look at my mother. "We have small children. Rogerio says it'll be safer away from the city. We're going to the suburbs, Brampton. We've saved up some money and—" The sun beat down on my head. I tried to run my fingers through my hair but my mother gently slapped my hand, afraid I would mess up the way she had set it in the goop. "We have to think of what's best for us," Senhora Machado said.

My mother shifted the lace veil from the back of her head to cover her face. "Vamos, filho."

My parents didn't talk to Terri and me about what had happened to Emanuel, but they didn't try to hide it from us either. It had been four days since Emanuel's body had been found and just over a week since he had gone missing. The day after his body was found, my mother started bringing the newspaper home with her from one of the waiting rooms at St. Mike's. She began to stack them at the foot of her night table, always folded to a story about the murder.

The newspaper reported that Emanuel was killed only twelve hours after he was kidnapped. The police said there was evidence to suggest the killers had choked him, injected him with drugs, and when that hadn't killed him they'd held his head under water in a sink. The police had found Emanuel in a green garbage bag hidden under a pile of junk on the rooftop. He had been wrapped like a mummy in electrical tape. A man called Saul Betesh—the same one who had lured Emanuel with the promise of a hamburger and a quick buck—came clean. He had turned himself in and told the police everything. That's how the other men were caught in a town called Sioux Lookout. They were hauled off a Vancouver-bound train. Parts of the story still didn't make sense to me, like why they had chosen Emanuel, and what they wanted from a twelve-year-old kid.

Once on Dundas Street, we made our way toward St. Agnes Church for the funeral. The funeral procession was snaking its way through our neighborhood. Not Emanuel's neighborhood—the Regent Park housing project—but *our* neighborhood, the respectable Portuguese one in the city's west end where the Jaques family should have lived but couldn't afford to. Some people were mad that Padre Costa, the priest of St. Mary's Parish on Portugal Square, hadn't allowed the funeral Mass to be held in his church. He blamed the media attention the boy's death had received, said he didn't want a magnifying glass held over the Portuguese community. We all knew that he made decisions based only on his own greed, and if there wasn't anything in it for him, Padre Costa rarely saw the need to help. My father and uncles said Padre Costa could keep his Lincoln Continental and his false conviction, but he would pay for giving in to believing the rumors that Emanuel had known what he was doing when he agreed to go to Saul Betesh's apartment. Padre Costa went as far as to tell some members of the congregation that he had no doubt sin was lurking in the minds of countless boys in the neighborhood. He wasn't going to support hustlers in his church. I worried he meant Ricky, but there was no way he'd know. I was sure Ricky wouldn't have blabbed stuff to Padre Costa during confession.

It looked like people had been gathering outside St. Agnes's since early that morning, hoping to get a good view for the seven-thirty Mass. I looked for Manny and his parents in the crowd. Chances were Ricky wouldn't show up. He'd be home waiting for his dad to come back from the night shift.

I saw Peter's red scarf. He kept his eyes on the sidewalk and walked against all the black figures heading toward the church. I resisted the urge to call out to him. It wouldn't be right here.

Word had spread that the mayor and a group of other important politicians were inside the church, in reserved seats. Television and radio crews were trying to work their way into the crowd, sticking microphones in people's faces, but the result was always the same: a polite nod, a raised hand, and a silent shuffle.

Men, women, and even some children were covered from head to toe in black. We walked steadily as one as if we were all on a conveyor belt stretching along Dundas Street.

The crowd stopped in front of the church and stood, waiting.

I was boxed in, squished against a man whose suit smelled of old books and Aqua Velva. He wasn't very tall. I could feel my mother's grip loosening. The crowd was pressing in and I could see the white of the inside of her arm between two people as she held on. It would have been easy to let go of her hand.

The organ music began and the shrill voice of the church's singer crackled over the speaker system they had placed outside the church. The lights and bunting, the same kind that bordered Senhor Agostinho's used-car lot on Bathurst Street, sagged against the front of the church; the Festa do Senhor da Pedra had been rescheduled out of respect for the Jaques family. My father chuckled when he heard my mother explain this to us. "It's because the priests don't want to lose money!" he said. "Always priests and money!"

I got stuck between two adults who now separated me from my mother. I had to push hard for them to move. My mother looked down at me and tried to smile. Terri kept shifting from one foot to the other—balancing herself on her platform shoes, and then crossing her legs, her face scrunched up in pain as if holding in her pee. The fingertips of one hand were covered in bandages; I still didn't know how she'd explained that to my mother. She whispered in my mother's ear. My mother sighed, then nodded. Terri pushed her way back through the horde. One man refused to give way. She nudged her shoulder into his chest. I heard the faint trace of "Perv!" and saw Senhor Batista's grin. He breathed in his cigarette and blew a steady stream through the black hole in his throat.

Senhora Gloria stood beside him. In her brown flowing robe she looked like St. Teresa, or Obi-Wan Kenobi. She was the holiest person I knew, but that hadn't stopped her from guiding my finger onto her flesh and holding it there.

I caught a glimpse of Agnes standing behind her mother before the crowd closed in again and blocked my view. Last year she'd been as flat as an ironing board. Then one day it seemed they just appeared, glorious breasts about the size of pomegranates, and it was wonderful. I loved pomegranates.

Ten minutes passed—I counted 163 honks into handker-chiefs—before Edite appeared, squeezing herself between Senhora Gloria and Senhor Batista. She dragged my sister beside her. Terri looked pissed. Senhora Gloria's face tightened as if she had sucked a lemon. Aunt Edite always dressed hip-pyish. My father said it was a sure sign she was a communist.

"I think I have an extra veil in my—"

Edite touched my mother's hand to stop her from looking for it. She shook her hair in the morning sun and stretched her red lips wide. "I spent half an hour," Edite told her, "flat-tening my hair with an iron. My hair *is* my veil." My mother tried to get Edite to go with her to church, but Edite always refused. She passed the Catholic test in other ways. She could repeat Bible sayings: *It is easier for a camel to go through the eye of a needle than for a rich man to enter the kingdom of God*, or *He that is without sin among you, let him first cast a stone.* These phrases usually ended the conversation, forcing the topic into other areas: the price of mackerel, or urging my mother, who didn't wear makeup, to make extra money selling Avon.

My mother looked at my sister. "Back so fast?"

"We ducked into Senhor João's fish market," Edite said. "He let us use the washroom—no need to go all the way home. It's like a circus here," she added. My mother pretended not to hear her.

A spell washed over the crowd. I saw the casket and understood why. It was small and glossy white. It seemed to float in the air, as light as Styrofoam over a sea of black. The brass handles flopped to the side, unused. Arms shot up to touch the coffin. People spread their palms and wiggled their fingers in the air like hungry children wanting something. The sniffles grew louder, the gurgle of sucking back snot. Some women had fainted in the heat and were carried out onto the sidewalk to be fanned. The smell of mothballs, cooking oils that had seeped into the fabric of their clothes, glycerine soap, and baby powder caked by sweat became dizzying.

The coffin tilted up at an angle. The crowd's arms carried the box across the blue sky and into the dark, incense-filled church.

I saw my father standing at the top of the steps near the church's entrance. He was dressed in a suit and held a felt hat to his chest. The sun bounced off his shiny head. I saw James there, taller than the rest and dressed in a tuxedo-printed T-shirt. He was about five feet away from where my father stood, his shoulders parting the crowd. I saw my father look back once, then again, and this time he nodded—a thank you, I thought, for James's help on the day of the pig killing. I could see my father moving his lips, speaking to James. James said something back and smiled. My shirt collar was digging into my skin. I closed my eyes and lifted my face to the warmth of the sun. When I looked back I saw Manny and Ricky had climbed the half wall of the church. Manny looked cool and relaxed in his shorts and Chinese slippers. Ricky stared at the wristwatch James had given him. They sat on the handrail beside James and my father. I could taste copper pennies at the back of my throat. My mother had said that today was a day for families, not friends. I poked my finger into the collar of my shirt and tugged. My mother drew my hand down and held it at my side.

— 8 —

A NTONIO! Come here and help." Edite didn't have a laundry room in her apartment, so she would come over and wash clothes in our basement, when she was sure my father wasn't around. "Damn sheets. Just hold on to the end until it comes through the other side," she said. "Don't pull, though. I don't want to break the wringer and have your dad blame your mom."

A tip of white sheet peeked between the two rollers of the wringer washer. She dunked her hands into the machine, the water up to her elbows. She fed the wringer again, then patted her hands dry on my mother's apron and pulled a cigarette from her pocket. She lit it, took a deep drag, and blew out the smoke like it was the thing she needed most in the world.

A small radio sat on a shelf, in front of three framed pictures: Pierre Trudeau, the Pope, and JFK. The radio was set to the Portuguese station. They were broadcasting live from Toronto City Hall, with José Rafael's voice battling static to deliver its message. *Nine days since little Emanuel was found dead and nothing so far. It's time, I say. We can't sit back any longer. That's what we've done, and look what happened!* He made it sound like the community had given up.

After the funeral, my mother had locked the front door in the middle of the day. She saw Billy, Senhor Matos's son, punch his own father on the front lawn. Senhor Matos was afraid Billy'd go to prison if he kept running downtown and beating up the *paneleiros*—Portuguese slang for homosexuals. Other people were drawn into it. I overheard my mother telling my father that it came to blows and nasty things were said between neighbors. If I hadn't been a prisoner in my own home, I would have run to the front yard to catch a bit of the rumble with my own eyes.

"My Johnny was able to wash his own clothes at your age. He'd just pop them into the machine."

I turned up the volume on the radio.

"Then he'd press a button. Not like these washers you have up here."

"My dad says dryers are useless—they waste electricity. Clotheslines in the basement are good enough."

I could picture Rafael's spit showering the microphone. We were proud and we worked hard. We did so quietly without bothering anyone. Rafael blamed the police and the politicians and the homosexuals for what had happened to Emanuel, one of our own. *Where is our voice?* he roared.

"Edite, do you believe that stuff?"

"What stuff?"

"That homosexuals are to blame for what happened to Emanuel."

Edite shoved her cigarette butt into the pipe where all the gray water from the wringer washer drained. "Bad people did a bad thing. They're to blame, no one else. But Antonio, don't get caught in it."

"In what?" I asked.

"Don't be afraid, that's all." She blew her bangs into the air. "It's when you're afraid of the world that bad things happen."

I looked into the tub of the washer. The load was almost done.

Edite leaned in and her breath tickled my skin. "I can tell you're itching to get out of here. Before you go, though, I want to tell you something. Remember, when you fight monsters, be careful that you don't become one. Do you understand?"

"Is that a proverb?" I asked.

"Yeah, the gospel according to Edite."

I hugged her, and lingered in the smell of smoke trapped in her hair. She hugged me back and wouldn't let go. I wriggled my way free, ran up the basement stairs, three at a time, then burst onto the veranda and jumped down the stairs in a death-defying bound.

The march had begun Monday afternoon. Our neighbors walked out their front doors and basement entrances onto the street. Senhora Gloria wore her wool dress but without the headband. Instead her hair was pulled back into a bun. She beamed hate rays at me because of what I knew about her. I turned away, pretending I hadn't been looking. My uncle David had decided to take a vacation day and was in shorts, black socks, and sandals. He topped off his outfit with an oil-stained *Kiss me, I'm Portuguese* T-shirt. I ducked behind a parked car, afraid he'd make me walk with him. He closed his gate and walked down the street, toward the crowd that had swelled. Senhor Anselmo stopped cutting his lawn and, with grass clippers in hand, joined the march.

At first I walked on the sidewalk, but then I followed everyone else's lead and began walking on the road. Beside me were strollers filled with crying babies, and old people with canes dressed in their Sunday best. A man in a wheelchair rolled himself along. I heard a little girl tell her grandmother she would skip rope all the way to City Hall, and as she began to skip she created space around her like a bubble. I waved up to Mr. Wilenski sipping from a tumbler on his porch. He wore sunglasses and a Chinese hat, like the ones people pictured in *National Geographic* wore when they worked in the rice fields. Mr. Wilenski and Mr. Robins lived together. They were always kind to us. After fishing at their cottage, they would often offer my mother the bass or trout they had caught. She accepted the gift with a smile and thanks, but then she'd order me to bury the fish in the backyard for fertilizer. We only ate ocean fish. The sea salt was what kept it healthy and free from disease. My mother explained once that Mr. Robins and Mr. Wilenski were brothers. I never told her I knew they had different last names. A couple of jeers were aimed at Mr. Wilenski. One guy cleared his throat and horked a greener toward him. Mr. Wilenski fumbled with his chair, then stumbled inside, slamming the door behind him. I walked along carefully now, more aware. People came down their walkways and through their front gates to merge with others that passed by in a rising jumble of roars. These were the same people who only a day before had been so sad at the funeral. Now they punched the sky with their fists.

A man held a placard that read TAR AND FATHER THEM. Photographers and television cameras were recording the march, recording the spelling mistake for the rest of the country to see. As we turned left onto Queen Street, chants for death battled it out with the honking horns of cars trapped in the jam of people. One driver in a Gremlin yelled, "Get off the fuckin' road!" A group of men and women, including

Senhora Rodrigues, who delivered homemade cheese to us every Saturday morning, swarmed the car and began to rock it. I recognized many of the men, even though I didn't know all their names, who pounded their fists on the windows the driver had rolled up in a panic.

People came from all directions. A Chrysler Cordoba, statues of Mother Mary and one of Jesus strapped to the grille, led the parade.

I kept dodging in and out of the crowd, looking for Manny and Ricky. We were blood brothers; we should have been marching together. A forest of signs read HANG THEM and DESTROY THE DIRTY PIGS. At first, I thought they referred to the murderers. But one placard flashed above the crowd read KILL THE FAGGOTS, and I knew. Edite had told me people were too ignorant to know the difference between a homosexual and a pedophile, and neither did they care. People called for the return of the noose and a clean-up of Yonge Street. Police officers on their horses became the next target in the calls of "Where were you?" mixed with accusations of "You don't care about the Portuguese."

I couldn't miss Manny in his pylon-orange T-shirt. He had managed to climb halfway up a telephone pole, in front of Brown's Short Man, where my father had bought the suit he wore for my First Communion and my sister's confirmation. I cut through the crowd and sidestepped my way onto the sidewalk. Manny was waving at me, pointing to a spot across the road, just north of the Kentucky Fried Chicken. I climbed atop a garbage can and clambered up the pole, stopping just below Manny's dirty toes hanging out of his sandals. This time I could see my mother, her hair covered with a kerchief, getting out of a Mustang. A man held the door open for her. His ginger hair was parted far off on the side. He wore sunglasses and a sport jacket with patches on the elbows. It was Dr. Patterson. I had met him before, when I had visited the hospital. He let me reach into the jar on his desk, which he filled with candies wrapped in foil. He was my mother's favorite doctor. At Christmas he wrote her long letters that he folded in cards, together with crisp fifty-dollar bills. I snuck a read of his letter the year before. He wrote about Africa and working with children in some of the poorest countries. I hated those Saturday morning commercials, with all the starving children, their faces like skeletons and their balloon stomachs. They would lie there, usually in their mother's arms or cradled in the lap of a white-skinned volunteer. In slow motion they shooed the flies that buzzed around their heads or landed on their faces. The commercials asked people to send money to somewhere on Sparks Street in Ottawa. I always felt guilty when I changed the channel.

Dr. Patterson swung the car door shut and it looked as if he was leaning over to kiss my mother. My arms turned to rubber and I thought I was going to fall to the concrete. I closed my eyes, heard my heart beating fast. I took a few deep breaths and counted to five. If he kissed her it would only be a peck on the cheek, just a thank you.

I opened my eyes and saw my mother walking up the street, away from the crowd. He jogged around the front hood, jumped back in, then swerved at the corner and peeled into the laneway.

"Who was that?" Manny asked.

"Who?" I slid down the pole and ran back into the street. I tried to lose Manny, hoped the crowd would swallow me up, but every time I looked back I could see he was there behind me, stuck like Krazy Glue.

My mother had warned me over and over to watch out for strangers, not to take anything from them or go with them if they asked for help. *Abre os teus olhos*, she kept saying, *cuidado*. I had kept my eyes open and seen her with Dr. Patterson. I didn't know who to trust.

At last I stopped. "Where's Ricky?"

"He stayed back. Doing a favor for James."

"What kind of favor?"

"Who knows?"

I was grateful Manny didn't ask about the doctor again. "Don't you care? Doesn't it bother you that James showed up just over a week ago and we don't know anything about him?"

"I know he's not a faggot, if that's what you mean."

"Yeah, but we don't know where he came from. What he wants from us."

"You sound weird."

"How?"

"I don't know. Kinda jealous that Ricky's there and you're here."

"I don't know what you're talking about."

"Look, I just like going over to his place and staring at all the tits he's got plastered on the ceiling. A sky full of tits. That's all I care about."

"I get that. I just don't—"

"Who cares. Don't tell me the old farts have gotten to you. That Emanuel kid was fresh off the boat. We're not like that. Anyone tries something with me—" Manny made a karate chop and jabbed his knee in the air like he was aiming for someone's balls, "he'd get it where the sun don't shine."

There must have been thousands of people at City Hall when we arrived, more people than those that filled our neighborhood streets for the Festa do Senhor Santo Cristo parade in the spring. Manny couldn't resist flying some paper cups, newspaper, and then plastic bags over the subway vents. It was a competition— whose object could go the highest and stay up the longest— garbage kites without string. They floated twenty or thirty feet, hovered, as if taking in the whole scene, before suddenly twisting and dipping in midair. I pictured my mother getting out of Dr. Patterson's car, how she looked with lipstick on, something I had never seen before. With every coffee cup I let go, my nervousness lifted away, until I was sure what I had witnessed was nothing. *The streetcars had probably been blocked by the march. He was just giving her a lift. My mother would never do anything wrong. She went to church and she meant it, not like Senhora Gloria.* Manny stretched his Bitondo's Pizzeria T-shirt, letting it fill like a balloon with the gush of air that blasted up through the grates.

"One of our children has been killed." José Rafael's voice was picked up by the microphones on the stage and amplified across Nathan Phillips Square. "How many times did he cry for mommy or daddy . . . how many times did he scream"—at this point Senhor Rafael switched to English—"*leave me alone?*"

"Bandidos, bandidos!" the crowd chanted. I looked at all the angry people, mostly men who were out of work, others who had left their jobs in their construction gear or janitor uniforms, shouting like my father did after I brought him the wrong screwdriver from his toolbox. I needed to pee.

They were all waiting to hear from the mayor or some municipal politician to tell them their plans. They weren't there for fancy words or promises to bring back the death penalty or strategies on how to clean up the city so it was safe again and people could feel protected. They wanted vengeance. They wanted to string the killers up in someone's garage and slit their throats like slaughtered pigs.

I shuffled away from Manny, moving along the edge of the reflecting pool—its green bottom dotted with pigeon shit. In the winter it would transform into a skating rink. José Rafael saw the crowd growing restless. He urged everyone to continue their march to the legislative steps of Queen's Park. One man tried to climb over in front of him to get to the stage. Another guy tore his shirt open and started thumping his chest with his fists. By now I was in the middle of it all.

"Kill them!" shouted one man who carried a sign that read DEATH TO ALL SEX CRIMINALS, and he chopped his free hand through the air.

The shouts began to swell. I made my way to a large concrete planter near the side of the stage and climbed up. I looked back over the thousands of bobbing heads to where I had left Manny. He stood atop the vents, still tossing garbage into the air. I looked again at the crowd. People shook their signs and huddled together toward the stage: STRIP THE STRIP and TODAY EMANUEL DIES TOMORROW OTHERS MIGHT DIE TOO.

I couldn't hold on any longer. I jumped down and ran behind the stage, pulled open my zipper, and peed against some plywood. I looked over my shoulder before I signed my initials, A and R in streams of yellow cursive.

Minutes later, Manny caught up with me. "Hey! I was looking all over. Where'd you go?"

"I needed to pee." I looked across Nathan Phillips Square. The crowd was breaking up. Some broken posters and signs and stuffed dummies that looked like the killers or the politicians, I wasn't sure which, was all that was left behind. The city garbage trucks would get it all cleaned up and in a couple of hours you'd never know there had been a demonstration. My father said nothing would change until people started working again—work made people forget. My mother said the problem was everyone worked too much.

"Are you heading over to Queen's Park?" Manny said.

"No. Are you?"

"I'm gonna stick around," Manny said. "I've got my eye on some good ones." He pointed to his butt. He had come prepared: his file and snips peeked out from his back pocket.

"You need help?" I asked.

"James says I can't let you help."

"Why would he say that?" I said.

"I don't know, but I saw him talking to your dad the other day. At the funeral. Maybe your dad asked him to protect his golden boy."

"Screw you!" I said as Manny disappeared around the corner.

It was getting dark when I wound my way back to my alley. I thought of how freaked out my mother would be, my having been gone all this time. But I'd let her sweat a little longer. James's garage door was open just enough for me to see a sliver of light. I knocked before raising the door higher, surprised by my own courage.

"Anyone here?" I asked, stepping into the garage. The small black-and-white TV was on, its bunny ears bent and taped together. The picture was fuzzy—a bunch of mosquitoes on the screen. I could hear his steps on the boards above.

James climbed down the ladder in his bare feet. We were alone. I thought Ricky would be there; he had a way of making me feel seven feet tall and bulletproof.

"I don't need a babysitter to watch over me—I can take care of myself."

"I know that."

"You're not my father."

"I know that too. I also know you're a smart kid," he said. "Edite told me."

"Edite?"

"She asked me to keep an eye on you, that's all. Your friends too. She interviewed a bunch of us who work on the strip. They're closing it down. The head shops, the massage parlours, the dance clubs. Edite's writing about it for the paper." He explained things calmly, and I could feel my heartbeat slowing down. He moved closer to me. I heard the faint sound of tobacco burning as he took a drag. He bent down to pick up his paintbrush.

I closed my eyes for a second. James smelled of armpits.

"You're a special boy, Antonio," he whispered, taking another step toward me.

"Antonio!" Edite called out.

The light of the garage illuminated Edite, who stood tall in the lane, all dressed up in wedge shoes and her shawl tied around her waist. "What are you doing here?" I caught the concern in her face. James whistled and she cracked a smile.

"Your mother's worried sick. You need to go home right now," she said, all the while looking at James.

I walked my bike home, but before going in looked back. Edite's body had relaxed, slinked against the garage doorway. I could hear James still urging her to come in. For a moment, it looked as if she would. Instead, she turned and walked up the laneway.

My lungs were filling up with a burning fire—no room left. My mouth was dry, my throat blocked, and yet their voices grew nearer, louder. "Treat you good, like one of the boys. Have some fun, lots of play with our adult toys." The alley seemed to stretch forever. I saw Senhora Gloria leaning against a garage door, her eyes smeared with black mascara. She lifted her skirt to show the dimply flesh of her leg. I ran past her. When I dared to look back I saw my mother instead. I stopped running and turned toward her. I was safe; she wouldn't let the men catch me. I tried to call out to her but my voice was gone. I took off again, cupped my ears to stop the giggling and laughter. That's when I saw Ricky crouched at James's feet. James was handing him five-dollar bills. I stopped. Suddenly, the men who were chasing me touched me with their large hands. I felt them tearing at my shirt, tearing at me. I cried for help but again no sound.

The orange numbers glowed 1:20 a.m., then flipped to 1:21. I sat up in bed, with my arms crossed over my knees, hugging them to my chest. If I was quiet, didn't move, the trembling might go away and I would hear my house breathe. I tried it for a minute or two, but I couldn't stop shaking. I heard the smash of glass breaking. I ran to the window and saw two stretched shadows running down Palmerston Avenue.

A glow came through Mr. Wilenski's broken window. I drew the curtains and jumped back into bed. This time I pulled the clock radio under the covers and pressed it to my ear. I took in the scratchy static and the world got quiet.

9

A HOT PLATE WITH two elements sat atop a stripped drop-leaf table. Ricky poured some hot water from the kettle into a mug. He stirred in a spoonful of Nescafé, careful not to clink too loudly, then tucked the spoon in his back pocket. Biting his lip in concentration, he climbed up the ladder and left the mug on the floor of the loft.

"James likes to wake up to a hot cup of coffee," he told me.

In the days that followed the march, my parents tried to keep me in the house, but it was a losing battle. Everyone slipped back into their routines. The newspapers no longer carried pictures of Emanuel, and stories about the march had disappeared from the six o'clock news. We all pretended everything was okay. I guess we figured if you pretended long enough it would be. I wasn't sure if I trusted James, but I played along. Manny and Ricky were spending all their time in his garage and I didn't want to miss out on anything. Besides, Edite told me she thought my father had spoken to James, asked him to keep an eye out for me, the way everyone in the neighborhood was expected to. I was pretty sure that even if he had, my mother knew nothing about it. She never once asked me about James. Meanwhile, James made us feel his garage was pretty much our own. We could use it as long as we took care of it and of him. Manny had been sneaking James's clothes home, wrapped in a plastic bag and tucked under his arm. When his parents went to work, he would shake the bag into the washer. He'd bring them back, still damp, to be strung along the clothesline that James had tacked along the peaked fold of the loft. He never asked, but I snuck James food from our fridge. My mother cooked the week's meals on the weekend—roasts and large pots of soup and stews that were full of cabbage, sausage, and sweet potatoes. If a little was missing, no one would notice.

It was ten o'clock and we still had not heard James's thick-soled feet on the floorboards. Ricky climbed up the ladder again and peeked into the space. "He's not here. You think he's okay?"

"He's fine," Manny said, and sat himself down at the breakfast table, his eyes glued to the map he had flattened there the night before.

I went over to have a look. "What are you doing?"

"The richer they are, the better the bikes," Manny said, his finger tracing his route for the day.

"Hey, Ricky, wanna go down to the fort park?" I asked. Before Emanuel, before James, we would go down to the park at the foot of Bathurst, where the city had created a mini construction site for kids to play and build. My dad hated it. *I no come to Canada for you to work in construction*, he had said when he found out where we were going. I didn't care; our fort was almost finished when Emanuel disappeared.

Ricky looked around the garage. "I got to go home, do some things for my dad," he said.

"What should I do, then?"

"Look pretty." Manny lifted his eyes from his map. "Sit back and look pretty, that's all."

"What the hell does that mean, dipshit?"

"Don't get all worked up," Manny said, raising both of his middle fingers.

"Stick them up your ass and rotate," I said.

Manny pushed his chair back. Ricky came to my side and blocked him.

"You're the lucky one," Manny said.

"What's your fuckin' problem?" I said.

"Don't play stupid. You got your aunt and your dad sniffing around, telling James to look out for you. You're no better than us," Manny said, his face close enough that our noses almost touched.

"You jealous?" I said, my eyes glued to his.

"Nah. The way I see it, I'll do my part and James'll let me spend as much time in here as I like," Manny said.

The roar of a familiar engine made him brush past me and lift the door. Manny's brother, Eugene, was cruising up the lane in his red Trans Am, a golden phoenix rising from a bed of flames across its hood. Eugene's fuckmobile, Manny called it. Manny said Eugene had no problem finding someone to get into it. Eugene was twenty-one, like James, and had been working in construction ever since he dropped out of school at sixteen. Eugene could afford a Trans Am and, according to Manny, an engagement ring for Amilcar's sister, Lygia, who was seventeen.

The car stopped in front of the garage and Lygia rolled down the tinted window. She had recently permed her hair with one of the home kits they advertised on TV. Manny had once walked in on her, half-naked in his bathroom when his parents were at work. He couldn't stop talking about her tits for a month. Lygia flicked open a compact and fixed her curls.

"What are you guys doing?" Eugene called, the furry dice swaying from his rear-view mirror.

"Hanging around," Manny replied.

Eugene nodded, trying to take a look inside the garage. "Later!" he called out. His car farted a couple of times up the laneway before the roar took over.

Through the Trans Am's cloud of dust, we didn't notice James walk up beside us. "Hey, boys!" he said. He had a faraway look about him, like Moses in the movie *The Ten Commandments* after he witnessed the burning bush. James had draped his T-shirt through the side loop in his painter pants, which were barely hanging on to his hips.

"I made some coffee for you," Ricky said. "Probably cold now but I can warm it up."

"Thanks, little man, but I just need some sleep."

"Where were you?" I said.

He stretched his arms and rose on his toes. "You guys promise to keep a secret? I came across this Indian girl who got her face smashed up by her pimp, so I helped her out. Took a few bucks and got a motel room so I could clean her up, keep her safe for a little while. I must have crashed. Before long, this chick's got her hand in my pants like she's lookin' to pay me back."

"So what happened?" Manny was practically drooling.

"Will she be okay?" Ricky asked. I thought Manny was going to slap him.

"Things'll work out. I could use a shower, though. A real scrubbin'." He picked at his groin, adjusted his cock. "Damn hose I hooked up from the backyard just trickles over my head like cat piss."

"Why didn't you shower in the motel?" I said.

Manny looked at me like I was a moron.

"Didn't think of it, I guess," James said.

"Well, no one's home at my place," I said, my scalp tingling. "You can take a quick shower in the basement."

Manny's eyes got huge, and Ricky's mouth made a perfect O.

The minute I said it I wanted to pee. I wasn't allowed to bring people into the house without my parents there, not even my friends. But I couldn't take it back. Manny'd never let me forget it.

James tossed his T-shirt into the corner of the garage and emptied his pockets: crumpled bills mixed with coins and a couple of Sheik condom packets. We had seen the wrappers before, windswept against the fences in our lanes, but those were always empty. "You sure?"

I nodded, trying to look uninterested. He reached in his back pocket and placed some cherry bombs and a string of firecrackers on the counter.

Manny stared at the firecrackers but didn't move.

"Now, boys, you better not blow up the joint," James said. "Antonio, lead the way."

James ducked through the doorway and came into our damp basement. He trailed his fingertips over my father's workbench, along the shelves stocked with Mason jars and tin cans. He stopped to look at the photographs that lined the paneled walls and started to fire questions at me. *How long had we lived in the house? How high did I think the basement ceiling was, between the joists, of course? Who lived here before and how many bathrooms were there?*

"How old were you in this one?" he said, pointing to one of the photos.

"Probably one or so," I said.

"It's a nice family shot." My mother sat on a chair with me on her lap dressed in shorts and a vest and tie. My father stood behind us, looking tall in his suit, one hand on the back of my mother's chair, the other on Terri's shoulder. She stood in front of him, wearing a tartan dress, bobby socks, and shiny shoes. She was the only one in the photograph not smiling.

"You can't go upstairs," I said, without needing to.

"Can I ask you something?" James said. "What's that Portuguese word I hear in the laneway sometimes—sounds like *feel you*?"

"Filho?"

"That's it."

"Son. It means son, but my uncles and aunts call me it too. Manny's dad calls me filho. I think it's a way of saying I belong to them, to the neighborhood. It means they care, I guess."

"Nice."

I felt my mouth getting pasty and my joints were achy.

"What's that thing over there?"

"It's a bidet." I turned the faucet on and the water shot up out of the spout in the center of the bowl. "All Portuguese houses have them."

"I've never seen a drinking fountain in a bathroom before."

"It's to wash yourself. You know, between your legs," I said.

He started laughing, hard. "I grew up with a shithouse, man, fifty yards back from the house. And here you all are." I looked at him, filling the bathroom space with his body. He turned on the shower and began to unbutton his pants.

"I'll get you a towel."

Keeping watch upstairs by the living-room window, in case my sister came home, I heard James trying to mimic Rod Stewart's voice—"Tonight's the night, gonna be alright." I looked over at Mr. Wilenski's house, forcing myself to think of something other than James singing in my shower. A large sheet of plywood covered their window. I wondered what Mr. Wilenski was planning to do. My father said they'd be moving soon. "They better move. If they no move, lots of people make troubles for them." Getting people right was one of the things my father was proud of.

The shower finally stopped running. I raced downstairs just as James appeared from a cloud of steam: barefoot, damp hair, his underwear tucked in the front pocket of his jeans, which he hadn't buttoned up to the top.

"That was the best damn shower I've had since I left home."

"Where do you come from?" I asked.

"Why do you want to know?"

"I don't know," I said. "Just curious, I guess. Where did you grow up?"

"A town. Up north."

"Why did you come down here?" I asked. The fog in the bathroom was beginning to clear. I reached for a hand towel to dry the shower door.

"There were no jobs where I'm from," he said. He shook his head a little, wiggled his fingers in his ears. "Traveled around a bit. Moved all over the place before settling down. This is where it's happening, little man." I caught his reflection in the shower door. He buttoned up the last two buttons of his fly with one hand, staring at me as he did. I wanted to rewind to James's garage, except this time I'd keep my damn mouth shut. "You wanna know something?" he said, flinging the towel at my face. When I whipped it off my head he was standing right in front of me, smiling. I could hear his breathing and I wanted to close my eyes. "Where I come from we don't wash our asses in drinking fountains." James laughed as he messed up my hair.

"Were you making that story up?"

"Which one?"

"About the Indian girl who got beat up." When James had told the story I couldn't shake the feeling he was just trying to impress us.

"It went something like that." He checked himself in the mirror one last time. "We should scram before you get caught in here with me. We don't want people to talk."

We made our way back from the cool of the basement out into the backyard. I felt relieved to be outside again. I was crouching down to raise our garage door when James's hand grabbed hold of my shoulder. "I won't forget this, you know."

"It was nothing," I said.

"Okay, filho," he whispered, before strutting into the sunny laneway. Manny and Ricky were standing outside James's garage, waiting. Manny must have lit some firecrackers already—the smell of sulphur hung in the air. When they saw us coming, they ran down the lane to meet us. As we approached his garage, James raised his arms into the air. "Now, where's my coffee?"

Then we heard a scream. "Help!" It was Edite. I squinted upward and could trace her shape on her landing. She was pointing toward the alley that cut onto Palmerston. "Help her!" We all ran in the direction Edite was pointing and found Senhora Gloria standing over Agnes, pounding her fist into the girl's head. With the other hand she whipped the braid across Agnes's back. The garden shears were lying on the ground. We watched, our feet glued to the ground. Agnes had curled herself up like a pill bug and sobbed into her bare legs.

"Puta! Why you go and treat us like this?" Senhora Gloria yelled from deep inside her guts. "You can die on the streets. I don't care. You hear me?" Her Portuguese was slurred. "If it's the last thing I do, I'm going to rip that sin out of you." Senhora Gloria's red face looked our way but she didn't care about the audience. "You is good for nothing!"

Agnes opened up and laid her cheek against the fence, her chin up in the air exposing the soft skin of her neck. Senhora Gloria picked up the garden shears and sprang toward her. Edite's scream channelled through the laneway, threw Senhora Gloria off for only a moment. "Puta! You're a disgrace!"

James leapt into action like a superhero. He grabbed Senhora Gloria just as she was about to lower the shears. He squeezed her wrist until the shears dropped to the ground. He kicked them away, and Ricky picked them up and took off.

"I no want you in my home. Mentiras! Ungrateful girl. Mentiras! You know how hard I work? How hard we work for you? And you do this. That baby will be a bastard! Perdida. Tas perdida!" She spat at Agnes and missed, before turning to stagger home.

My mouth opened but the words didn't come out. I closed my mouth and tried again. Still nothing. It didn't matter, really. What would I have said anyway? The idea that Agnes was pregnant—that some guy had done things with her—was beginning to sink in. Once again, James had saved the day, while I could only stand there and watch.

10

I RODE MY BIKE DOWN to the Bathurst streetcar loop. Along the way there seemed to be more boarded-up stores. There were men outside the Paddock Tavern who should have been at work. I avoided the Princes' Gates because it was the busiest entrance to the Ex, our city's equivalent of a country fair, which ran for two weeks every August. I made my way straight to the Bulova clock tower, the tallest building at the Canadian National Exhibition, past the smoking carnies collecting tickets, moving cranks, levers, pushing buttons with their tobacco-stained fingers. A few of them were on break and had gathered along the side of the wooden rollercoaster, the Flyer, where a bunch of generator cubes rested on wooden blocks. Everything was hooked up to miles of rubber tubes and electric cables the same way my grandmother had lines connected to her before she died.

One of the guys bent down and crushed his cigarette butt into the asphalt. He lifted a container of water over his head and let it drip over his oily hair, shaking off the beads like a wet dog. The guy caught me staring. He cupped his crotch with one hand, jiggled his package a bit, and then blew me a kiss. I ran away. I kept looking over my shoulder to make sure he wasn't following me.

Always the same dirty men and tattooed women working the game booths. They drew you in with promises, "Hit the black dot and win a prize!" "Everyone's a winner!" They smoked their cigarettes under a sky of stuffed pink elephants, gigantic teddy bears and snakes with felt tongues, rubber bats and monkeys that dangled from long, sharp sticks, engraved mirrored plaques with western-styled letters next to a bottle of Molson—the kind of thing I'd try to win if we had a basement bar in our house. There were framed posters of Ann-Margret kicking up her heels, the Dallas Cowboys Cheerleaders, and a smiling Farrah Fawcett with her nipples poking against her red bathing suit. The food stalls sold hot dogs and fries. The smells of fried onions and popcorn mixed with the candy smell of Tiny Tom doughnuts. The candy floss hung upside down from the ceiling like blue and pink clouds. Corn dogs were arranged beside candy apples, all glossy red in their glass cabinets.

Today was Children's Day, the only day during the two weeks of the fair when kids got in free. Most years the place was crammed with a crush of kids my age, but today the grounds looked empty. Most of the kids I saw were with their parents, holding hands. Attendance numbers were down, even though city officials and politicians had been going on and on about how safe the city was. But the more they said it, the more it sounded like it wasn't true. Edite said that fear had infected the city like a cancer.

I sat underneath the Bulova tower. The clock read 11:08. My friends were late. They were supposed to meet me after Ricky got his dad into bed. I had told my mother that we'd be coming as a gang and that we'd stick together, even when we went to the bathroom. Staying around the house or playing in our laneway was one thing, she said—at least the neighbors could watch out for us—but going to a place like the Ex with all those people was just too dangerous. She refused to change her mind, even after I pointed out that she was always working, and that she would never be able to take me to the Ex herself.

When Edite had called to say she might pass by the Ex and wondered if my family would be there, I told her—in a voice that made it sound like my life was over—all the reasons I had already given my mother for letting me go. She told me to put my mother on the phone. When my mother hung up, she went to her purse. "Here," she said, and handed me twenty dollars. "It's your birthday present." I kept the bill damp and crumpled between my sweaty palm and handlebars the whole ride down. I wasn't sure if Edite had told my mother she would be going to the Ex too, or if something else had changed my mother's mind. I wondered if maybe she knew I'd seen her with Dr. Patterson. Maybe the money wasn't really a birthday present. Maybe it was meant to keep me quiet instead.

I climbed up on the stage to get a better view, and in the distance I saw Ricky floating in the air. A closer look and I could see him sitting on James's shoulders, taller than anyone else. A stuffed snake was coiled around his neck, and he bopped up and down with every step. He looked safe, like no one could touch him.

James had taken Agnes in to live with him. He told us to stay away. He said we needed to give her some privacy. That was a week ago—a whole week without meeting in his garage. The first couple of days, we went back to doing all the things we used to do: catching grasshoppers, racing across roofs, and rolling old tires down the laneway until they crashed into garages and we'd take off running. Despite the ban, I was still sneaking food over, enough for James and Agnes now. And Manny said there were things James still needed him and Ricky to do.

"What things?" I asked.

"Nothing really," Ricky said.

"I'm not sure what he has for dickless wonder here." Manny sucked on his cigarette. "But James has to support Agnes and her baby now too, so I got a few more bikes to hawk, that's all."

Ricky said he needed to steal more of the stuff James needed from stores like Woolworth's and Senhora Rosa's. He was good at it. He was small and could get in and out quickly. What it was that James actually did was still a bit of a mystery to me. Edite said a lot of guys like James came to the big city to work the streets. Hustlers. She said they did things to survive. I told her Manny said James was some kind of gigolo. I left out the part where Manny said James took care of horny old women who would throw him fifty bucks to do things their rich geezer husbands couldn't. "Manny says he saw it in a movie," I added.

"I'm sure James *sometimes* meets with women," Edite said. "Do you know what I mean, Antonio?" I nodded, even though I wasn't sure. "Deep down James is a good kid who just needs people to see the good in him, that's all." That part I understood. He was taking care of Agnes, while I was just a useless dipshit.

"So this is it?" James said, sneaking up breathless as he twirled Ricky down from his shoulders. Manny leaned against the tower and picked his hair.

"Agnes isn't with you?" I said. I had hoped she'd come. I wanted to win her a teddy bear or maybe buy her something.

"She wasn't up to it. Still needs to rest."

"What do you want to do first?" Ricky asked.

"It's Antonio's birthday," James said, a smile stretched across his face. "Let him choose. Me, I don't have much of a stomach for rides. But I saw here"—he unfolded the brochure he'd picked up at the entrance—"they have a Scottish World Festival. How 'bout that?"

"Why?" Manny shot out. "I want rides, not a bunch of men in skirts."

"Kilts," I corrected. I knew we'd all go with James, if that was what he wanted to do.

"My father was Scottish," James said. "But I didn't grow up with any of it, just wanna see how it makes me feel."

James sat glued to the burly men tossing their logs and hammers. With every winning toss he would jump up and yell. Meanwhile, Manny scanned the stands for distractions.

Three girls sat a few bleachers below us. Two of them had flipped hair, and the one that sat in the middle wore her hair in a ponytail. All three of them wore tight hip-huggers that went so low you could see the dimples above their ass cracks. Manny kept trying to throw popcorn down their pants. Whenever they turned around, they looked right past him, straight at James. He was wearing a tank top and a pair of jeans he called loons. The flares covered his wedgies. He stood over six feet tall but he seemed almost seven feet when, after the hammer toss, he bought himself a felt top hat with his name spelled in exaggerated silver sparkly loops.

"How about lunch?" he said.

"Can we come back to see the horses?" Ricky asked. "I want to see the Clydesdales."

"Yeah, great," Manny said. "The smell of horse shit right after lunch."

James grinned down at me. "Hey, how about I win you something for your birthday?"

"Nah, I don't need anything."

"Not even that poster of Farrah?" Manny said. "I'd love to have that hanging on my bedroom door."

I was drawn to the framed poster of Evel Knievel standing beside his motorcycle. The deep V-neck of his flared collar exposed his hairy chest, and he wore a cape like a superhero. I kept thinking when I grew up I wanted to look just like him, with big hockey-stick sideburns and cool shades.

James went over to the first game he saw. He spent at least ten bucks trying to get a softball into an old milk can. The carnie kept offering two balls for the price of one, then telling him he was close and couldn't lose.

"Let's go, James," I said, tugging at his undershirt. "It's fixed."

He handed the carnie a couple of quarters. His hand covered the top of the ball. James closed one eye. He flicked his wrist up and the ball moved in a perfect arc and landed right in the mouth of the milk can, only to pop back up and out.

"Aghhh," the carnie moaned. He came up from the counter with a small pink snake. "Here you go, bud," he said, "goes with that other one your friend has wrapped around his neck."

James reached up and yanked at the leg of a giant teddy bear. The bear fell and practically knocked the guy over.

"Hey! What do you think—?"

"Don't fuck with me, brother." James's fist had knotted

the guy's T-shirt right under his chin. With his free hand James scooped the large bear toward me.

"Happy Birthday, Antonio."

The Food Building was a huge warehouse filled with kiosks. Voices boomed "Free coupons!" "Ten-cent spaghetti—cheese extra!" I saw funnel cakes arranged into towers, schnitzel piled into hills alongside kielbasa and pails of sauerkraut. The smells of curries coming from a Caribbean place tickled my nose and made me want to sneeze. We walked around snacking on samples. Every so often a pigeon would swoop down from the rafters, shit on the floor or tables before picking up crumbs or french fries and flying back up to its perch. It was hard to decide, but I ended up getting a burger, fries, and a Pepsi because I took the Pepsi Challenge at last year's fair and I chose Pepsi.

We paid for James's lunch. He had wanted to pay for us, but we said he was *our* guest and we knew he had spent most of his money on winning the damn bear. We found a spot of brown grass outside and sat with our food in our laps, careful nothing could touch the grass or the goose shit.

Manny slurped on his spaghetti. "I didn't bust my ass so you could throw cash away on a toy for Antonio."

James ignored him. "It was a nice thing you did, giving your bear to that kid," he said to me.

"Well, I saw the way she was looking at it and thought she might like to have it," I said. The truth was I didn't want to drag a huge stuffed animal around with me all day.

"You're a good kid, Antonio. See that, boys? You just need to be good and the world will be good back to you."

"And I won't keep handing over cash so you can play house with Agnes." Manny always said things out loud that I wish I could. "You said if we helped you with the rent we could use the garage any time."

"It's just for now," James said.

"You know who the father is?" Manny went on. "It's her stepfather, Senhor Batista. She's a slut who opened her legs for him," he said. "Part of the wedding agreement."

James got up and with one hand lifted Manny to his feet by the neck. "Who the fuck told you that?"

I pulled at James's belt and T-shirt. Ricky wedged himself between Manny and James, trying to push Manny back with his body.

"You little shit! Answer me, who told you that?" Spit was foaming in the corners of his mouth. Manny's legs dangled like a puppet's. His face was red. I rammed my shoulder into James's side and he let go. Manny dropped to the grass, taking Ricky down with him. Coughing and wheezing, he rubbed his neck.

James bent over and yelled in Manny's face. "Who told you that?"

"I overheard my father tell my mother last night," Manny said. "You fuckin' crazy or something?"

James leaned closer. "What did he say?"

"Senhor Batista was drunk and bragged to the other men about doing it with Agnes. It was his bonus for marrying a divorced woman—something like a two-for-one deal."

James cocked his elbow and was about to backhand Manny, but Ricky sprang from the grass and ran into the crowds.

"Ricky!" I shouted. "Wait!"

He was too small to see and all I could do was follow in his direction. I was happy to hear James panting alongside me, and Manny bounding up behind. In the dizzying heat, I broke through near the Grandstand, its aluminum bleachers packed with people, their heads to the sky watching the air show. I heard the slam of jet noise and I covered my ears. A spooked police horse was calmed by the officer riding him. "I know where Ricky is!" I ran ahead. I could hear the thud of feet behind me.

In the dark, cool space, the smell of horse shit mixed with that of straw. Flies buzzed. Horseshoes clopped on concrete. The metal stall gates clanged.

At the end of one of the rows, I saw Ricky stroking the massive animal. I moved closer—the blue ribbons nailed to the stall door—and saw the horse's cock almost reaching the ground. "Ricky," I whispered. James and Manny were suddenly beside me. I took a step toward Ricky, but James's arm shot out, his hand spread out against my chest to stop me.

The horse looked to the side, its head down.

James drew in his breath. Ricky nuzzled the horse's chin and leaned his shoulder under its massive barrel chest. "It'll be okay," Ricky whispered. He stood on his toes, reached way up and patted little clouds of dust from the horse's neck. "Everything will be okay."

11

M Y FATHER HAD BEEN out all day excavating Senhor Melo's basement. My mother and Aunt Edite sat on the crushed-velvet sectional as my sister painted their toes. Edite had ordered a whole kit from Avon and signed my mother up to help her make some extra cash. Worm-picking season would be over soon. School was a few days away, and after my shitty time at the Ex, that first day couldn't come any faster. Manny and Ricky and me would get back into our routine, we would forget about James and leave Emanuel's murder behind us. It had been five weeks since his body had been found, but people still kept their windows shut and their doors locked. Our neighbors, who once lugged their lawn chairs up onto our porch to chat and share stories, remained behind their closed doors. Fights were breaking out all around our neighborhood—broken fences, property line disputes, mean gossip—old hurts freshly opened. And there were arguments about whose kids were being raised properly and whose were doomed.

On my lap I cradled a bowl full of limpets in their flat-tened, cone-shaped shells, a delicacy fresh from the Azores. They had only recently come into season, sticking to the rocks along São Miguel's shore. The ones that were covered in hairy algae creeped me out so I tossed those to the side, but I cut the rest. Their pale yellow flesh squirmed, their edges ruffled as I slashed the muscle that attached them to their shell.

"Slow down, filho. You know how much those things cost? Your father would kill me if he knew."

I had to eat them with buttered cornbread to stretch them out. Senhor João, the fishmonger, charged a hefty price for Azoreans to smell and taste the ocean. Home, my father always said.

"Eat up, Antonio. It's your birthday," Edite said.

"I bought a cake for you," my mother said. "I know it's late, but with work and everything . . . anyways, Senhora Estrela made sure the ladies at the bakery made it with extra icing." The mention of cake and I couldn't help but notice my mother's breasts coned like party hats.

"Twelve. I remember when my Johnny turned twelve."

"Ouch! Filha, you're tearing my skin with those things."

"Mãe," Terri whined, "I need to push back the cuticle so the polish goes on evenly."

"No color. Just a clear coat or a very pale pink. You know how your father gets."

"Where is he?" I asked, my mouth full of limpet and bread.

"He said he was running late. He should make it home for some cake. We have to finish soon. I don't want him to walk in on us like this."

"Relax, Georgina," Edite said. "It's okay to be pampered every once in a while. You need to take care of yourself."

My mother said, "The city hired a man to close down the sex shops. It's all we talked about at work today. They're going to clean it all up."

"Craziness," Edite said.

"I read the politicians are scared they won't get re-elected," Terri said, crouched at my mother's feet. "They're freakin' out." She had been wearing the same Bay City Rollers jeans with their red tartan cuffs for the whole week, ever since she scored tickets to the concert. Suck up, I thought. Anything to impress Edite.

"Nothing good will come of it," Edite said. "Now the owners are forcing the girls who work for them to sign an affidavit naming politicians they've serviced."

"Edite!" my mother said, shaking her head as if to shush her.

"What? They're old enough."

After the Ex, I had gone to Edite to ask her about Agnes and Senhor Batista. I thought she might know the whole story. She always did. She tried to explain it to me, how it was that a father, even a stepfather, could have done that to his kid. But she couldn't explain it to me in a way that made sense. She was so angry that the right words just weren't there, she said. She did manage to say that she wished she could cut off Senhor Batista's dick. I asked Edite why Agnes couldn't live with her. Edite said she had offered but James got protective; he said he'd be the one to take care of Agnes and the baby.

I wanted to shock my mother with what I actually knew. About James. About Ricky. About Dr. Patterson. About Agnes. But then I figured my mother already knew who fathered Agnes's baby. She said nothing because they had their lives and we had ours.

"It's going to be a war zone," Edite said.

"Even the inmates at a prison gathered over three hundred dollars for the I Give a Damn Fund," I said. "It's thirteen thousand dollars now."

Both my mother and sister turned to me. Terri smiled; she knew Edite was feeding my curiosity about the murder case. Limpet juice ran down my chin. I dabbed my mouth and chin with my bread.

"Money isn't the answer. It doesn't change anything," Edite said quickly, before my mother's concern about where I had learned such a thing could form into questions. "We should all try to think happier thoughts," she said.

My mother looked from me to the picture of Jesus that hung over the TV. The image would blink at you depending on where you were standing. His chest would close, the skin sealed over his heart, then open as he blinked. I would shake my head back and forth just to see him blinking, the scar healing, over and over.

"I heard Senhora Gloria and Senhor Batista are going back home," my mother said. "They're not feeling very safe here. The city's changed. They've decided to go."

"I guess that's a happy thought," Edite said.

The limpet I was chewing got stuck in my throat. I gagged and coughed.

"Yes, it is," my sister said. "Senhor Batista is a pervert."

"What about Agnes?" I said.

"Senhora Rosa says she has gone to live with her father." Agnes's father had beat Senhora Gloria so bad that she slept with a knife under her pillow. That wasn't a reason for divorce in our community, and according to my father, Senhora Gloria got her marriage annulled—which meant they were never really married—only after signing a hefty cheque to the archdiocese. So Senhora Gloria had left her husband because he was abusive, and yet she would leave her daughter with him? That's how concerned the neighborhood was about their children's safety? Hypocrites, I thought, knowing it was the correct use of one of the words I had studied in the dictionary.

"Mr. Wilenski's house is still up for sale," my mother said.

"Poor man. They're both so spooked they won't tell anyone where they're moving to. Everyone's afraid—"

"Fear is a terrible thing," my mother said quickly.

Edite lit a cigarette. My mother fanned the air. "At least there'll be a wedding soon," Edite said.

"Who?" my mother asked.

No way James would marry Agnes without telling us. He didn't have to marry Agnes; it wasn't his baby.

"Eugene Daniel is going to marry that girl from the Continent," Edite said. "She came up to me flashing her diamond ring. He bought it at Peoples Jewellers, the one at the Dufferin Mall, was all she said, twisting her hand in the sun to get the little twinkle."

Terri laughed. "What an idiot."

"They're young and they'll survive," my mother said. "What's love if it doesn't jump over a few hurdles?"

A large, meaty limpet bounced in my mouth.

"Mãe, you need to get rid of the hair on your legs," Terri said, her face contorted in disgust. "It looks horrible when you wear panty hose. This isn't from Avon. It's Nair with baby oil."

"No! Once you do it you have to keep doing it. And the hair comes back thicker. I don't have time for that," my mother insisted. "I *work*."

"But they look like angora leg warmers."

Edite nodded to my sister, who opened the bottle of Nair and began to rub the sickening smell onto my mother's legs.

"If you're going to sell Avon to all those women you work with, you need to look the part." Edite gently punched my mother on the arm. "Besides, you never know when you'll meet a handsome man. A girl needs to be prepared."

"Don't talk foolishness, Edite."

"You never know when a nice man, oh I don't know, maybe a *doctor*, will take a fancy to you." Edite giggled, nudging my mother's elbow. My mother couldn't look at me; I knew it was shame that flushed her face red.

The tension broke as my father entered the room. Edite threw a blanket over my mother's legs while my mother scrubbed at her cheeks and lips with a tissue. Without a word my father slumped into his chair. He removed his hat. A thick red band encircled his head. He had little pills of spit in the corners of his lips, one on each side.

"What's wrong, Manuel?"

"They took everything," he said in Portuguese, softly, "everything."

"Manuel?"

"Robbed me. All my tools—at least a thousand dollars' worth of tools from my truck." His eyes were bloodshot. When my father got drunk he fell into a mood deeper than the one that got him drinking in the first place.

"But you're okay, right?" my mother asked.

"Nothing good ever happens," he said, shaking his head before drawing in a breath and blubbering into his hands.

I looked down into my palm. I cradled a limpet shell, ashamed of my family, in that room, at that moment. My father crying. My mother, her legs burning with hair-removal cream, unable to go to him to comfort him and tell him it was all going to be okay. Edite, who knew everything, but couldn't seem to stop any of it from happening. I stabbed my knife into the limpet's flesh. It was a big one and the muscle tightened hard, then relaxed. I slurped up the meat, sucked the juice, and rolled it all with my tongue before swallowing.

The blues and purples swirled in the empty shell. The glare from the TV bounced into the shell and something took shape—slowly, at first—the image of a man with sad, droopy eyes and a crown of thorns digging into his head. I looked up to the blinking picture—a carbon copy. It had to be a reflection, a trick of the eye. I tilted the shell away from the TV's glare. I shifted again, all the while holding my breath. Jesus's face remained.

I dragged myself along the carpet. I placed the limpet in my mother's hand. She looked a bit confused by my offering in the middle of my father's crisis. "Mãe, look!" I said.

"Not now, filho!"

I reached up and cupped her cheek in my hand, directed her face down to look at what lay in her palm.

She dropped to her knees. The blanket slipped from her legs, patches of hair coming off with it. She raised the shell to her lips and kissed it. I scanned the spinning room, saw everyone looking at her as she swayed. Her lower lip trembled as she made the sign of the cross, whispering her prayers up to the light fixture.

"A miracle!" my mother wailed, her entire body trembling. "Pai Nosso, que estais nos céus, santificado seja o Vosso nome . . ."

My father shakily got up and picked up the shell from her outstretched hands. He looked at it, then at me. "It's a sign," he said. "A sign!"

"What are you talking about?" I heard Edite say.

"It's what everyone's been waiting for," my mother whispered.

"The record!" my father shouted. The album's sleeve was already in my hands. I bent over the stereo and lowered the album onto the turntable. I cranked the volume to high. I opened the drop-leaf panel, the light in the mini bar lit, and I poured my father a shot of *aguardente*. "Make mine a double, Antonio," I heard Edite say. I could not look back. The handle, with its taped penny for added weight, swung over the record and into the fine grooves.

My sister grabbed the bottle from my hand as she brushed past me. She filled each shot glass to the rim. "Look what you've done now," she whispered. She bundled the shot glasses in her hands and turned to offer them to everyone.

I walked over to the window. I drew the sheer curtains aside, looked out onto our empty street. JFK's inaugural speech began to thunderous applause. *We observe today not a victory of party but a celebration of freedom* . . . The record was scratchy. The hairs on my neck rose, standing at attention as my mother's prayers and my father's tears crowded the room. The window was sweating. I made ticks on the glass with my finger—twelve candles with flickering flames atop each. I sang "Happy Birthday" in my head and pretended to blow them out.

＊

Trapped Star^s

*"He tells himself, 'My flower's up there somewhere . . .' but if the sheep
eats the flower, then for him it's as if, suddenly, all the stars went out.
And that's not important?"*

ANTOINE DE SAINT-EXUPÉRY

— I —

T HE MORNING AFTER I saw Jesus in the limpet shell,
my father closed himself into the small room at the back
of the house he called his office. He opened the door only to
take the cigarettes he'd sent me to buy from Senhora Rosa.

When Senhora Rosa gave me the change, she held on to my
hand, closed her eyes, and whispered something in Portuguese
that I didn't understand. She wouldn't let go. Senhora Rosa
knew. She had plugged herself into some wacky game of
broken telephone. My hand became scorching hot and she got
all bug-eyed. I pulled my hand away and ran straight home,
locking myself in my room for the rest of the day.

The very next day Senhora Rosa knocked at our door. Her
arthritis was gone, she said, her gnarled fingers straightened.
I saw her standing at the door, looking over my mother's
shoulder. She was trying to push herself in with outstretched
arms, reaching for me. "She's nuts," I had said to my mother
after she almost shoved Senhora Rosa out the front door and
locked it. "Her fingers still looked crooked to me."

Senhora Rosa's visit had given my father an idea and he ran
off to the local lumber store on Dundas Street. He returned
with new tools, two-by-fours, and sheets of plywood all
stacked in the back of his truck. He paid for everything on
credit, which made both my mother's eyes twitch. Everything
we had, we had paid for with *cash-money*—a Portuguese

expression that embarrassed me. My father disappeared into the garage.

The phone rang. My mother let it ring a few more times before picking it up.

"Hello?" she whispered. "He's right here, Manelinho," my mother exhaled, handing me the receiver.

"What's up?" I asked Manny.

"Can you meet at the garage?"

"Mãe, Manny's inviting me to go play at his house."

"You're going straight there? Are his parents at home?"

"Yes."

"Okay, just be home by six. Your father wants you home by then."

"I'll meet you there, Manny."

I walked up the street toward Manny's house. My mother came onto the veranda and pretended she had to sweep the path. I opened Manny's front gate and checked to see if she was watching. She stood at our fence, looking straight at me and not even hiding the fact that she was tracking my every move. I made my way through Manny's backyard, climbed up to the roof of his garage, hand-dropped into the lane, and looped back to James's garage.

I told Manny about Senhora Rosa. He rolled around laughing on the floor. I couldn't get a word out of him. He got so loud that I was sure he'd upset James; it was our first day back in the garage since he'd taken Agnes in. Manny kept making the sign of the cross and then holding his balls and curling up and rocking. While Manny was busting a gut, Ricky wanted to know everything, every detail, and when I had finished he whispered in my ear, so close that it tingled,

"You think I can borrow the limpet tonight? I'll bring it back, I promise."

James remained at the table. I heard Agnes weeping up in the loft. If anyone should have the limpet it was Agnes. "You just don't play with shit like that," James said, directing his comment at Manny. "It's not right."

It was the Saturday of the Labour Day weekend and my father had given me ten dollars—more than he'd ever given me before—to get my back-to-school supplies at Woolworth's. I came home with two bags full and ran upstairs to my room. I threw the bags on my bed and that's when I noticed everything laid out for me: soap, new clothes, a comb, and even some sandals. I had some sense of what I was expected to do, and thinking about it made me gnaw at my fingernails. I used the fresh bar of soap in my bath—goat's milk soap with a hint of mint. I dressed in a pair of linen shorts and a spray-starched shirt, fresh creases evidence that my mother had just ironed them. I wiggled my feet into the sandals and buckled them up. When I was done, I looked the part: angelic.

I sauntered along the path that led to our garage, past the rows of collard greens and hockey-stick teepees of beans. I took my time, tried to slow things down. The heat rose in waves to tickle the blue sky. I opened the door and stepped into the garage, blinking as my eyes adjusted. When I could see again, it was apparent my father had been hard at work. The brick walls were bare, the rafters and nails had been stripped of rope and jars and buckets. His hatched plan zoomed into focus.

"You like?" my father asked. The harsh light in the garage lit up his cheeks, and shadows dug into his crow's feet. He knelt on a makeshift stage, tacking in the last bit of artificial turf over the plywood. He wore his hat set far back on his head. In the summer humidity the concrete floor was still a bit sticky with paint. I lifted my foot and checked the bottom of my sandal.

"Is that where I sit?" I asked, pointing to the dining-room chair set in the corner of the stage. Two bedspreads, both white and made of heavy cloth, hung on pocket rods in the corner. The stage itself took up one entire corner of the double garage. My father's flourishes to make it look more like a church or a chapel hadn't been lost on me. Candles and some pictures, small and unclear, rested on a shelf. My father had taken a cookie tin and cut a slot in the top, and it dangled from a thin wire nailed to mortar.

"Sit down," he said. "Try it out."

I climbed up the two steps and sat in the chair.

"It'll do," he said. My mother had said it was my job to love my father. I knew I couldn't say no to any part of his plan.

My mother appeared in the doorway wearing her hospital uniform, the sunlight hitting her back, the rays spreading out around her as if she were a saint. A jumble of red was tucked under her arm. She stepped inside. All the hammering, the excuses we had been making to angry men who called wondering why my father hadn't shown up with his dump truck, demanding refunds, it was all becoming clear to her now too.

My father ripped the velvet from the crook of my mother's arm, cracked it in the dusty air, then held it by its gold tassels in front of me like a bullfighter. It was our Christmas tree skirt, trimmed with tinsel from a garland.

"This is your cape," he said, swirling the tree skirt in the air before letting it fall over my shoulders. His thick fingers tied the tassels together. His knuckles brushed against my chin as he did so.

He stepped back to take a look. The tinsel scratched my neck.

I could see my mother looking anywhere but at my father. "This is not what we talked about. It's not right."

"It's what they want. It's what they are looking for," he said.

"Not on the back of our son, it's not."

"Rosa Medeiros suffered from arthritis only a few days ago. Now she sits behind the counter and crochets like a young girl," he said.

My parents argued. Obviously they had forgotten that I spent years with my grandmother. Now I was glad she had drilled some Portuguese into my head.

"That woman should mind her store and that's it," my mother said, "not start these stories that make no sense. Manuel, yes, God shows himself in these ways, but he's just a boy," my mother said. "There has never been a sign before."

Was I a sign? I didn't feel any different. The night before, I had tried to test my powers. I pointed to the alarm clock in my room, focused real hard, tried to blast it with the electricity Senhora Rosa spoke of. I thought sonar waves might work better, like Aquaman, so I squeezed my eyes shut, concentrating on sending mental waves that would move my bed, just a little bit. Nothing. I tried something smaller. No use. Then it occurred to me that if God did give me some kind of superpower, He would want me to do good things with His gift. Blowing up a clock wouldn't count. Exhausted, I realized if it were truly a miracle, then God would have to let me know somehow. But maybe Senhora Rosa's hands uncurled because it was something she wanted so badly. Like when I trained my brain to dream about Agnes and she showed up in my dream the very same night.

"I built the stage and kneeler. We can direct the flow of people. They'll say a prayer, take a look at the shell, and drop in some loose change . . ."

"A carnival!"

"It helps them believe."

"In what?"

"Their prayers," he whispered. "You'll deny them that? And the money will be used to do good. Most of it, anyway."

"I've prayed every night for the answer and this isn't it."

"How do you know?"

"Because it's a lie. For us, for Antonio."

"But maybe not," my father said. "Believing heals. That doesn't hurt anyone."

"He's our son."

"It's you who goes to church. It's you who tells me about miracles. And yet when one happens, when the miracle is born under our roof, you throw it away like garbage."

"You don't even believe! Padre Costa is going to hear about this and—"

"I'm sure he will. And he'll come knocking for his cut."

My mother turned to go.

"Don't be foolish, Georgina," my father called after her. "You hear me? You knew what you were doing when you sewed that cape."

My mother turned her back on him, focusing her eyes on me. She'd make it all better; we'd manage to get this—the stage, the lights, the cape—dismantled by the end of the week.

"Plug in those lights!" he ordered, in English.

My mother hesitated for only a moment. In a daze, she bent down and took hold of the end of an extension cord.

Bang. Bang. Bang. Hands slapping on aluminum doors, gravel scuffing the soles of shoes. They were growing restless, kicking the garage door to be let in.

A newly hung chandelier, spray-painted gold, dangled above the chair, the glow casting a wonky circle around me.

I felt something pinching on the left side of the cloak. I patted it down and felt a tiny bump there. I lifted the left flap of the cape. Another medallion of St. Anthony dangled from a diaper pin, and with it was my mother's gold swallow, its forked tail slightly dented. I let the flap of the cape fall before my father saw it.

He was busy arranging the clay pots of begonias along the steps and doing another walk through the maze of velvet cords he had tied around the garage to guide those who would come to pray. Every so often he'd stop, rub his stubble with his knuckles, before adjusting the posts and ropes again.

When he looked at me now, there was a glimmer in his eyes, like he was proud of me. Even though I knew that I hadn't done anything to deserve it, it made me feel good. Maybe my father just wanted to spend time with me, as my mother had insisted when he first started talking about this whole thing. All I could do now was pray my friends would not be there when the garage door opened, laughing at my ridiculous outfit.

Bang. Bang. Bang. "Open up!"

My father now held a margarine container. He looked at me, his eyes so clear, so blue. He tipped over the tub and tapped a couple of times. The chunk of ice made a sucking sound before it plopped onto a silver tray that I recognized from our dining-room china cabinet. The shell was frozen in the block of ice, the image of Jesus looking like it was trapped under a lake.

My father cupped my face with his clammy hands. "Now when I open the door, you no be afraid."

"How long do I have to be here?"

"Things go very fast."

"I don't know what to say."

"You no say nothing."

"What if they speak to me?"

"You make like this," he said, tracing the four points of the cross in the air. A current of electricity ran through my body. "They come in and go around the ropes before they reach you. See this piece of tape?" With his toe, my father tapped a strip of duct tape he had stuck to the floor. It was barely visible against the painted concrete. "They stop here until I say okay. And then they move again."

"But what are they going to do?"

"They kneel, they will make prayers, they take a look at the lapa, and then they leave."

"That's it?"

"Maybe they drop some money in the basket at your feet. Just a little something for the church."

"And the candles?"

"Another little something more, to make sure God hears them." He adjusted my cape, then placed his hands on my shoulders. He pressed down hard, his way of announcing it was time. "You ready?"

I nodded. My eyes focused on the upside-down Jesus in the *lapa*.

"You is a good boy."

More thunder, as the aluminum door lifted up to the ceiling. My father's work looked junky now. I could see patches of exposed plywood where the fake turf had run short. A crumbling brick wall that held uneven two-by-fours displaying old black-and-white photos of me when I was a kid: catching a small wave at the beach, riding the antique cars at the amusement park, trying to cross the splash ladder at the playground.

Fifty people or so—old, young, men and women, a few children—walked in the way they walked into church, dabbing their fingers into some water my father had poured into a chipped teacup. The women covered their heads with veils and had rosaries tangled between their fingers. Some carried flowers in the bend of their arms. Some were in wheelchairs. The men had guck in their hair—shiny, like engine oil. They wore dark suits and stank of drugstore cologne. I heard one woman sing a high-pitched "Ave Maria," her voice then drowned out by others that joined in and harmonized.

A slender woman, probably in her late twenties or so, was the first in line. On my father's nod, she crossed the tape and threw herself down on the ground. Her veil flapped up like wings. Her arms spread out on the first step. The room turned quiet. She bowed her head in prayer over the block of ice, examining the shell. She looked up, the joy spread across her face.

"I've had four children," she said. "Not one of them born alive."

I glued my eyes to the shell. It could have been a picture of anyone. Who was to say it wasn't one of the hoboes that sat on the bank steps at Queen and Bathurst, or just a farmer with a long beard. I shouldn't have said anything. I should have thrown the damn limpet shell into the pile with all the others.

The swooshing blood between my hot ears was blocking what the woman was saying to me, what she was asking for. I steadied my wrist and lined my fingers, my palm to the side like I was going to karate-chop the woman's head. I was reaching back to scratch my itchy earlobes. But she caught me with her expectant eyes. My head was pounding, my throat dry. I slowly cut the sign of the cross in the air, the same way Padre Costa did up at the altar. The woman rolled her eyes back and collapsed on the steps. The crowd swayed and moaned in a wave of Alleluias.

My father helped her to her feet, almost dragging her outside for some air. I heard the scrape of her shoes on the concrete and the clink of money dropping into a tin can.

2

WHEN SCHOOL STARTED my mother made me promise to walk home with my friends, never alone, and within half an hour of the final bell, so that Edite could drop by to check up on me and my sister. She warned me not to speak to anyone about what was going on in our garage. *Do as your teacher says and it will be a good year.* She didn't have to worry, because no one spoke to me. The first day back, kids I had known since kindergarten parted to make a path for me in the halls, and they went quiet every time I came back into the classroom from the washroom with a buddy, which was a new rule—you could only go to the bathroom in pairs.

At recess, Odette Cabral walked like a cripple toward Sofia Nunes. Sofia touched her forehead like healers in white suits did on television and Odette stumbled back, cured and walking straight. Odette's sausage curls bounced as she giggled in her huddle. They knew I was watching and only turned away when their little play was over. At least Manny treated me like he always had. "Oh that beautiful boy, an angel really, came in for milk," Manny mimicked Senhora Rosa, right down to placing an imaginary kerchief over his head and tying a knot under his chin. "I touched his hand and a heat ran through my body. Like God had entered me Himself."

When we were alone, Ricky told me I had been given a gift. "God chooses people, you know. He chose you." He was serious, and I missed him. He had been pulled out of my classroom on the first day and placed in Manny's class. I was happy Manny would be there to look after him, or the other way around.

Our teachers didn't live in our neighborhood, but Manny said he overheard two of them talking outside the library about saints and sinners and the circus in back alleys, and so we knew they must have heard about the limpet.

"I don't care," I said. Our teachers didn't either, not really. They spent those first weeks trying to make sense of Emanuel's murder for us. From day one, every assignment, every class discussion, had a kind of sadness to it. Mr. Sowerby, my teacher, had picked some students to decorate the class bulletin board. They covered it with banner paper and bubble-letter headings: WHO? WHAT? WHERE? WHEN? WHY? And HOW? The biggest heading read, CURRENT EVENTS! We were expected to read the *Toronto Star* every day—my father eventually agreed to a subscription—and each morning one student had to bring in a news story and present his findings, the story dissected like a frog and carefully pinned under the headings on the bulletin board. The stories were all about Emanuel Jaques or Yonge Street or City Hall or immigrants. It was like Mr. Sowerby was telling us it was okay to feel like crap. We played along.

"Whose turn is it today?" Mr. Sowerby's glasses barely clung to the tip of his nose as he looked down his list.

"It's me," I said, not even bothering to sit at my desk as we all shuffled in. "I picked something from yesterday's paper." Mr. Sowerby sank into his chair. "The *Toronto Star*. Wednesday, September fourteenth." Mr. Sowerby looked pleased with my

presentation voice. "Fifteen charges face operator of sex shops."
I scanned the room. It was clear they'd all be listening carefully.

"WHO?" Mr. Sowerby yelled.

"Joseph Martin, forty-three. He managed Yonge Street sex
shops. He controlled Charlie's Angels body-rub shop."

"Massage parlour," Mr. Sowerby said, even though the
article clearly said body-rub shop. "WHAT?"

My paper rustled in my hands. "He was arrested."

"WHERE?"

"Toronto."

"WHEN?"

"Yesterday."

"The date, Mr. Rebelo."

"Tuesday, September thirteenth."

"Thank you. WHY?"

"Keeping a bawdy shop was one reason. It says he was—"
I looked down at the newspaper clipping, knew I had to get it
right, " 'living off the avails of prostitution.' "

"What does that mean?" Mr. Sowerby raised his voice.
"Tell the class."

"It means he was like a pimp."

Some of the kids snickered.

"Antonio, we don't use words like that. Agent. Procurer.
Even panderer can be used. We're still on the WHY? I'm waiting for a clearer reason."

"They want to clean up Yonge Street." I knew Mr. Sowerby
wouldn't like the vagueness in the way I answered his question. "It's about getting perverts off the streets and out of
business so that what happened to Emanuel doesn't happen
to another kid."

The class went quiet for the longest time. Then Mr. Sowerby invited comments.

Pedro's hand shot up. "My mom said that when those guys killed Emanuel they killed something inside of us."

"Is that true?" Mr. Sowerby asked the class.

"Nah. It's just made things a bit harder." Pedro laughed. "We gotta lie more."

"Antonio?"

"Yes?"

"Would you like to add something?"

"My dad put a bolt on our front door" was the first thing that popped into my head.

"Because your parents want you to be safe." Mr. Sowerby sounded so sure of himself.

"Something like that. I mean, at school we're never alone. Like when we have to go in pairs to the bathroom. But at home our parents still go to work every day and night because they say they have no choice," I said, "even though there are crazies out there like that Saul Betesh guy."

"We don't know anything about this man, Antonio," Mr. Sowerby said.

"I know he was adopted by a Jewish family and grew up with lots of money. And that when he was five he saw a psychiatrist."

Edite had managed to get her hands on some kind of psychological assessment from some cops she knew who were assigned to the case. I found the report on her kitchen table. Saul Betesh had been kicked out of every school he ever went to. He was aggressive and vicious.

"Is that in your article?" Mr. Sowerby said. "I don't want

neighborhood gossip. You need to stick to the article you selected."

The class got fidgety. I heard someone say *faggot*. Mr. Sowerby heard it too, I was sure, but he did that thing teachers do when they pretend not to hear something so they don't have to deal with the kid or the office.

"Calm down, class!"

"He was a homo." I made the word sound hateful, just the way I wanted the class to hear it. Still, I couldn't block the image of James coming out of the basement shower, steam swirling around his naked body. "That's why he decided to sell himself. He figured it was a good way to survive the streets."

"That's quite enough, Antonio." Mr. Sowerby stood beside me, nudging me to return to my seat, but I didn't move.

"He liked that feeling of power," I said.

I had half an hour before my disciples—the name my father jokingly gave them—were allowed in. The laneway had become off limits during certain times of the day. My father said there were people lurking out there, trying to catch me alone. I made my way over two fences and into Uncle David's backyard. The light sifted down through the leaves, their tiny shadows trembling in the breeze. We had waited so long for a breeze and it felt good. I sat under Uncle David's fig tree, where scarred earth hadn't quite healed. I imagined the worms and bugs eating away at the pig's guts, breaking them down until they became nothing more than the soil again. The branches of the fig tree had grown heavy with fruit since then. My uncle had smuggled the seedling into the country from his yard back home on the island. It had been carefully packed in his luggage with a wheel of Portuguese cheese, *chouriço*, and some live crabs. That was fifteen years ago. Every October a large hole the size of a crater was dug and the fig tree gently rocked, careful not to damage the roots, until it tipped slowly into the hole. The crown was bound with twine before it was laid on its side below. It was then covered with plywood and tarp before soil was tossed back over it to keep the tree protected from another harsh winter. In the spring, the men would meet—only the men—and the tree would be dug up, the bare branches reaching up to kiss the sun, as my mother would say.

My mother appeared, climbing up the basement-stairs walk-out into my uncle's backyard. She was dressed in a zippered housedress, her hair in large curlers smothered under her sheer headscarf. She ducked under branches and sat beside me.

I shifted my back away from her a bit and turned the page of my book. I caught a whiff of her Skin So Soft smell.

"You okay?" she asked, only after an awkward silence and the flicking of pages had worn her down.

"I just wanted to read a bit."

She looked over my shoulder to take a peek at my copy of *Lord of the Flies*. My mother motioned to my book with her chin. "What's it about?"

"A group of kids who find themselves all alone on an island."

"You'll never be alone."

I didn't respond.

"It's not easy for me, you know, leaving you and your sister at home by yourselves."

"I thought he'd show me off in the garage maybe once a week. Not every day!"

My mother took in a deep breath and switched to Portuguese. "Sometimes when I'm hanging up the clothes or working in the garden, just when it looks dark and it will never brighten up, the sky clears and the rays from the sun come shooting down to warm my shoulders."

"I don't like it when you talk in riddles."

"It means I *will* take care of you. I need some time." My mother's voice shook a bit. "Don't be afraid, filho. Jesus is watching over us."

I didn't say anything for the longest time. I wanted to believe her, but I knew she'd have to stand up to my father to make it stop. She needed to be brave, much braver than me.

"Is that why you put the swallow charm in my cape?"

She looked up into the canopy, and started to get up and pat the dirt off her skirt.

"It's the one that was on your necklace, isn't it? Who gave you the necklace?"

"It was a gift," she said. "It will all be over soon, Antonio. Trust me." She ducked under the branches and walked away.

"Mãe!"

She looked back. "I promise," she said, before descending the stairs into the basement.

My mother dragged me to church, to balance everything out, to show parishioners that I was a normal boy, but everything the priest said made me feel bad and dirty and that the world would end and gobble us up unless we prayed for forgiveness and salvation. I didn't want to believe him.

It must have been close to noon. Twelve to three o'clock were my Saturday hours. I could hear the sad voice of Amália Rodrigues, Portugal's greatest fado singer, blaring from someone's open window. The smells of barbecued sardines mixed with the smell of the morning's laundry. I looked up through the branches of the fig tree that closed in on me like a cage.

Later that afternoon, I sat on my chair in the empty garage. My father had started wearing a suit to greet those who came. And he had taken to dressing in his room, getting the knot in his tie just right. I could hear people outside, singing, praying, brushing up against our garage door.

Figuring out facts and fiddling with numbers made things easier for me. Fifty-one days had passed since Emanuel was found dead. Fifty-five days if you counted the four days he'd been missing before they discovered his body. It had been two weeks since Labour Day, nine full school days since my father first opened our garage door to strangers. During weekdays it was only two hours, or a hundred and twenty minutes—seven to nine. People came before setting out for their second jobs. My father had quit his night job cleaning the TD Bank. *Not enough time for everything*, he said. Each evening the crowds got bigger. People now came in from the suburbs: Mississauga, Brampton, and Oakville, places I had never been. My father said some had come from as far as Hamilton and Niagara Falls. A man had driven twelve hours from Fall River, Massachusetts. He wanted to see the limpet and kiss the feet of the *miracle boy*. He said it in front of everyone. He was certain I could tell him where his wife was hiding, where she had taken his little girls. People were getting crazier, and my legs got all soft and shaky every time I got in the chair. My father watched like a hawk.

One guy on the pilgrimage—that's what Edite called it—brought a pile of Wintario lottery tickets, as thick as a deck of cards. He scratched them at my feet, rocking and sweating. The crowd got angry, and my father pulled him out kicking into the laneway. Another man came to tell me he had lost his fingers in a meat grinder at a factory that made hamburger patties for a big fast-food chain. He flicked his tongue out of his mouth like a lizard after almost every word. His hands had been frozen cold so he hadn't felt a thing when he pushed the meat through the grinder. At first I thought he wanted me to pray for a way to get his boss and the company he worked for to pay for what had happened to him. Instead, he wanted me to kiss his ten pink nubs and pray for new fingers to grow. There were so many times that I wanted to run.

Every night they came. Many returned, frustrated that nothing had happened. My father explained their religion had taught them to be patient. Others went around professing they had been healed. They'd come back with another family member, claiming they themselves had been saved. When I heard these confessions, a lump would build in my throat and I began to believe myself. But I knew it wasn't true. How could anything they prayed for come true? I wasn't special. If I were, I'd know.

3

I STOPPED GOING TO Senhora Rosa's. Ricky told me she had a Polaroid of me on the scratchy glass counter by the register, a rosary draped over the picture frame and a prayer candle that burned during store hours. Instead, I went to Mr. Jay's store, which was just a block south of our house. All we knew about Mr. Jay was that he was Italian and his store smelled of old books and garlic and cat litter. A massive Pepsi-Cola refrigerator that sat in the corner of the store took up a quarter of the floor space. It was so deep we could easily fall into it reaching for pop or a Kisko Kid. Mr. Jay's assortment of Surprise Packs, chocolate bars, and lime licorice string was tossed around the sill of the bay window. I never bought chocolate bars from him, or wax skeletons for that matter: the chocolate and wax melted in the sun and it was a dirty job licking chocolate off wrappers.

"Hey, hey! The Jesus boy," Mr. Jay roared, his heavy accent not too different from Portuguese. "Or maybe St. Superboy." I placed a bottle of soda on the uneven counter and handed Mr. Jay a dollar bill. He gave me my change in pennies, seventy-five of them pushed across the counter, one by one, with his pointing finger. He wasn't even counting, just wanted me in the store as long as it took him to mumble a prayer under his breath. Where the hell was I going to get my Pepsi now? I looked out the window and was distracted by Peter ambling around the corner, his bundle buggy and red scarf trailing behind.

The minute I left the store, I turned up Palmerston, Pepsi bottle in hand. I scanned the rows of houses, looking for the flash of Peter's red scarf. When I was on my throne, my father kept our garage door open. Peter passed by once. I saw him clearly above the heads of everyone crammed in the garage, and I desperately wanted to be stuffed in his bundle buggy, carted away from them all. But Peter simply looked ahead and kept walking. Since then he had been showing up in my nightmares, moving toward me, his scarf flapping in the wind. Seeing him, even in my nightmares, made me feel safe: he was unchanged— someone I recognized. The men with no faces were still chasing me, but they would disappear the minute Peter reached me and his face eclipsed the sun, his tumor gone.

I ran a bit, looking over the hoods of parked cars, across the yards of the Chinese neighbors with their bean poles and flapping plastic bags all set up in their front gardens. But Peter had vanished.

When I got home, Terri was standing at the kitchen table, carefully wrapping a small block of cheese. She placed it in a bag and held it out to me. "Go ahead," she said. "There's some stew and bread in there for your friends." At first I wasn't sure if I should reach for it. Maybe it was some kind of trap. "I've seen you from the window sneaking out food after school." With one hand tucked in my pockets I played with the bulge of pennies Mr. Jay had given me. She dropped the bag on the table, then swiped my Pepsi from my hand and took a long swig. "You'd better take it over before Mom gets home." Terri's eyes got wide. "Think of the baby."

Edite knew where Agnes was staying. It pissed me off that she would snitch us out to Terri. But what if Edite hadn't said anything? What if Terri had figured it all out herself? If she had, it meant others would too. And James didn't want anyone to find out.

"Suit yourself," she said.

"Are you going to say anything? I mean, we're taking care of Agnes. Her parents may come back and punish her for ratting—"

"No, I won't tell. Agnes has enough on her plate. She's probably better off now that she's been abandoned. Senhora Gloria's a piece of shit for doing that. And that perv for a husband is an asshole. I just can't figure out what a guy like James is thinking, taking Agnes in. But then again I don't get what he's doing with a bunch of kids like you."

I didn't have an answer for her. I needed to go, deliver the food and warn James that Terri had figured it out. Usually I left the food in the backyard behind the garbage can, where James would find it. This time I'd risk delivering it in person, before my parents got home.

"Hey!"

"What?" I hugged the bag with both arms.

"Be careful," she said.

Only when I had made my way through our backyard and into the laneway did I allow myself to breathe.

It was too early for the worshippers to start gathering. Some people had left flowers and prayer candles at our garage door, the same kind we'd light at my grandmother's head-stone at the cemetery. Some were still lit.

Pressing my ear to the metal door of James's garage gave

nothing away. In the month since school had started, all the promised fun had vanished. When we were there James asked us to watch our language. He seemed to think Agnes was delicate. *The world can be cruel*, he said. Ricky had given James a large flannel sheet with cowboys and Indians going at each other. James had hung the sheet up along the fold of the peaked roof to create a floating wall. Agnes slept on one side. Manny told me he had found a cot mattress in the Patch, folded up like a jelly roll cake. He hoisted it up through the loft opening, all by himself. Manny knew which day to pick up the clothes and sheets, all crumpled and packed in a garbage bag next to the shiny blue trunk. Ricky was in charge of delivering James's rent money to Red on the first of the month. So far he'd only had to do that once. Ricky didn't make coffee any longer—the smell bothered Agnes—but I caught him once using Lemon Pledge around the garage, even though James just had a couple of workbenches, a scarred table, and a broken rocking chair Manny had salvaged from the laneway. When he thought we weren't looking, Ricky would drop money into the crock James kept on a shelf. Manny kept adding to the pot, not so secretly too, earnings from the bikes he stole then sold. James had shown Manny how to sand down the serial numbers with a file. He'd told Manny to spray-paint the bike frames—*You'll get more for them*—but that had stopped now, since the fumes weren't good for Agnes or the baby. I dropped the coins my father let me keep into the crock too. I made sure Manny and Ricky saw me do it, which wasn't the way I was taught; when the church collection basket came my way, my mother told me it wasn't nice to show people how much I was giving.

The handful of times I saw James, I'd ask him if there was anything more I could do. James told me I *was* doing enough, bringing food for him and Agnes. Once, he was in such a good mood he caught me by the waist near the Patch and lifted me into the air. "You got God on your side," he chuckled. "I can't take you away from that." He let me slide down his body till my toes touched the gravel. "But anything you need, just ask, man." My waist burned where his hands had grabbed me.

It started to rain. Drops were coming down hard, ringing across the roof and against the garage door like bullets. I looked over my shoulder before I lifted the door. I ducked underneath and closed the door behind me. I could barely make out Streisand's voice cooing her "Love Theme." I wasn't quite sure where it was coming from. The garage smelled of warm wood and socks.

"Did you forget something?" Agnes's uncertain voice spilled from the loft.

"It's me," I said. "Just brought some food over."

"James isn't here. He went to pick up some milk. He likes to warm it for me."

She came down the ladder wearing her slippers. Her hair was short and uneven, and her belly had changed, it bumped out in front of her from nowhere, it seemed.

"I haven't seen you come down in a while," I said.

"You haven't been around a lot." Agnes reached for some dishes and began to set the table. "I'm not sleeping very well. James is out most of the night. When it gets dark I go to my old house. I still have this." Agnes reached into her sweater and showed me her house key from around her neck. "I pick up small things. Things we could use but that won't be noticed if they're missing."

Agnes had brought her touches to the garage: a doily runner she draped over the table, frilly tea towels dangling from some nails above the water pail where we washed dishes, and a sewing machine sitting on the floor next to a bolt of fabric.

"I thought I'd sew a few things," she said, patting down the apron she had wrapped around her belly. "I don't want James spending any more money on me."

I nodded. She pulled out a chair and opened her hand to suggest I sit. Agnes was playing house, and she wanted me to play the game with her.

"Okay. Just a little after-school snack," I said in that *aw, shucks* tone that made me sound like a kid and that I hated. I thought of all the times I had wanted to be alone with Agnes, but this wasn't the way I had imagined it. I thought one day I'd be tall and she'd look at me differently, the way I had always looked at her. I fantasized that she'd run to me, her arms out wide, and I'd be able to lift her in the air and twirl her a bit and as she slipped against me her T-shirt would rise up. I dreamed she'd then take my hand and tuck it under her T-shirt, guide my hand up to her breast, where it would rest, my finger allowed to rub her nipple. I'd usually wake up at this point, drenched with sweat. I'd lie in bed thinking about the word *tit* and how that was the root word of *titillating*, or thinking of the word *areola*, which was the proper word for the whole nipple. Anything to get me back into that dream.

I watched Agnes's fingers untie the plastic bag. She removed the bread and cheese and lifted the Tupperware bowl onto the table. She unsealed the corner of the lid, closed her eyes, and breathed in the smell of beef stew. "It's still hot," she said.

"How come James is gone so much?"

She shrugged. "I don't ask."

"Don't you wanna know? Where he goes at night or what his plans are?"

Agnes ladled a bit of the stew into my bowl. "I don't think it's important. I just figure he sees us like a family. He's never had a real family."

The garage door lifted. Agnes flinched. Manny and Ricky ducked underneath the door. They were both soaked. With his foot, Ricky lowered the garage door behind them.

"What's for dinner?" Manny asked.

Agnes went to the shelf above the hot plate and brought down two more bowls. "Dry yourselves off." Manny grabbed a chunk of bread. I caught his wrist, squeezed hard. He dropped the bread onto the table.

"It's okay, Antonio," Agnes said. "There's enough for all of us."

"Is she kicking yet?" Ricky asked.

Agnes put her hand on her belly and blew a long bang off her face.

"You know the baby's a girl?" I asked.

"For sure," Ricky whispered.

Manny had sat in the rocking chair, adjusted the handle, kicked up his heels to the wall before gently rocking. "When is *it* coming?" Manny asked.

"February, late Feb—"

"You think it'll be normal?" Manny interrupted.

The way Agnes looked at him made it clear that she didn't need James to protect her.

I'd be lying if I hadn't wondered the same thing. Manny said the best we could hope for was a baby born cross-eyed or retarded or a hemophiliac, which was really bad because if it got cut or bruised it would bleed to death. I knew Senhor Batista was her stepfather, so there was no chance they were mixing blood. But when I thought of him mounting her—the hole in his throat wheezing as his breath misted over her face—I couldn't help but think of the crazy stories my grandmother told me about back home: Senhora Xica, who had been warned not to kill a chicken while pregnant, she gave birth to a baby that was half-human, half-chicken. It fluttered and banged its head under the kitchen table for an hour after it was born, until it died from exhaustion, my grandmother had told me with tears in her eyes. Or the story of another pregnant lady, who picked up a cat, then her baby was born completely covered in fur. Or another, who refused to listen to all the women in the village about wearing necklaces while pregnant, only to give birth to a stillborn, its umbilical cord tied neatly around its neck.

I marched over toward Manny, thought if I was close enough and needed to I could kick him in the teeth.

Just then James lifted the garage door. Manny stopped rocking. The hollows around James's eyes were gray and soft. He placed a jug of milk on the table and lightly ran his hand across Agnes's belly. She let her shoulders roll back.

"Manny, do something useful—fix that rocking chair for Agnes."

Agnes climbed up the ladder to the loft, her slippers slapping against her heels.

Manny hesitated for only a second before going to the workbench and pulling the toolbox from underneath. He lit a cigarette and put it in his mouth, then got right down to work, screwing in loose spindles.

James yanked the lit cigarette from Manny's mouth and crumpled it in his bare hand. The smoke escaped between his clenched fingers. The cigarette fell to the floor. He sat down at the table. Manny refused to look at him. James grabbed a hunk of bread and tore at it with his teeth.

"I've got a job for you, Ricky," he whispered.

"Is there anything I can do?" I offered. "My parents won't be home for a bit."

"This job's for Ricky." He grabbed my thigh under the table. I couldn't stop the boner that was beginning to press against my pants.

James let go of my leg and motioned for Ricky, who got up from his chair and came over to him. It was as if Ricky was waiting for a sign as James dunked some bread in the stew's sauce. Some gravy dribbled down his chin. "I like the food your mom makes. It makes this place feel like home," he said to me.

"I can get other things, you know. Wine, liquor, beer. People who can't pay money bring stuff like that when they come to the garage." I crossed my legs under the table.

James turned to Ricky, who had been waiting expectantly, and cupped his hand to Ricky's ear. He whispered something that made Ricky's face light up.

"I know where my dad stashes his booze, so if—"

"I don't want you to steal from your family, Antonio," James said. He squeezed my shoulder. "I got Ricky a little job on the side, something that'll bring in a bit of cash. You need to be patient. I have another plan for you," he said. I held my breath, tried hard not to let on he was hurting me.

— 4 —

Is your father home?" James said, standing at my front door.

At first I thought he was some kind of mirage. I hadn't slept well—the thought of what James had in store for me had kept me awake.

"What are you doing here?" I said. "You can't be here."

James stubbed his boot against the swinging door. "Your father wanted to see me."

"James! Come inside." It was Friday morning, too early for my father to be in a happy mood, but he reached out his hand and James shook it. James wore a clean shirt and his jeans had a crease. He had shaved and had his hair parted down the side. "You know James, Antonio."

James held out his hand. I froze. I wasn't sure what was happening. This wasn't the way it was supposed to be.

"Antonio! Shake the man's hand. James is going to be the new driver for Rebelo and Son Ltd."

James grinned. "That's right, sir." James looked straight at me. "I can drive the heck out of anything, and I've been around trucks all my life. If you need the help, well."

"That's good." My father locked the door with the dead-bolt. My father was much shorter than James but it didn't stop him from patting James on the back and guiding him toward the kitchen. "My wife she working. I make the coffee. Antonio, go get ready for school."

The morning sun warmed my back but my feet were cold on the ceramic tile. Had I missed something? I had overheard my father fighting with my mother in their bedroom a couple of nights back. My father had replaced all his stolen tools and my mother yelled that the dump truck still wasn't paid off, and my father wasn't helping matters by spending so much of his time in the garage. My father insisted he had a plan. At the kitchen door, James turned to me and winked. James had a plan too.

I ran up the stairs as fast as I could. I had felt this way once before. Last winter my bike hit a patch of black ice on a busy street and slipped sideways. I hurt my wrist trying to break my fall, but all I kept thinking about were the cars and trucks that were behind me that could hit the same patch but they wouldn't be able to stop. I remember closing my eyes so tight my body shook. I think I prayed harder than I've ever prayed and was answered with a loud honk. It was all I needed to give me the time to drag my bike to the sidewalk.

I got dressed, slung my Adidas school bag over my shoulder, and headed out the door. I made it to Edite's in record time. I found her spare key where she told me it would be hidden. I needed a place to feel safe, which is what she said her apartment could be. Just as I was closing the door, I saw her stumbling into the kitchen.

"My dad hired him. James. He just came to our house and my dad gave him a job."

"Take a breath, Antonio. It's okay." Edite's hair was matted like a bird's nest. She hadn't washed her face. In the morning light the lines she had drawn around her lips and eyebrows were uneven. She touched the edge of her mouth where the lipstick smeared. She raised her hand to my forehead and I ducked.

"But what does he want?"

She stood at the kitchen counter. "It won't be so bad, will it? You have nothing to hide?" Edite said. Again, the image of James appearing from a cloud of steam flashed in my head: bare-chested, drying his hair in a towel, his jeans unbuttoned. "You kids meet up and take care of each other. You're safe. I think that's all your mom and dad care about."

"They don't know I go there, do they?"

"Relax." She pulled out a cigarette. "Antonio, look at me." Edite grabbed my wrists and whipped them like reins. Her voice became calm and soft. "I saw James yesterday at the bar and he told me your dad had asked him if he was interested in some work. Your dad says he can't keep up with all the calls. Ever since word's gotten around that you're a healer, he's been getting more business. Now he thinks he can run his little dog-and-pony show and have someone else take care of the real work for him."

I wrenched my hands away. "I gotta go to school."

"Ah, look, Antonio. I didn't mean anything by it."

I stood at the door, my hand resting on the doorknob.

"It was a rough night, that's all," she added, laying her hands on my shoulders and turning me around. "My words aren't coming out right. Sit down. I'll make us some coffee."

"I'll have tea."

Her eyes were dark, mascara smudged into the hollows.

"You don't look so good," I said.

"Tell me about it." She gave me a hug and lowered me into a chair.

Edite smelled of unwashed clothes and tobacco. "When do you need to be at school?" She plugged in the percolator, then loosened the belt of her robe and tied it again, cinching it at her waist. Her breasts jiggled under her robe. I could trace the outline of her nipples. The word *high beams* came to mind—that's what Manny would have called them. I looked away.

"A boy needs a healthy breakfast. Just give me a minute," and she shuffled into her bedroom. I scanned all the magazines and newspapers, the books she had piled on one of the chairs and along the kitchen wall on the floor. I took deep breaths, tried to match my breathing to the percolator, which had begun to pop and wheeze. Every so often she would yell or curse, like she was tripping over things. *It'll all be okay. James working for my father doesn't have to change things.* Edite hopped into the kitchen on one leg, holding her toe with her hand. Her hair was pulled back by one of those Alice in Wonderland headbands, her face all red as if it had been scoured with hot water. She poured coffee into two mugs, the grounds swirling on the surface. "Shit," she mumbled.

"It's okay, coffee is good."

"Isn't that what you asked for?" She stabbed at the sugar bowl, managed to chisel off a couple of chunks, which she plopped into the mugs.

"You should put some grains of rice in the bowl. Rice-A-Roni even." She looked over at me. "The sugar bowl. My mom says it sucks up the humidity." The lines on Edite's forehead vanished with her first sip of coffee. "The humidity gets sucked up and the sugar stays loose."

Edite sat back in her chair and licked her spoon. "How about the rice?"

"What do you mean?" I said.

"The rice . . . how do you make sure the grains of rice don't fall in your coffee?"

I had never thought about that. We'd always had rice in our sugar and I just thought everyone did the same thing. "I guess you have to be careful. Mom has a sugar dispenser she bought at Kresge's."

"Your mother thinks of everything." Edite brought the spoon down from her mouth and twirled it in each mug. I wasn't going to say anything about sharing spoons. We didn't do that either. She stared out the back window. Her collection of Red Rose animal miniatures had grown to twenty-three. Some were doubles my mother didn't want. Edite's were lined up on the windowsill, a way of keeping count of her time here, I figured. It was her favorite part of being in Canada, she had said, the tea that comes with figurines.

"What's all this?" I asked, pointing at the stack of papers on the table.

"I was up all night poring over documents, psychological assessments, interviews with people who were friends or worked with some of the men accused of killing the Jaques boy. I'm helping out one of the reporters. I have a couple of police friends that are slipping me some juicy bits. It's hard to get this information. Everyone in our newsroom is just too polite so they asked me to use my American know-how to dazzle a few answers out of them."

"Who are the reports about this time?" She'd kill me if she knew I had shared that secret information about Saul Betesh with my class. There was a pact between us—a pact I felt guilty for breaking—that allowed her to share information if

I kept it to myself. I still needed to ask for it, though, like poking a bug to get it to move.

"One of the accused, this Werner Gruener, came to Canada from Germany when he was seven. He grew up in a small town." She whispered it like it was a bad thing.

I sipped the coffee. It was strong and bitter, despite the sugar, and I was tempted to ask for a smoke too. Manny had been smoking since he was ten, and I knew Ricky smoked in secret, though every time I asked him he denied it.

"His parents were very religious." Edite pointed at me. "Always a problem. Anyway, he grew up with a head filled with good and evil and thoughts of eternal damnation." She laughed. "Hell, you know about that."

Fuck off, I wanted to say, wanted to run out of her apartment, maybe kick over a chair on my way. But I nodded instead. Edite dug under some magazines and old newspaper. She pulled out a clipboard and flipped a couple of pages over.

"His father left them when Werner was eleven years old, took off somewhere, just disappeared. Shortly thereafter, his mother had a mental breakdown. He was thirteen. No, fourteen." Edite tapped the report before she laid the clipboard on the table. I reached over to see it for myself. Her hand swooped down and pinned the clipboard to the table. I tucked my hand under my ass, as if she had slapped it.

Edite picked at a fleck of tobacco that clung to her lip.

"Did he help murder Emanuel?"

"Well, he opened the door. Ran down two flights of stairs when he heard the doorbell and opened the door for his friend Saul Betesh and the boy, Emanuel." She laughed again, a smoker's laugh.

"What's so funny?"

"This Gruener guy was pissed because all the knocking interrupted his favorite show, *Three's Company*. He heard the knocking just when Jack was trying to juggle two women on the same date. According to the report, he kept repeating he missed the best part."

Edite reached back to the counter and brought the percolator to the table. I tried to read the report upside down. She poured herself some more coffee—tar black—and was about to do the same for me. I placed my hand over my cup.

Edite got up and leaned against the kitchen wall, her coffee and a cigarette in the same hand, and looked out the window.

"What do you and James talk about?" I said.

She brought her mug to her mouth. I could hear her gulp. She looked over her shoulder. "He's trying to make ends meet. He's determined to take care of Agnes."

"Why can't she come here?"

"I offered. She said she wanted to stay with James."

"Why?" I asked.

"Why does she choose to stay or why does he want to take care of her?"

"Both."

"She's had it rough and so has he. He says she's the closest thing he's got to a family." Her voice sounded like it was going to crack. "That's why the baby— My head's pounding," she said, before plopping herself back down on the chair.

"Can I get you something?"

"I want you to listen to me," she said. "James is a good guy. A bit rough but he means no harm. He won't hurt you," she whispered, before kissing her finger and plinking me on the nose with it. "Jesus, I'm tired. I didn't sleep very much. I was out all night looking for him."

"Who?" I asked.

"My Johnny," she said.

"I thought you said you spent last night—"

"What?"

"You told me you were looking over the reports."

She pressed her temples, made small circles with her white fingertips. "I'll go back to bed. I'll just have a refill and a smoke." But she never moved toward her bedroom.

"I better go," I said.

"Let me write you a note."

Edite tore off a blank corner of the newspaper, then got up to look for a pen. I stared at the coffee grounds sticking to the inside of her mug.

SATURDAY MORNINGS were quiet at our house, except for the sound of our screen door slamming when Senhora Rodrigues delivered her fresh cheese. Before cleaning, my mother went to Czehoski's on Queen Street for Polish cold cuts and to Future Bakery for sliced rye. She'd do her banking before heading to Kensington Market, where all the rest of her grocery shopping was done. My father started the morning early with a basement excavation job. He'd be home for lunch and then get ready for the afternoon disciples. My mother called them visitors, which made them sound like friends or family. James was going to take over in the afternoon, dumping the truck's load of dirt in one of the city's landfills.

I stood outside James's garage in the morning, breathing in through my nose, out through my mouth, the way we were taught in gym class.

The light in the garage was powdery. My eyes inched over a bicycle frame that hung from a hook, across to the hot plate, to a few baseboard heaters, unplugged and piled against a wall, over the shiny blue trunk and up to the window in the door that burned in the morning sun.

James stepped out from behind the curtain. "I know why you're here. You want me to quit."

"Why didn't you tell me?"

"Would it have made a difference? I thought you were old enough to understand."

"What do you want?" I said.

"Extra cash. The baby is on the way. When your dad offered me a trucking gig on Saturdays I didn't think twice. My hope is he'll like my work and he'll offer me a few weekdays too. Look around you. This ain't no way to live, especially with a kid. I want to get something better for me and Agnes and the baby."

"But *we're* helping you."

"Yeah, I just don't want this to get messed up."

"What do you mean?"

"Like, we gotta keep an eye on Manny, for starters. He's getting sloppy. If that little prick gets caught stealing bikes, it leads the cops back to me. And then what? Who's gonna take care of Agnes?"

"So tell him to stop."

"I can't."

"Why?"

"You know how much a baby costs?"

"Well, Ricky and me can—"

"Ricky is a problem too. You and I both know about Ricky and what he does. He can't get caught down on his knees," James said. Dribbles of pee blotted my underwear. James took a step toward me. "He was doing this shit long before I came around. You just need to know that I'm offering him a kind of protection, that's all." Instantly the room turned hot. I couldn't look at him because all I kept wondering was what else he knew. "Ricky came in here crying the other day because at the billiards, Amilcar's dad, Poom Pooms or something, bent down and peeked through the hole."

"What did you do?"

"Let's just say I'm taking care of it."

Next thing I knew I was pounding my pedals along Queen Street, racing so fast that I passed a streetcar, James's last words—"Don't leave!"—pulsing in my head.

Sunday morning, I woke to the sound of stones being thrown at my bedroom window.

I pressed my face to the mesh screen and yelled through clenched teeth, "Are you nuts? What time is it?"

"That thing freaks me out," Manny said, glaring at Jesus on our lawn.

My father had spruced Jesus up by applying Spackle to its chipped nose and painting its flaking face. The sacred heart, the size of an India-rubber ball, burst through Jesus's robes, shiny from a fresh coat of glossy red nail polish. My father had also cut some Plexiglas in the outline of the tub, caulked and screwed it in place, trapping Jesus in a sweating coffin.

"Manny, it's seven in the morning on a Sunday."

"I like to work early," he said. "Listen, if you don't want to come, let me know. Believe me, I like working alone." Before he even finished the sentence I had started to get dressed. I didn't need him to get any louder and wake up my parents. I slipped on my shoes when I got to the front gate, then followed Manny to the mouth of the laneway opposite ours. This was not our territory. It was Amilcar's. "Follow my nose. It always knows," Manny sang in Toucan Sam's dorky voice.

"I don't like this."

"Then stay home!" Manny shot back.

"I'm coming."

"Hey, is it true about the vampire lady?" Manny asked.

"What did you hear?"

"Is it true, then? Did she stab you?"

I rolled down my tube sock.

"I don't see anything," he said.

"It was a sewing needle, but man, did it hurt. See, it's a bit red there."

Manny looked unimpressed.

"The place went mental so my dad closed the garage early."

"What did she look like?"

"Old, hunched over and wrinkly, wearing a long black dress with a black shawl and kerchief tied under her chin."

"That describes every old lady in our neighborhood."

"Yeah, but I never saw her before. Turns out her son had driven in from Buffalo to bring her to me. Anyways, she spoke in whispers, not in English but in Italian, I think." There'd been something different about the old lady. Her eyes. Her eyes burned like someone's much younger. They were caramel-colored and her pupils sparkled. If I told Manny that, he'd think the heat in the garage had rewired my brain.

"So what happened?"

"She bent down to look at the lapa but her hand and chin moved to my feet, like she was going to kiss them." Manny made a disgusted face. "That's when she pricked me."

"I heard she bit you."

"No. My dad heard me yell and he drew her back but not before she swiped some blood from my leg and sucked her finger."

"That's crazy, man."

I had him hooked now. "My dad dragged her out as she licked her lips and kept chanting something."

I didn't tell Manny that my eyes had locked with the old woman's and I had seen things that scared me. They weren't objects or places, but more of a feeling that made me think of James and Emanuel Jaques and my parents. It was hard to explain . . . it seemed like the person I was now was not the person I would've been if Emanuel Jaques had not been murdered, if James hadn't dropped into our world out of nowhere. I'd never have the chance to be that boy again. Manny would think I was delusional if I told him any of that.

"Where's Ricky?" I asked, willing myself to shake it off.

"You know he can't leave till his old man gets home from work and crashes."

Manny walked slowly, bending down to stuff his pockets with stones. So I did the same.

Ricky's father was a phantom. Since Ricky's mother took off, the only time his father left the house was to go to work. When he got home he'd sit on the couch in front of the TV drinking wine until he passed out. Ricky waited for him with his breakfast: five eggs, sunny side up, splotched with piri-piri sauce, five pieces of buttered toast (one for each egg), and a *caneca* of coffee, black. Everything had to be perfect, just the way Ricky's dad liked it, right down to the way the ashtray was angled on the breakfast table. "Or else—" Ricky had said once, letting the threat hang. Ricky tried to sleep when his father did, and woke when his father went to work. He almost never went to school, and James called him Hoot. Ricky would tell us things he had heard or seen in our backyards or laneway when everyone else was asleep.

We never dared set foot inside Ricky's house. His father's belly, according to Ricky, was the size of a beach ball, but the rest of his body was thin and the skin hung off his shoulders. I imagined he was like the beast in *Lord of the Flies*.

"Did you finish the book we got?" I asked Manny.

"Yeah, it should be called *Flies on Shit*."

"I liked it."

"I don't get it."

"What don't you get?"

"I just don't think that's the way it happens. They're stranded, right? They're far away from any kind of rules. So the first thing they do is they make their own laws. That's stupid right there. You're finally away from them all, all their fights and lies, and then you go and make the one thing you hate—rules." Manny shook his head. "Doesn't make sense."

"Look at us. We're in an enemy laneway trying to steal bikes. Look at your brother, he's creating his own rules by marrying Amilcar's sister. Your parents are flipping and—"

"Don't talk about my brother."

"I'm just saying—"

"I know what you're saying. My brother doesn't steal, he doesn't kill."

"My father killed that pig. We *are* animals. Just like the kids in the book."

"Your father didn't kill the pig to survive. He could have just gone to the butcher or the grocery store. He did it because he's a *pork chop* and it's the kind of thing they did back home." Manny climbed up the downspout like a monkey. He scrambled along the roof before sitting on his bum and looking over the laneway. Silence as he fished out a cigarette from his hair and lit it. "But you're right. We're all animals," he said, looking down at me and spitting his laser spit through the side of his mouth. "We do things because we can. Why does a dog lick its balls? Because it can. I'll show you."

"What, you're going to lick your balls?"

"I'm going after the big one," Manny said.

"Manny, don't even think about it," I said.

"Look, you don't want to be here, fine. Just don't go on talking about what's right and wrong, rules and all that crap. Do you ever hear yourself? Do you ever look yourself in the mirror after your dad's ripped off a bunch of people who believe in you?"

"You're an asshole."

"I'm an asshole? I don't sit on some throne and have people kissing my stinking feet."

"Fuck you!"

Brilliant light, like the tail of a falling star, shot across the crisp morning air. The flash was bouncing off the frame of Amilcar's bicycle, *the big one*, a ten-speed that had been stripped and chromed. Manny knew he could get at least fifty bucks for it.

It was too easy. Amilcar wouldn't have just left his bike there. It was a trap.

Manny crept up the laneway, signalling me to stay back, but I followed. He lifted his feet, careful not to kick the gravel. Amilcar was nowhere. Manny got close enough that he touched the bike, brushed the handlebars the way the models did on *The Price is Right*.

In one fluid motion Manny had hopped on the bicycle and thrown the kickstand up with his heel. I heard rustling behind the tall, narrow gate that divided the two garages. I saw Amilcar through the slats, leaning against the cinder block of the garage, his pants dropped to his knees. It looked like he was taking a leak.

Manny looked back only once, punched the air with his pinky and index finger spread wide, like he was at a Kiss concert. He gave out a kind of primal cry, and then broke into a song about choking the chicken on a Sunday morn.

I looked back and caught Amilcar scrambling through the gate. He had pulled up his pants but his buckle was still undone. He spat from the corner of his mouth and his cheeks bounced up and down. He was fast. Manny had already turned at the elbow in the laneway. He'd be far gone by now, but Amilcar had seen who it was. He wheeled around toward me.

I raced up Palmerston, pumping my arms, my legs burning, past the entrance to our laneway. I looked over my shoulder. Amilcar was gaining on me.

I reached the synagogue at the top of Palmerston and turned in the laneway. Amilcar was getting close. This is it, I thought. I'd never make it to James's garage. Amilcar would catch me and beat me to a pulp.

I turned into the neck of our laneway. I stopped and bent over to heave. Only spit came out. I grabbed at my heart, tried to calm it. I thought of all those people who came to be healed because they believed. It was a joke; I couldn't even save myself. I leaned against a garage door and shut my eyes tight. The door wobbled a bit, then opened, and I stumbled into darkness.

"Where are you, you little shit!" Amilcar yelled. "I'm gonna cut your fuckin' head off."

Through the gaps in the boards I could see Amilcar in the laneway, banging on garage doors, turning handles. I guided my hand up the door, slid the latch to lock it.

"I'm going to kill you! You better not go to sleep because I'm going to hunt for you, you faggot."

I looked around the garage, the mold and dampness from the packed earth tickling my nose. It was too dark to tell whose garage it was. I tasted the copper of my blood. I must have bitten my lip when I fell in. I looked out again. Amilcar was close enough that I could hear him breathe.

"I know you're in there," he whispered, before banging twice on the garage door with his fist. "Come out or else—" He tried the next garage and pounded at its doors before heading to the next one.

"I really don't care," I heard myself saying, much louder than I had expected.

"You're in there, aren't you, you little faggot." He rattled the handle of another garage, then tried to kick the door down. "I'm coming for you and your friend, shithead."

My breath filled my ears so I couldn't hear anything else. That was, until the pop of a firecracker snapped my attention. I looked out with one squinted eye and saw Amilcar leaning against the opposite garage, a string of firecrackers in his hand. A cat, splotches of ginger against white, rubbed itself along his shin. Amilcar grinned, exposed the dark gap between his front teeth. He separated a firecracker from the row and brought the end of it to his mouth, the way you would suck the icing off a birthday candle or moisten a joint—something Manny had shown us once when he had stolen one from his brother's glove compartment. The cat mewed and wove between Amilcar's legs in a figure eight. Its tail was erect, quivered. Amilcar bent down to pet the cat's head. With his other hand he drew the moistened firecracker from his mouth and screwed it into the cat's ass. The cat only raised its rump to let him. I held my breath till I thought I would burst. Amilcar flicked his Bic, lowered the flame to the wick. The spark lasted a mere second before it cracked. The cat popped off the ground and dashed in circles screeching, dragged its hind legs up a wooden fence and disappeared over the top. Its screams faded into the distance.

"And I'll do it to you too," Amilcar said.

I inched backwards, into the garage, watching through the crack as Amilcar's figure got smaller and smaller until it was gone.

I looked at the old garage door I had fallen through. It was wooden and swung out to the sides.

I tried to swallow. My knees trembled and I could feel the tears building. Then I heard the scratch of a match.

I turned to see a flickering of light over the hands of a man. The flame rose to his face. "Might as well sit down." He tilted his head, cupped the flame, and lit a cigarette.

"Peter?" I said his name out loud without trying to.

He wouldn't look at me. "You need to wait it out," he said, his voice new and strange.

I stood there without making a sound. Outside the sun was bright, but Peter's garage was shadowy and cool. I heard the scratchy nails of squirrels racing across the garage's rooftop. Peter moved around quietly, lit some candles he kept in punched tin cans. From what I could make out, the inside of the garage was decorated in plywood and tarpaper. Though the garage was dark, he didn't trip over anything, as if he knew every inch of the place. The candles lit up hundreds of books on shelves, piled high or their spines packed tightly. Paperbacks and old faded hardcovers, all of them brought there in his bundle buggy, I figured.

"You can talk?" I whispered, smacking my tongue in my dry mouth, trying to whip up some spit.

Peter nodded.

I felt lucky, like I was the first one to hear him. But then I thought of all the nasty things that had been done to him, things he suffered without once complaining or fighting back. I thought of all the names we had called him.

He turned to reach for something and I could see the lump on the side of his head, pushing his ear out like in a child's drawing. My dreams had been wrong. He held a Coca-Cola bottle, popped off the cap with a flick of his thumb and offered it to me. He raised his hand and rubbed the lump a bit. He caught me staring and dropped his hand.

"Does it hurt?"

"No," he said.

"Is it filled with pus?"

He shook his head, rubbed the frosted stubble on his neck.

"You can drain it. I once had a blister. I popped it with a pin. I disinfected the pin with a match. My blister wasn't that big but—"

"It's my ticking clock. Close to my ear so I'm sure of when it's time."

"For what?"

"For that which is inevitable."

I liked the sound of the words coming out of his mouth.

"How come you never talked before?"

"No one asked me anything."

As Peter maneuvered his way through the room, my eyes followed: hot plate, cot, red scarf draped over the handle of his bundle buggy, an old washbasin and jug, like my grandmother's, sat in a wired holder beneath a narrow mirror, and a small record player—the portable kind. The basics.

Peter brushed his fingers across the spines of his books the same way I rattled a stick along the spindles of a wrought-iron fence. He stopped and tilted a book toward him far enough that it dropped into his hand.

He held the book out to me. "Go ahead," he urged with his chin. "It's a gift." I reached up and held the cloth-bound book with both hands. *The Little Prince.*

Again, he lifted his hand behind his ear as if to scratch, then stopped. "You share the same name," he said. "Antoine . . . Antoine de Saint-Exupéry."

I tried to calm myself by running my fingers across the raised letters of the author's name. *He knew my name?*

"What's it about?"

"It's about a boy like you." Peter held his breath. "I worked in a library." He raised his meaty hands in the air, palms open, as if he was supporting their weight. "They were weeded from stacks or left in boxes on garbage day."

"Have you read all of these?"

Peter nodded. He stepped closer to them, his nose almost touching them, to take in their smell, as if it was a drug that made him calm and happy.

"I don't know why they come to see me," I said, unsure why I was confessing to him. "I don't have any special powers."

"They come because they need someone or something to explain the world to them. What they *expect* to feel when they kneel in front of you is what they *want* to feel, nothing more. You don't need to be frightened by it."

"How do you know?"

"Most of them are looking for a miracle. They're desperate because they've tried everything else and they have nothing to lose."

"They believe I can make their fingers grow back or make their cancer go away."

"Believing feels good."

"You want me to try it on you?"

"I don't believe. It's all lost. Gone."

"What? What's gone, Peter?"

His eyes welled up. "My name is Adam." He reached for his red scarf, slowly wound it around his neck. "And you should go now," he said.

— 6 —

A COUPLE OF DAYS LATER, right after the final bell rang, I took a different route over to James's. Everything was about staying alive, mixing things up, avoiding the laneways where Amilcar might be hiding. He had changed schools. After he failed last year his parents switched him to Charles G. Fraser, which wasn't a catholic school. Manny told me he hardly ever saw him; he had a job in Kensington Market, stocking shelves at Melo's Grocery Store.

Agnes told me I would find James at the park. She looked shabby. "Every morning I make sure I've got all the things he likes all ready for him. His coffee, the newspaper, toast with butter and jam. He likes apricot." She sounded tired, the way she went through the things she did for him, the things he liked. "But he's been coming home mad because they're not giving him as much work. He says he's getting too old for his kind of work." I wondered if she knew exactly what it was James did downtown, and if she did I wasn't really sure she'd tell me. "Thank God your dad gave him that job. It helps." She stopped to look up at the TV. "People are staying away. Even from the new mall. They're afraid. James says he sees gangs of boys, some of them from our neighborhood, gathering down there and beating the crap out of other guys, the ones they think are queers."

For weeks the rumors had been spreading that Manny's brother, Eugene, and Amilcar had been involved in some of

{ 164 }

the beatings. Most Portuguese in the neighborhood were just glad homosexuals were being scared off. I had even heard my parents say as much.

"Does James scare you?" I asked.

Agnes placed a candy in her mouth. "He makes me feel safe." She turned and looked straight at me. "He touches me so gently, it makes me want to cry." She drew her hands to her belly. "I didn't want to keep it, you know, but James said we'd make a perfect family. He said he'd take care of things." I caught a whiff of her minty breath. "He'll take care of us all." She tried to twirl her hair in her finger. It would have worked if she still had her long hair. "You better go. Alexandra Park. He's there with Manny. They've been together all day."

"Do you want to come?"

Agnes shook her head, then grabbed a rung on the ladder and climbed up.

I made it to the park in record time: one minute, twenty-seven seconds. The faster I rode my bike, the slimmer the chance that Amilcar could ambush me from some nook or hideout along the way. I took in the rattle of dry leaves, the way they crunched under my tires, and thought of my mother and how she scoured our walkway and sidewalk with bleach trying to scrub away the rusty stains left by the rotting shells of horse chestnuts. Last fall I had suggested we try cooking them. I was certain the thought had crossed her mind too. We gathered a few handfuls and my mother roasted them in the oven for a couple of hours. Their shells blistered and cracked. But the insides stayed green and bitter.

Manny's hair was the first thing I saw. I pedaled harder and found James slouched beside him on a park bench, a brown paper bag in his hand. At Manny's feet was a bottle of *aguardente*—Portuguese moonshine. They both held joints pinched between their fingers.

"What's wrong with you guys? A whole lot of help you'll be if Amilcar comes after me."

They looked at each other and burst out laughing.

"I'm outta here!" Anger burned my face. They were too stoned or drunk to notice.

"No, no, no, no," James said. "We've got to talk, little brother. Let's just talk this through."

"What are we going to do? I'm a walking target and so is he." I pointed to Manny, who fluffed it all off like he didn't care. "It's been a week since you stole the bike. Amilcar's waiting to pounce, I know it."

Manny spat over his shoulder. The bike had been sold; he'd given half of it over to James and pocketed the rest. Not a penny for me.

"Remember, protection, baby." James smiled, his eyes blistery red.

Adam appeared in the distance. He walked across the park's baseball diamond. I hadn't told anyone his real name. Even when Manny pressed me on how I managed to get away from Amilcar, I hadn't mentioned being in Adam's garage. It felt good to keep something from them. The only thing I told them was what Amilcar had done to the cat. Manny still wasn't as freaked out as I thought he should be. As I was.

Adam veered close to the other side of the path when he saw us, his red scarf trailing behind him. He looked straight ahead, made sure he didn't look our way.

James caught me looking and followed my gaze. Suddenly,

he was on his feet and crossing the path to the other side, purpose in his step. "Hey, bud, what you got in there?"

Adam moved onto the grass.

I shot a glance at Manny, who just grinned.

"Let me take a look," James said.

"Don't!" I said, running after James, but he ignored me.

Adam tried to walk faster to avoid James, but James shadowed him. If Adam turned, James blocked him. Every time Adam tried to sidestep, James pursued him.

"Check what's inside!" Manny shouted.

Adam's stubbly face glistened with sweat.

James flicked at his ears with his fingers, snapped Adam's scarf against his face. Adam didn't flinch.

"Stop!" I yelled.

"Holy shit, man. What's that thing behind your ear?"

"Let him go!" I wanted Adam to walk away but he was just standing there, looking like he didn't have a care in the world.

James laughed. "You should keep that thing covered up," he said. He grabbed the red scarf and wound it around Adam's head like a turban. Then he whipped the red scarf off Adam's head. Adam spun like a wooden top. He wobbled a bit before he banged into his bundle buggy and fell over it. The cart tipped and books, newspapers, and magazines spilled from the garbage bag lining. They lay scattered on the path and in the dry leaves.

James fell to the ground, lying down on the carpet of books.

"Books? All he's got are books!" he yelled back to Manny.

Adam was on his knees and with his bent arm he tried to scoop everything back into the upturned cart. James got up, allowed Adam to collect the books and magazines that had been underneath him. Adam was almost done, reaching for the last of the books on the ground, when James stepped on his hand, crushing his fingers under his boot.

"I'm serious, Manny. You gotta check out the alien bubble on this dude's head."

"Leave him alone!" I shouted, punching James in the chest, then grabbing his overall straps and yanking him hard. It was enough to get his boot off Adam's hand. "You're an asshole!"

James turned to face me, his eyelids no longer heavy.

"Let him go home," I said, calmer this time.

The Dickie Dee Ice Cream bike passed. There was a transistor radio duct-taped to the handle, the antenna extended two feet out. In that moment the world froze. We all stopped to watch it pass us by. The Dickie Dee man smiled and waved, flicked the row of bells on his handlebars. It was late in the season to be selling ice cream. He had come from nowhere. The distraction allowed Adam to scramble to his feet. He was already on his way. The cart was missing a wheel and the axle carved a white line into the cement path. Adam was whistling the Dickie Dee tune, and he never looked back.

James held the red scarf taut between his white-knuckled fists.

"Give it to me," I said.

James's eyes would not meet mine. His hands relaxed. He unwound the scarf and placed it in my hands.

"It belongs to Adam," I said. "His name is Adam."

I knocked a few times on Adam's garage door, but no one answered. I managed to push the garage door open enough to shimmy the scarf in, piece by piece. I was almost done when the door gave. I stepped in and adjusted my eyes to the space.

Adam returned to his chair and sat down.

"Thought you'd want this," I said.

He reached for the scarf, lifted it to his face. He took a whiff—long and deep—then slowly wrapped the scarf around his neck.

Adam had pulled his cot closer to the stove with its long tin stovepipe. The cot was neatly made, an extra blanket folded at the foot and a crisp pillow at its head.

"I gotta go," I said. I had to be home by five o'clock. I was nearly at the door when Adam started talking.

"Twenty-three years ago, last week. Hurricane Hazel." He looked up into the blackness of the ceiling. "This was my daughter's scarf. She was three." A smile stretched across his face. "With every jump she thought she could take hold of the clouds. There wasn't much time. There was no place to go. Things flashed in my head but—" He stopped to catch his breath. "The house got dark and the thunder cracked louder than anything I thought possible. Furniture shifted with the crash. I thought my wife and daughter would be safe under the kitchen table. Our windows blew out." He held his hands up to his throat, as if a cold wind was ramming down his throat. I inched closer to the door. "And then it stopped. Everything was quiet. I looked up to the sky where our roof once was. Half the house and the backyard had slipped into the river. They were gone."

I turned to go. I didn't want him to see my tears welling up. I wanted to take a step into the laneway, but instead, I placed my forehead against the wood, looking straight at the flaking paint. "How come you weren't afraid? James was going to beat the crap out of you and it was like nothing, like you didn't care."

"I have nothing left to be afraid of," he said.

I kept my forehead pressed to the door as I took hold of the handle and turned it slightly.

"The moment you're afraid, you close your eyes," he said. "That's when the earth opens and swallows you up."

It was October sixteenth, the Feast of St. Luke; the clock in my room read 6:40 p.m. "Get over here!" I heard Terri yell, traced her voice back to the rear room on the second floor. "Look," she said, pointing out the window with its clear view of the laneway. "You're a star!" she laughed, "in New York and L.A. . . ." I elbowed her lightly. There must have been hundreds of people, some holding lit candles, huddled outside our garage. Others lingered in a line that stretched halfway up the lane. Their black dresses, veils, and hats made my skin prickly and hot. I imagined whiskered faces of men and women planting kisses on my knees, some tickling my toes with their lips. The room spun. I wanted to close my eyes and lie down—go to sleep until it was all over.

"Look!" Terri said, tapping the window. Ricky stood on the peaked roof of our garage like a funny gargoyle. He leaned into the sky, raised his hand and waved. His smile was kind. *Everything's going to be okay*, it said. *Tomorrow, after school, we'll be riding our bikes through the laneway like we always did.*

The house was hot because my father had turned on the furnace and my mother had roasted chicken and potatoes for dinner. I passed through the kitchen; the walls were sweating—house tears, my mother called them.

I could hear my mother and Edite downstairs. From the landing I could only see their legs and laps as they folded laundry. Edite had a glass of wine at her feet. My mother never drank.

"I want to forget him. Start fresh."

"Can you?" Edite asked as she lifted the glass of wine to her lips.

"Nothing happened."

"Nothing?" Edite giggled.

"I love my family. I'm not going to throw that away."

"When are you going to be honest with yourself, Georgina? You deserve more."

"I have my children to think about. It's not that easy."

"There's a way you can have it all, you know."

The floor creaked as I shifted my weight. Their voices grew softer.

"I'm going," I said, loud enough so they wouldn't think I'd been spying.

"Okay, filho," my mother said. I wanted her to stop me.

As I walked down the narrow path to the garage door, my thoughts bounced around. *It's the right thing to do.* Another step. *Soon, Pai will be happier. Mãe will love him again.* I moved closer, almost there. *He's giving it to the church. Adam said I didn't have to be afraid—they just needed to believe in something. Just don't close your eyes.*

When I stepped inside the garage, I was met with a flurry of hands signing the cross. Some people genuflected. Then they tried to touch me, my hair, my cape, anything. After the needle incident my father had pushed the ropes farther from the door. He stood in his pressed suit at the front of the line, holding the rope in his hand, traces of worry across his face. Things had become bigger than he'd expected.

I stepped over the frozen limpet and sat on the chair. I looked at the crowd in the garage. There were more people outside, mumbling the novenas of the rosary. Everyone's thumbs keeping count to the rhythm set by Roy Orbison, who sang of candy-colored clowns and sprinkles of stardust.

My father nodded, then unhooked the rope.

The first person in line, an older man with few teeth, shuffled along the floor with his cane. I guessed that the two women at his side were his daughters. They held his elbows and lowered him onto his knees. He whacked their shins with his cane to shoo them away. "She needs to leave me," he said in Portuguese. "My wife haunts me," he whispered, as if she might be listening. "My wife's been dead for fifteen years. I was always afraid she'd go to another man's bed in the middle of the night. That's why I beat her. Now it's my turn not to sleep."

My father had suggested ways for me to speed things up. At the thirty-second point, I could press my thumb to their foreheads and whisper a prayer, "even if they're still talking," he said. Or I could wave the sign of the cross in the air to get the crowd going and encourage lingerers off their knees. "Whatever works," he said, and I knew he didn't care. My father raised the handle again, before setting it down on the record with a pop and scratch. The baseboard heaters had been turned on; ribbons of orange glowed at the foot of the walls. I was getting drowsy in the heat.

The man sobbed. One of his daughters tried to get him up, and he swung his cane and hit her thigh. She stepped back. He wasn't going anywhere. I felt the crowd getting restless. I saw my father urging me to do something. I slowly reached out my hand. I wanted to close my eyes, but I fought the urge.

My thumb pressed to his forehead and I made a tiny sign of the cross. The man grabbed me by the wrist and kissed it, wet kisses, his stubble prickling my skin.

Minutes dragged on for hours. People kept falling at my feet, but the line never seemed to get any shorter.

I stood up, struggled to untie the cape at my neck. The sounds drowned out. I swallowed my spit to see if my ears would pop, but the stale air in the room was making me sick. I only saw sombre faces, the crowd swaying in unison. I wanted to close my eyes, but Adam had said when you close your eyes you get swallowed up. It was only when I lowered my face that I realized it was James. He had made his way through the crowd and was kneeling in front of me, a fisherman's cap on his head, his blond ringlets poking out from under the rim, his blue eyes looking up at me.

My eyelids flickered and then the light went out.

I wasn't sure how long I was passed out. Someone was fanning my face, the circulation of air giving me the breath and the strength to open my eyes once again. "James?" I whispered. The faces in the crowd were blurry. "Where's James?" My father stood up and looked over the crowd. I could have said something then. I said nothing. I scanned the room of faces for James. The visitors had parted, stepping aside for someone to enter.

"Padre Costa," my father said, ears red as the priest came into focus and stood in front of the limpet and me.

"Manuel, it's been a while," Padre Costa said. He lifted his heels for a second, then stood again, smiling like the Cheshire Cat. "Antonio." He nodded. I wanted to throw up, but I managed to sit back in my chair.

We all knew how conceited he was. He must have been at least sixty but he still used Grecian Formula and had his teeth capped. According to Manny, he tanned in the rectory's backyard in a Speedo. He prided himself on knowing scripture but he would often get names wrong or mixed up. No one dared correct him. It wouldn't have made a difference.

"I was wondering when you'd drop by." I was thankful my father had found his voice.

"I received a visit from one of our parishioners the other day, one who understands the sacrifices made and the hard work that goes into heading such a faithful congregation." He swept his hands back to indicate the people behind him. "'Have you heard?' this trusted friend asked."

"Heard what?" my father pushed harder.

"Of the gift. The miracles Antonio Rebelo performs. The effigy of Jesus in a lapa."

He was so close I could smell his strong cologne as he whispered in my father's ear. "There is nothing here, Manuel. I won't let you profit in the name of Jesus."

My father looked him square in the face, then whispered back so that no one but Padre Costa and me could hear. "How much do you want?"

"For my blessing?" Padre Costa answered. "Half."

My father grasped Padre Costa by the shoulder and squeezed hard. "Never."

The sound of a guitar strummed and Roy Orbison's voice grew louder. Padre Costa spun around, shook my father's hand from his shoulder. The music blared from the speakers. Someone must have, intentionally or otherwise, cranked up the volume, a repetition of *It's over . . . It's over . . . It's over . . .*

"Shut it off!" Padre Costa yelled, holding up in his clenched hand a wooden cross the length of a pencil. He raised it above his jet-black hair, high up in the dusty air. "Heavenly Father, they gather here in your name but they are misguided. Let us pray. Heavenly Father, your forgiveness will lead your flock."

My father maneuvered around the crowd and reached under the chair for the limpet. He scrambled to his feet, wrapped the block of ice in my cape, and tucked it safely under his arm. He opened the door that led to our house.

"Antonio!" I got up from the chair and brushed past Padre Costa. "Take this and go inside!" My father passed me the block of ice. "You'll be safe inside."

The people who remained in the garage looked hungry, as if they wanted to lunge for the *lapa*. Touch it; kiss it. They could have all rushed at me and torn me apart like savages. But Padre Costa had challenged them to choose and they were undecided.

"Now, Antonio!" my father barked. I stood there, stunned, until he pushed me out the door and closed it behind me.

7

Down in the basement, I lifted the lid of the box freezer. Light filtered out and lit up my hockey pajamas. My father had told me that the light shut off when the lid was lowered, but I didn't believe him. Since I could remember I had toyed with the idea of climbing in and lowering the lid, just to see. But what if I couldn't open it again? I'd freeze between the rump roasts and the pork ribs.

My arms dove into the freezer and turned some frozen quail over. The birds clicked together like rocks. I saw the butcher paper marked *Rosbife*. I lifted the package out and unwrapped the paper, but then I heard a sound, someone walking to the bathroom. My father's clammy feet smacked on the ceramic tiles in the upstairs hallway. I waited for a flush, the sound of water gushing down the pipes buried behind the wall. My father returned to his bed.

I held the block of ice and spat on it. I rubbed the frostiness off the surface. The limpet shell floated in the middle of the block. It had lost some of its color, so brilliant when it was fresh, like gasoline in a puddle of water, it was now gray and murky, the actual outline of Jesus and the shaded features had faded. People see only what they want to see. My mind filled in the blanks, traced the figure of Jesus wearing his crown of thorns.

I heard my father in the hallway again. He stopped at the top of the stairs. I carefully tucked the block of ice under my arm like a football and straddled the lip of the box freezer. It was going to be tight. The basement light flickered on. I looked around the room one last time, saw my father's white feet appear on the top step. I took a deep breath, slinked into the freezer, a piece of meat jabbing at my ass. I lowered the lid until I heard the sucking sound of the seal. It was pitch-black.

I panicked. *What if my father looked in the freezer? How would I explain it? What if he didn't leave? I'd have to come out or else I'd freeze. What if I couldn't lift the lid from inside?* I couldn't hear if my father had left but I knew I couldn't stay in there longer than a minute or so. I decided to count from one hundred backwards. As I counted down I thought of hot things, the beach and the sun. I was so scared I wanted to pee. I thought that might warm me up only for a little bit until it froze against my skin. I was almost at one. I took in a deep breath and pushed up on the freezer's lid. He had gone. And then it hit me: I had to get rid of the shell. I wasn't quite sure how to do it. I couldn't flush it. I couldn't hide it. Shivering, I tucked my tongue between my clicking teeth. I placed the shell back in the open freezer. For now. The glow from the freezer spread across our table. I saw a purple ring soaked into the tablecloth. I shivered as I traced the ring with my finger and tasted the wine on my tongue.

On my way home from school, I saw Adam coming out of Future Bakery. "Hey!" I yelled. He didn't walk away like he used to. He reached into his bundle buggy and offered me a bun like a magician would pull a rabbit out of his hat. I smiled.

I shifted the weight of my backpack and waited for him to say something. When he didn't, I tore into the hot bun. His lump looked bigger, more purplish. And yet he remained so calm; the only still thing as the wind rattled everything around us. Adam grabbed the handle of his cart and turned away from me. He raised his steaming bun in the air without looking back. A goodbye, I thought.

I smiled all the way to James's place. I found him chomping on bacon, tearing at the *chouriço* he had pitched on a fork. I hadn't brought the food over but I recognized it as our dinner the night before. Ricky sat cross-legged on the rug and folded the laundry.

"Why are you here? Aren't you sick?" James said, sopping up liver sauce with cornbread and stuffing it in his mouth, a little bit of gravy pooled at the corners.

"Who brought the food over?" I asked.

"Your sister," Agnes said. "I saw her leave it in the usual spot. I explained to James that maybe you weren't feeling well and you sent her over." Her eyes got big, urging me to play along. "You must have forgotten." She resumed humming in her rocking chair, which didn't rock; she had placed some stones under the runners, secured the chair so it stood reclined but firm. The housedresses she wore, all dark with tiny floral prints or polka dots, had been stolen from her mother's house and could barely zip up. She looked much older than fifteen. She watched James eat.

Strips of orange hissed along the garage floor. November meant the baseboard heaters would be on for most of the day. I sat on the trunk across from James. I could feel the lock pressed up against the back of my knee.

James side-saddled his chair, pointed his fork at me. "What did you tell your sister?"

"Nothing. She's not stupid you know."

"You don't have to bring food around anymore. Tell your sister that too," he said. "I can take care of things." He lowered his eyes, brought the meat on the fork to his mouth, and chewed it slowly.

"Just wanna help," I said.

"That's very nice of you, Antonio—" Agnes began before James raised his hand to shut her up. She pushed herself out of the chair and went to the ladder, but then changed her mind. Instead, she went to the counter, picked up a wooden spoon, and stirred red Kool-Aid in a plastic jug.

"You need to drink milk!" James said, slapping the table with his open hand. His voice softened. "For the baby."

Agnes stopped stirring. She placed the wooden spoon back on the counter. She returned to her rocking chair, lowered herself slowly into the seat, and pulled the blanket up to her chin. Her knuckles formed eight bumps on the blanket as she held tight.

"Why's he in a bad mood?" I whispered in Ricky's ear. James was always with Agnes or Ricky or Manny, and I could never catch him alone to ask him why he'd come to my garage. I had a feeling his shitty mood had something to do with that night.

"I'm not sure," Ricky whispered back. "Hey, you still mad at Manny?"

"What do you think?" I couldn't help the suckiness in my voice. "The shit dresses up in a velvet cape and goes out for Halloween with a cross on his chest flashing a damn lapa he's made out of cardboard. Asshole."

"He was only kidding."

"Have you seen your friend?" James said. "Adam, is it?"

"Who's Adam?" Ricky said.

"He'll be okay." James got up from his chair and stood in front of me.

"I'm sorry," I said. I knew I had to apologize for passing out the night he came to the garage. He came to visit me to be absolved for what he had done to Adam, for letting the anger in him bubble up to the surface. It was embarrassing for both of us.

James placed his hand on my shoulder. "Let's all go see a movie, huh? My treat."

James stepped over to Agnes and whipped the blanket from her. He looked like a whole bunch of electricity had just been shot into him. He teased Agnes, tried to help her up and dance a kind of jig with her.

"You go," she said.

He wouldn't take no for an answer, tried to twirl her. Ricky kicked the trunk with his heels, giggled like a little kid.

"I just want to take a hot bath at the house," Agnes said. "I'm always cold."

"Go," James said, spanking her bum. "But wait until it's dark, okay?"

"I can't come," Ricky said. "My father hasn't been sleeping well." He started to fold the clothes again, carefully pressing the creases down with his hand. He had two piles going: one was James's and the other belonged to Agnes. I fought hard to not think of the way Ricky handled their clothing. These were the things that touched Agnes's skin and brushed against James's body. "He gets up a lot during the day and he likes me to be there, just in case he needs something."

Senhor Anselmo and his brother were painters at the College Park Shopping Centre and had both been told they

weren't needed any longer. I had overheard my father telling
my mother that Poom Pooms, Amilcar's father, had also lost
his job. Things in the city were slowing down. My father
blamed it all on Emanuel's murder—it had poisoned the city.
My mother said it was a curse.

James turned to me. "That makes it you and me, kid."

Edite was coming over tonight to look after us. My mother
had taken another shift, and after my fainting spell my father
suggested we shut the garage for a couple of days until I got
my strength back. I knew Edite would cover for me.

"What about Manny?"

"He's out for the day. He's doing a little something for
me." He wiped his hairy forearm along his chin and cheek and
flung his parka over his shoulders. His eyes peeked out below
the fur-trimmed hood and you couldn't rub out the smirk on
his face. Ricky had gone with him to the army surplus store
to buy the coat. Ricky said James had been impressed with all
the zippers and hidden pockets. Sold.

"You're growing fast," James said, a bounce in his step as he
looked down at my feet.

My cords were short, a good two inches above my ankles. I
was taller and felt stronger. My throat had been sore, at times
I squeaked, and I had noticed that hair was growing in places,
fine golden hair. My big toes pushed at the suede of my Roots
Earth shoes.

We got on the eastbound streetcar at the corner of Bathurst
and Queen. James guided me to the back. He plopped himself
on the long back seat, stretched out his legs as if the whole
streetcar was his.

I looked out the window, up to the needle tip of the CN Tower. It was just over a year ago that a helicopter had hovered above the tower, dangling its final piece, and the city froze. Manny, Ricky, and I had stood in the middle of our street. People got out of their cars like zombies and gathered together to look up. The tallest free-standing structure in the world. We could do anything now.

The streetcar rattled along the tracks: Resendes Fish Market, Shoppers Drug Mart, Army Surplus, and Duke's. Woolworth's had signs announcing it was shutting down. In between we passed rows of stores that had already closed. For Sale signs were plastered everywhere. We passed Spadina Avenue and trundled toward University Avenue, past City Hall and Nathan Phillips Square, now empty, the rally long forgotten, nothing changed. The skating rink would open soon. A few kids were walking along the subway grates, their jackets puffed up with air as they threw their hats up into the sky. I counted how long the hats hovered in the air before veering off and crashing into the sidewalk. "I'm sorry I passed out the other night," I said as we approached our stop. "I saw you and I don't know . . . things kinda closed in on me."

"It's okay."

We got off at Yonge.

"I was surprised to see you there."

"Forget it," he said, flipping his hood over his head.

"Why'd you come?"

"Doesn't matter now," he said, walking away to the intersection. We walked up Yonge Street, across from the Eaton Center and all its glass. "Imperial Six okay?" James said.

"What are we watching?"

He didn't answer.

As we crossed Shuter Street I looked over my shoulder to glance at Massey Hall. The Good Brothers had played there last week. Terri only blared disco through the house, practising the latest steps printed on the inside cover of K-tel's *Disco Dynamite* album. I liked Queen, whose concert at Maple Leaf Gardens the night before had sold out. James didn't know they were my favorite band. I didn't tell him because if he knew he'd find a way to get tickets, and then I'd feel like I owed him. Besides, I'd feel doubly bad when I turned him down. The concert was at night and my mom would never have let me go.

"The Terrace roller skating rink is down there." I pointed east. I could see the north wing of St. Michael's Hospital. It had been a long time since I had visited my parents at work, my father proudly ushering me past the huge statue of St. Michael before taking me to every department, parading me in front of all the nuns who ran the place. He had been the housekeeping supervisor. Things hadn't worked out. That was three years ago, before he bought the truck.

We finally arrived at the outdoor square, underneath the Imperial's marquee panels.

"There's *Star Wars*. It's still playing," I said. "Or what about *Close Encounters of the Third Kind*?" I stared at the poster of the big spaceship with all its lights coming over the horizon.

Soon we were sitting in the theater, a large bag of popcorn between us. When I reached for my drink under my seat, my cheek rubbed against James's arm. The hairs on my head tingled and I twitched, the static in my legs and down to my toes felt like swarming bees. The last time we were alone was in my basement. I tried to watch the movie. Our hands touched as we dug for popcorn. I felt a pinch in my groin. The second time it happened the pinch turned into a knot. By the third and fourth time I found myself thinking about when to dig in so that our hands *would* touch. I tried hard to focus on the screen—on the actor in the movie looking out into the suburban neighborhood he lived in, and everyone going on with their everyday lives, as they always had. Then James leaned in against me, his shoulder lowered to touch mine. I closed my eyes and then something exploded in my head, the image of blood being spilled a few buildings away. Emanuel's blood.

The bag of popcorn tumbled into the aisle and I ran through the corridor, down all the stairs, heard James coming after me. I made my way outside and ran until I found myself in front of 245 Yonge—the windows of Charlie's Angels now completely boarded up. I looked up to the rooftop. Then I bent over and puked into the gutter. James was there. He rubbed my back with his hand, small circles. Some cars honked their horns. I wished he would stop.

I wiped the spit from my cheek, tried to breathe through my mouth so I wouldn't have to smell the sourness of my puke. "Leave me alone! I'm fine."

James put his fists in his coat pockets.

"Hey, kid, that guy bothering you?" one man yelled from his car.

"Just leave, James."

He punched a telephone pole. The honks kept coming.

"Leave!"

He began to walk up Yonge Street. He turned back a couple of times but that was it. I was afraid to be alone so I followed behind him and saw him kick a mailbox over. I imagined catching up to him to tell him I was sorry for ruining the movie, sorry for behaving like a little kid.

I was just a few paces behind when James crossed at College Street and began to walk west. It was five o'clock and starting to get dark. I was cold and wanted to go home. A van drove up beside James, slowed down. James stopped, leaned in to the open window to give the driver directions. I came up behind him and saw the driver, a man in a suit, the knot of his tie bigger than my fist. "A hundred for the both of you," I caught the man saying.

"Fuck off, buddy." James kicked the van's side as it sped off.

A shiver ran through me; my teeth chattered. "I want to go home."

"So go home. I didn't bring you here—you followed, remember."

"A little young, no?" a voice ricocheted off the building next to us.

I followed James's look to a boy who sat on a huge city planter. We crossed the road. The boy's jeans were so tight you could clearly trace his dick in his bulge. He threw back his parka hood and his hair was dyed a yellow blond. He was a teenager, his face covered in acne. A long feathered roach clip dangled from his ear, rested on the shoulder of his jacket. He was so skinny.

"You got it wrong," James said, nodding at me to follow him.

"Not like you to turn down an offer." The guy spoke as if he was chewing gum.

"I'm not workin'," James said.

The guy expelled a burst of air in a short, sharp hiss. "You're getting too old for this. They want fresh meat."

"Come on," James urged, grabbing me by the hood and spinning me around.

The guy called out, "Leaving them all for me?" as we began to walk south to Dundas Street.

I sat in the streetcar seat in front of James, who said nothing. I opened the window and stuck my face outside, like a dog, breathing in the air and cooling my head. We were heading west, toward Spadina, and James didn't have any nails left to chew.

"It doesn't mean anything," James finally said. I pressed my forehead to the window the way my mother did when she sat on the worm-picker. "I was seven when my mother left." His elbows stretched across the seat over my shoulder. He leaned in. I shifted away. "She said she was going to find my father, bring him back home. I was so excited. Just thinking about it, those words, *my father*. I waited. Never had a family like yours. My grandfather was the only other person to take care of me. He hadn't wanted my mother to go. He had said that's how he lost *his* wife, to the flash of the big city." I leaned my head against the streetcar window. "I kept thinking of how my mother'd come home with her arms full of toys and my father, who I had never met, would walk in behind her. It's what kept me going, you know? I practised my reading so I would impress my father when he came home. I was ten, I think, when I realized they would never come." I heard him swallow his spit. I couldn't bear to look at him and I was sure he wouldn't continue if I did.

"My grandfather was a crazy bastard sober, turned devil with a bit of drink. He bought this dog, didn't allow me to give it a name. 'Go feed, Dog!' he'd yell, which meant throwing scraps at the thing because it was chained to the tree all day long." James stopped. The streetcar swept along Dundas Street, past Chinatown. There wouldn't be much time for James to finish his story.

"One day—I was fifteen—I came home and before I could even make my way through the front door, he tackled me, wrapped a chain around my ankles. It happened so fast. He dragged me through the snow and tied the chain to that same tree out back." We had stopped at Kensington Market and the Project, the buildings all uniform like piled bricks. "*What the fuck is he doing?* It kept going on in my head like a skipped record. *What the fuck is he doing?* Then I saw him come from the front of the house. That beast of a dog was pulling him forward. 'Make a man of you yet, boy, not a fuckin' crybaby.'"

I saw James's reflection in the window. He was someplace else.

"He let go of Dog. I covered my face, but he went at my head, tore at my thigh. I kicked. Then I punched. 'You got to fight dirty if you ever gonna make something of yourself, boy.' I reached for its collar, held its head in the snow. *Get it off!* That's when it got loose, lunged at me and dug into my face. 'Fight back! Because if you don't, the world's gonna swallow you up and spit you out.' The dog was yanked back, clear off its paws. 'Get him, you little fucker!'" James said, softly.

"BANG!" James jumped off his seat as he said it. I jumped with him. Even the streetcar driver looked back at us. "My grandfather shot into the air. Slung the rifle over his shoulder and went back into the house with his dog. Bastard."

I traced the pink scar along his jaw with my eyes. "I tied a rag around my head. It kept the blood in check and held the skin in place."

"How did you get away?"

"That same night I set a trap, one of those nasty things that look like the jaws of a shark, with all those teeth. I hooked some meat on it and dragged it close enough to the barking dog. He went for the meat and the trap snapped shut." James clapped the air for added effect. "Clear took its fuckin' head off."

"And your grandfather?" I asked, lowering my voice. The streetcar was in front of Sanderson Library. I reached up and rang the bell.

"He was there. He could hardly stand. He crouched in the snow and patted the dog's head. Its body was five feet away. He stood up, old bastard. Started clapping—loud and slow. Then he laughed. Said, 'I'm the only family you got, boy.' And that's when I ran as fast as I could, straight at the miserable geezer. I rammed into him so hard he fell backwards, right into the tree and the rusted nail that waited for him."

James looked at me. I nodded as though I understood his pain, even though I didn't. All I felt was an emptiness in my stomach.

"When I left that night, the snow had almost completely covered him. Frosty the fuckin' Snowman. But the old bastard sat crouched against the tree, giggling. He was fuckin' demented."

James raised his knees and hugged them, drew his sleeve across his nose, then into his mouth. "Never told anyone before." He hugged his legs tighter and looked out the streetcar window. "It's our stop," he said.

8

2:11 P.M. . . . I had been getting to the garage later and later. I was doing it on purpose. My father knew it and was losing patience. Earlier that morning, I lay curled up in bed, unable to move, flashes of the moustached man in the van offering us money; the pimply boy waiting in his tight jeans; the cars turning the corners, slowly, before taking another turn at the next block. *Faggot*, Manny's voice said in my head. Padre Costa had been over to our house two nights in a row. He threatened to shut things down. I closed my eyes and willed him to make it happen, to make my father hand over the *lapa*. If I squeezed my eyes tighter, harder, Adam appeared, a great big grin traveling across his face as he rolled his bundle buggy along the alley. *You can do this. Just one more time. There's nothing to be afraid of. Just one more time.* I stood naked in front of the full-length mirror that hung behind my bedroom door. My body was covered with red dots the size of fleas. They were itching and I scratched my stomach and my arms until they had become hot. It started happening after I passed out in the garage. I thought of telling my mother because it would be a good reason to get me out of performing. I knew it would work, but then I'd hate to think of how my father would blame my mother—how he might think I was a sissy for going to her and complaining about a silly heat rash. The thought of having my costume touch my skin made it worse.

Underwear, then pants. I bristled when I picked up the starched white shirt from behind the chair. My skin felt hot. My throat burned. "Antonio!" my mother called. I could hear the concern stuck to her voice. I wanted her to come up, sit on my bed, and tell me to think of the nicest place in the world, and to imagine myself there. Like she used to. I put my arms in the shirtsleeves and then flung the cape around my shoulders.

"Antonio!"

Coming, I mouthed.

The crowds weren't thinning out. I was sure three hours had passed when a woman wheeled the boy up to me. "My son, Nelson," she said. The boy was around my age. He had an egg-shaped head and a tuft of tangled black hair. His mouth was open and all I saw were teeth. His limbs were thin and stringy and his body was bent the weird way you could bend a pipe cleaner. It looked like he was straining his neck, his head lolled to the side, almost off the leather backing of the chair. His mother held a rag to his drooling mouth.

"I had four girls before I get pregnant with Nelson. The day they take me to the hospital my husband tell me to make sure is a boy or else no come home." I could tell she was embarrassed about speaking English. I heard grumbling calls to speed things up. "I bring our son home. My husband is happy. A son! But I know everything is not right, not like my other kids. My husband no want to hear anything from me. He say I was a louca—crazy woman. My son is weak. He no take care of himself. I see he is not like other boys. Not strong. My husband see this too. My husband say is better for us to finish him." She heaved. Nelson tilted his head up to the rafters as if gulping for air. Again she wiped the drool from his chin. The crowd lowered their eyes and turned silent. It dawned on me what *finish him* meant. I tried hard to freeze my face, hide my fear. I turned to my father, the tears welling in my eyes. There was nothing I could say or do. It was all a lie.

"Help him, pelo o amor de Deus, you can help my son."

"I can't," I said.

My father climbed the steps onto the stage and stood beside me.

"I can't," I said. "Please, Pai, I can't."

The woman reached for my face. She dabbed the tears from my eyes and cheeks. She brought the handkerchief down and stuffed it in her son's shirt, rubbing it on his back. It was hard to breathe. Bursts of air squeezed through my sandpaper throat. I fumbled with the knot of the cape, gave in and tore at it as a warm trickle of pee ran down my inner thigh. The snapped tinsel powdered the air with sparkles. The crowd broke into song, *Alleluia, Alleluia*.

I had recovered from scarlet fever. My mother blamed my father, said it was brought on by exhaustion. A week of rest was all I needed, my father said.

His wine press had been assembled where my chair had stood. The rest of the garage remained the same. In a matter of hours my father could have the whole damn thing running again. The sweet smell of grape juice filled the garage. It was the smell that reminded me that winter was on its way. We were late this year. My father had bought the last thirty crates of grapes, and according to my uncles, he had waited too long—too mushy, they said. It was my job to remove the nails and staples from the empty crates. There was no one around. I saw the hammer lying on the ground. I dragged a stool from the corner and got to work, piling the slats of wood into small bundles that my father would use for tinder when we smoked the *chouriço*.

"You is here." My father entered the garage from the laneway. His sleeves were rolled up to his elbows and his arms were dark with matted hair, stained purple with grape juice. "You find the hammer okay?" he said. Other than letting me know his sister wouldn't be coming to stay with us until next summer—the delay, unexplained—few words had been shared between us in the week since the worshippers had been left swaying in disbelief. The last thing I saw was how frightened they looked before I collapsed on the stage. The situation was getting out of hand, and my father was smart enough to know when to let things rest. "This is a ship! I am the captain!" he had argued with my mother that night. My father lit a cigarette and looked at me with one eye through the smoke. He headed to the wine press and torqued the ratchet head a few times. "I'm at your uncle house. I helping them to bury the fig tree." His voice was soft, almost pleading. I didn't say anything. "We have to bury it now before the freeze." I couldn't face him either. "The lapa's gone," he said.

"What do you mean, *gone*?" My voice was strong, and it surprised me.

"Someone come in through the basement window and steal it."

"If you're lying—" I stood up, tall and straight. I couldn't back down. I waited longer than I needed to, waiting for him to lunge at me. He looked small.

"Filho, I did it for you." I stared at the pile of crates and wiped my nose and eyes. He cranked the large metal bar of the ratchet, and then he reached down for a jug of last year's wine and raised it to his lips. He took a deep swig, enough to make the jug gurgle. "Pronto, I go to your uncle's house now." He swiped at his mouth with his hand. The drip of grape juice turned into a thin, steady stream that pissed into the bucket.

I traveled up the lane straddling the thin river of watered-down wine. It looked like our houses were bleeding. Red ran down the spine of the lane, all the way to its ass. That's what we called it—where the sewer was at the bottom of the lane close by my uncle David's garage. Senhor Anselmo was hosing down his garage after making wine. So were Senhor Rodrigo and Senhor Benjamin. They acknowledged me by tilting their hats as I walked by.

Once on Markham Street, I beelined to Mr. Serjeant's house. I walked along the narrow stretch at the side of his house through to his backyard. I opened the door that led into his garage. James stood facing his canvas, a gallon of paint in his hand. Agnes sat on her rocking chair and smiled. A Swanson's TV dinner balanced on her lap.

"Are you feeling better, Antonio? Would you like something to eat?" Agnes said. Her face and arms had plumped up. I tried to avoid looking at her belly. James looked at me for a second before turning back to his painting.

"No, thanks."

I noticed Mr. Serjeant's trunk was opened. Its brass lock had been broken off. The rim of the chest was covered in ruffled fabric and the inside was lined with quilted material, a balloon print. There was a small yellow blanket folded neatly in the bottom beside a tiny pillow.

"It's early, I know," Agnes said. "I like yellow. And the baby will like the balloons."

"It's pretty," I said. *Pretty* sounded like the wrong word—a girl word. There was something creepy about a crib with a lid. "My mother says it's bad luck to prepare anything before a baby is born. She told me that when I was born she let me sleep in a drawer in her bedroom, just for a couple of days, until my father could set up the crib." I could tell from the look on Agnes's face that it didn't come out the way I wanted. I turned to James, who kept painting. He swung the tin of paint a bit and then splattered the canvas in the same way that Padre Costa blessed the congregation with holy water.

"It's over," I said.

Still James did not turn around. He put down the tin of paint. He smudged the paint in swirls on the canvas. "Your aunt says that dreams and nightmares are like cleaning out the trash. You wake up with a fresh mind." He stopped to light a cigarette. "No worries. No troubles."

I heard creaking and saw Agnes climbing up the ladder, her belly rubbing against each rung before she disappeared into the loft.

"Painting does the same thing," James said, blowing smoke out his nostrils. He faced me now, his curls fighting their way out from underneath his painter's cap. "Edite's a good lady. She doesn't judge." He reached for the rag dangling from the loop in his jeans and wiped his hands, picking at the webbing between his fingers.

"Does she know what you do?" I asked, lowering my voice.

"I'm not a faggot, if that's what you're thinking. It means nothing. You're not a kid anymore, Antonio. There's lots of stuff in this world that ain't pretty."

"I know."

"Do you?" James said. "Look, Edite helps us out a bit, that's all."

"And what does she get from you?"

"I fill her in on what's going on downtown. I give her information."

"About the murderers?"

"Something like that. She's working on a story in the lead-up to the trial."

"There's nothing about the trial in the papers or on TV anymore."

"Wait until the trial begins. But Edite's not really interested in the trial. She's investigating another kind of story."

I kept my mouth shut. I didn't want him to think Edite kept secrets from me. I was mad that she didn't trust me enough to tell me what she was really working on, though.

"She's interested in what makes people tick," James said. "Edite's brave, you know. She's more interested in how Emanuel's murder has affected the gay community, how they've all been made out to look like animals. It's the kind of story most reporters are afraid to tell."

James came closer to me, placed one hand on my shoulder. His hand was hot. I shook it off. "The world is full of monsters," he whispered. He put his hand on me again. This time his fingers dug in. "I'm not one of them. I look after you guys." He let the cigarette butt slip from his fingers and drop to the floor. He spread his arms wide, as if daring me to take a step back. I was ready to push him away, punch him if I needed to.

"The limpet's gone," I said. James's face betrayed nothing. "Did you steal it?"

James looked stunned for a second, but then I thought I saw something, the tiniest flinch, the quickest blink. It *was* him; he had put an end to it. My mother and Edite had made promises, but it was James who had saved me. I took in his smell of tobacco, sweat, and turpentine. I pressed my lips to his chest, but pulled away at the sound of the garage door opening.

"You should see them," Ricky said, slipping under the door like a crab. "I've never seen Manny in a suit. I followed them all the way to the door."

"What are you talking about?" I said.

"They were going to meet Lygia's parents to talk about Eugene and her getting married."

James flicked a switch and the disco ball started turning. "Isn't that the way you Portuguese people do it? Meet before a marriage is set?"

Climbing down the ladder, Agnes slipped on a rung but regained her balance.

Near the basin at the rear of the garage James stripped down to his waist. He splashed water on his chest and under his arms, dragged a face cloth he had patted with soap along his skin. Droplets of water splashed onto the baseboard heater coils and sizzled. Agnes turned away as he unzipped his jeans and reached down into his groin to clean with the cloth. I watched from the corner of my eye. James caught me looking. He reached for a towel and tossed it over his shoulder. He placed his hand on his belt buckle. Ricky turned to face the garage wall.

"I've got to get dressed," James said. "You mind?" I could feel my dick getting hard. I turned around and stood next to Ricky.

The bulge pressed against my jeans. I tried imagining starving kids in Africa with their bubble bellies and the flies that swarmed around their mouths, and what things would be like if my parents were killed in a car accident and I was left alone to live with my sister. And then my grandmother, waxy and scrawny, lying in her coffin. Anything to force my dick to go limp.

"You can turn around now," James said. "Don't you have to be somewhere, Ricky?"

"I almost forgot. I'll go now," Ricky said.

"Everything going okay?" James asked. Ricky nodded and left. Agnes reached up behind her, and without looking at James, she rested her hand on his chest.

"Antonio?" James said, as I zipped up my coat and tugged it down as far as I could. "Follow Ricky to Red's. Just stand back and keep an eye out for him. Don't let him see you," he added. "Will you do that for me?"

"Sure," I said, before dipping under the garage door. I figured Ricky was just dropping off the rent or some money to cover the electricity bills. Red lived all alone in a big brick house on Markham Street, three stories high and just a few houses down from Ricky and Edite. I climbed over Red's fence. He had a lawn, not a vegetable garden. A bluish light from a television shone from the basement window. I crouched down, off to the side of the house. I saw an elongated shadow, which shrunk and then turned into Red as he came into view. He was probably twenty feet away from me. He walked over to an easy chair, the kind with a handle on the side, reclined, and a footrest magically appeared. He had a beer in his hand. His flaming red hair turned a strange color in the television's light. Ricky walked by him. He carried what looked like a roll of toilet paper and a bottle and placed them on the floor beside Red. Red plunked his beer bottle on an angle between his legs. He loosened the knot of his robe before lifting the cable box from the floor and resting it on his knee. The long wire that stretched to the TV was tangled under his feet. Ricky positioned a small stool in front of Red's recliner. He sat on it facing him, between his spread legs.

What the fuck has James gotten him into? I thought. I wanted to pound on the window, make enough noise to have it all stop. But my feet felt like they were stuck in wet cement, my arms just tubes of air.

Ricky sat on the stool. Red stared at the TV, watching *Tom and Jerry* in the freaky glow. Every so often a slice of Red's belly would jiggle with laughter. Ricky remained quiet. Red then reached down with one hand and drew his robe to his sides. His dick was hidden in his bush of red pubic hair. Ricky picked up the bottle of baby oil and lathered his hands. My mouth went chalk dry. Ricky was about to place his small hand on Red's bush but Red's fat hand came up and slapped Ricky in the head. Ricky almost toppled over. I thought about calling the police. I knew what the police would do to men like Red, but I didn't know what they would do to Ricky. Ricky righted himself, blew on his hands and rubbed them together. Red's head fell back as he closed his eyes and spread his legs wider.

I waited in the cold, crouched against the brick wall next to the basement window. I couldn't watch anymore. Spit gathered in my mouth like a puddle. I fought not to swallow because I was afraid all the spit would gush into my stomach and that would make it worse, trigger the vomit. I sank into the fog that had settled near the ground and tried to breathe in the frosty air. *James was sending Ricky in to do this shit. Making him do the same shit he did. The world was full of monsters and he was one of them.*

I heard the side storm door open. I slunk behind the garbage can. Ricky wiped the snot from his nose with his sleeve. He zipped his jacket up to his chin and looked up to the sky. His breath made small puffs in the night air. He turned and walked between the houses, toward Red's front yard and onto Markham Street.

I followed. I saw him turn into his walkway. He looked so small. He shut his gate and disappeared onto his porch. I wanted to make sure I heard his front door closing behind him. I crossed over to the sidewalk and hid behind the trunk of a maple tree. I tucked my face up to my eyes in my jacket and breathed hard to keep warm. I waited until his bedroom lights went out. It was all I could do.

9

Even the December air couldn't erase the smell of cat piss and dog shit in the Patch. A mattress covered in brown stains leaned against the brick wall of a garage. It seemed like everything got sucked up into the Patch, like it was a gigantic magnet for diapers, shampoo bottles, broken chairs, squashed lampshades, and I don't know how many shoe boxes. It was early in the morning and the clouds in the sky looked bruised, as if they were about to burst. Even though James did the one thing everyone else promised— destroying the *lapa*—I hated him. And after everything I knew about him, I hated what my body did when I so much as thought of him.

Up the lane, Manny's garage door opened. He stepped into the laneway and rolled the door behind him. He walked a bit faster, and then jogged, when he saw me. "Kinda early for you, isn't it?" He horked up a good one, shot it five feet away, then dug into his Afro for a cigarette.

"I couldn't sleep."

Manny kept bouncing on the spot to keep warm. He looked at me through his squinted eye as he flicked his Bic lighter, then took a drag and blew the smoke out through his nose.

"Getting fuckin' cold," he said. "What's up with you?"

"Where did you learn to do that?"

"What?"

"Blow through your nose like that."

"Watch this," he said. He took another long drag and tilted his face up to the sky. He poked his tongue slowly into the smoke and blew out in puffs in perfect O's that wobbled as they got bigger. "James taught me."

"What else did he teach you?"

"What's that supposed to mean?"

"I don't know. You tell me."

"Okay, I'll tell you. You got a lot of hang-ups when it comes to James." Manny tipped the mattress down. Some potato chip bags and chocolate bar wrappers flew up into the air and tumbled in the wind, until they wedged against the fence. "Problem with you is you think too much," he said.

I lifted the cuff of my jeans and drew the knife from my sock. The minute I had heard my father's truck revving that morning I got out of bed, dressed, and opened the drawer of my nightstand. Shoved at the back was the knife my father had given me when I turned ten. My father said he had carved the handle himself. A big wooden fish with fat lips twisting along its length. A grouper, he said. I held the knife in the air, and the glint of the blade caught Manny's attention.

"What's that for?"

"Just because."

Manny grinned. "You first."

I had brought it out before and we had taken turns in the Patch throwing it down at each other's feet, trying to stick it into the packed soil, as close as possible to our toes.

Our shoulders touched, back to back, before we each took ten giant steps forward, like we were preparing for a shootout in a western.

"Go on," Manny said. "The first to jump away is chicken shit."

I held on to the tip of the knife, reached over my shoulder, and flicked it with my wrist. It bounced off a brick or something and skipped like a stone in water. It stopped a couple of feet from Manny. He went over to pick it up.

"You ever wonder why James is here?" I asked, just as he was about to throw the knife. I saw him mouth *Fuck*.

"What, you think he stabbed someone or maybe you think he killed a guy?" Manny grinned, flicked his wrist quickly. The knife whistled past my shoulder. I ducked but kept my feet stuck.

"You're an asshole, Manny."

"What does it matter anyway?" he said.

I picked up the knife by its cold blade. I stepped back to my spot and flung it. "I think we should stay away from him."

The knife hit the frozen ground, twisted, then slid across and stuck in the sole of Manny's boot.

"Ohhh, that was close," he said, bending over and wiggling the blade until it came loose. He straightened up, pinched his cigarette butt between his thumb and forefinger and flicked it to the ground. "What's got you so pissed?"

"I don't want to play anymore," I said.

"Even-steven. After my turn you can call it quits." Manny licked his bottom lip, raised his arm, and threw hard. It landed a foot short but it was too late, I had already jumped away. "Chicken shit!" he howled. "Listen, James is harmless."

"You don't know that."

"What is it you know that you're not telling?"

"I know too much."

"Look, I know what James does," he said. "You think I'm stupid?" Manny turned his back to me. "It's the same kind of shit Ricky's been doing at the pool hall for a long time."

"You knew? Why didn't you say anything?"

"The same reason you didn't."

"Doesn't it kinda freak you out?" I said.

"I fuckin' hate it. But as long as James doesn't touch me and as long as he knows that I won't do the shit Ricky does, I'm good."

"So why do you steal bikes for him?" I asked.

"I don't know," Manny said, turning around and jabbing his heel into a puddle covered in ice. "I guess he's there for us, and he lets us use the garage. It's kinda like paying rent, a payback."

"You don't owe him anything, you know."

"He took care of Amilcar for us. Blackmailed his dad about something, got his dad to agree to beat the shit outta him if he even looked at us."

It took a minute for it all to sink in. Even though Amilcar was no longer around, the fear of him stuck to me.

"What's Ricky doing out so early?" Manny said, pointing at Ricky running down the laneway to meet with us.

"You okay, Ricky?" I said, trying to make the words sound normal, but I could hear in my head that they hadn't come out right.

"I saw you, Manny," Ricky said, out of breath. "Saw you following your mom and dad and your brother up to Poom Pooms' porch."

Manny lit another cigarette.

"It ain't gonna happen." He took a deep drag. "Eugene's not good enough. That bastard. Poom Pooms's hair was all done up like some kind of old Elvis. He reached his hand out to my old man and said, 'You understand, don't you?' Fucker!"

"They can still elope," Ricky said. He reached up, took the cigarette from Manny's lips, and took a drag. I had never seen him smoke before. Manny grinned and Ricky tried hard not to cough.

"My brother left a hole in the drywall bigger than his fist before taking off." He took his cigarette back. "He hasn't come home yet. Shit, man, if you could have only seen the hole."

"My dad didn't come home this morning," Ricky said. "He should have been home by now." Ricky looked around the laneway as if he was looking for a clue. I took a step toward him and he stepped back.

"You're better off," Manny said. "You don't have to clean your old man's ass now."

"Shut up, Manny," I said. I took another step toward Ricky but he held up his hand to stop me.

"No, it's okay. I'm going home now to wait a bit more." With his blinking eyes and twitching lips, he looked like he was about to cry right there. "I made his favorite breakfast." He ran back up the lane.

Manny threw his cigarette down and turned to follow, but I pulled him back. "Let him go," I said. "He'll figure things out."

"You're right. Anyway, you and me, we need to have a bit of fun."

"Edite's away this weekend. Let's go hang out there," I said. Manny's smile grew big.

Edite had told me she'd be out all weekend looking for

Johnny. Manny thought we should raid her fridge, take everything over to James's. I knew her fridge would be empty, but there was always a jar of peanut butter and a box of Ritz crackers in her top cupboard.

As I opened the door, Manny tackled me and we both fell into Edite's kitchen, laughing. Manny sat up on my chest, holding on to my coat.

"Everything's going to be okay." I said. "With your brother, I mean."

Manny stopped laughing. "I know." He flopped off me and sat with his legs crossed on the kitchen floor. I got up and opened the fridge door. "Thanks," Manny mumbled. I pretended not to hear him.

There was some beer and a few cans of Tab in Edite's fridge. I knew James would like the beer, so I left them behind. Let him get his own beer. I'd sneak a few cans of Tab back for Agnes. James said Edite had been helping them out. She wouldn't mind if I did the same. I scooped as many cans as I could into my arms, wedged a cold can of Tab under my chin, and kicked the fridge door closed.

"What the hell!" I yelled. Manny stood in the kitchen, his pants dropped to his knees. The can of Tab fell, hissing and spitting fizz all over the floor. Manny's coat was hoisted and held under his chin. He had his pecker pinched between his fingers.

"Double digits, buddy," he said.

"What?"

"Seventeen pubes. Count them."

"You're nuts." His dick was a lot darker than mine. It was bigger too.

"Got a few fuzzin' up those too." He giggled. "Sprouting like weeds." He flopped his dick up, pointed it toward his belly button to expose his nuts.

"Pull up your pants and help me." I bent over to pick up the can, trying hard not to look at his dick. "Get the dishcloth from the sink."

"You a man yet?" he said, bumping into me as he reached for the can I had placed on the counter. He sucked up the hissing foam.

"Shut up!"

He flung the dishcloth at my face. "How many times do you whack off? My record is seven. Of course I get about a hundred stiffies a day. If you get less than that there's something wrong with you. My brother says you gotta stretch it and use it, kinda like exercise. If you don't it'll dry up and fall off. If you want I can lend you some of my brother's *Playboys*. He's got a whole bunch in a box under his bed."

I thought of James, but then I thought of my dead grandmother and once again it did the trick. I got a grocery bag from the kitchen drawer and started stuffing the cans inside. Manny watched me, sucking the pop from the dented can. I stepped on the dishcloth and dragged it across the floor.

"Help me clean this up. And stop making that horny sound, you're freaking me out."

"What sound?"

We both turned to each other. Groans were coming from the bedroom. Manny zipped up his fly and stepped out into the hall.

"We gotta go, Manny."

He was lurking outside Edite's bedroom. The door was

open a crack. He looked back at me as I approached, placed a finger over his lips.

He picked up an empty bottle of Canadian Club. "Looks like your aunt had herself a bit of a party," he whispered.

Edite lay under a mishmash of blankets. Her head and long legs stuck out of the bed, along its sides. There were empty or half-empty bottles everywhere, mostly wine. She shifted a bit and her sheets slipped off her shoulder, almost far enough that I thought her nipple might pop out.

"Let's get outta here," I said, sweeping my arm back to get Manny away from the door. I heard the faint sound of the shower. That's when I looked down at all the clothes and newspapers and garbage and saw a pair of men's black boots, the kind cops wear, tucked under a chair. I shoved Manny back, tried to trick my brain into erasing what I knew I had seen.

The whole way down the laneway Manny kept clicking his tongue.

"Shut up, Manny."

"What am I doing?"

"You know what you're doing."

"I know what I'm *gonna* do. I'm going home to break my record." He grabbed at his pretend penis and stroked it. He looked at me as if I understood. I swung at him but he dodged my arm and ran away laughing.

"Freak!" I yelled, walking faster, half jogging down the lane. My cheeks were getting prickly from the cold. I wanted to go straight home but then James was standing in the middle of the lane, outside his garage, blocking my way.

"What's that all about?" he said.

I stood in front of him. I wasn't going to tell him anything.

"I'm just going home." I tried to go around James but he stepped in front of me.

"Shit happens, Antonio. I didn't send you to follow Ricky to get some cheap thrill. Shit happens and I guess I thought you could handle it."

"Handle what?"

"Forget it."

"You can't send him to Red's anymore."

"Ricky isn't doing anything he wasn't doing before I got here."

"What you do is one thing but—"

"And what is it I do, boy, that's got you all in a knot, huh? I took care of that little shit Amilcar for you—called him off. And I closed down that circus your father had going."

"I never asked you to do any of it."

"I did it for you."

"Where's Agnes?" I said, noticing she wasn't in her rocking chair.

"She slept at her parents' last night. She wanted to sleep in her old bed."

Strings of colored lights throbbed in the garage. They hung from nails and hooks, were tucked between joists. There wasn't much thought to where they were placed. It was clear James had tried to cram in as many as he could.

"Agnes'll be back soon. Just needs to rest. It's not safe for her to climb the ladder anymore. I tried bringing her things down, set her up nice and cozy down here but—"

"What if she doesn't come back? What if she's gone?" I said, looking at a section in the strand of lights that hadn't come on. It only took one blown bulb and the whole string

wouldn't light. You'd have to go through the whole thing, jig-
gling the bulbs one by one until you found the bad one.

"What did she tell you?" He came toward me. "Agnes is
coming back."

"How do you know?" Goosebumps crawled up my arms at
the sound of my tough voice.

James caught me by the arm and yanked me into the
garage. He was strong and it happened quickly. I wondered if
those men had done the same thing to Emanuel. I tried to
stop shaking. I focused on the feeling of the electric heater
searing my ankle. James let go to lower the garage door.

"Sorry. I'm sorry, Antonio. I shouldn't have—"

I still had the knife tucked into my sock. I could stand up
to James. We could take care of Agnes ourselves, I thought,
without all the crap he dished out.

"We're all we've got," James said, his voice softening.
"Each other. Agnes and I are family."

I nudged the garage door open a couple of inches to allow
the cold air to gush in or the hot air to escape.

"We're a family," James said as he removed his T-shirt. He
was doing it on purpose, I thought. "We stick together."

"I've got a family."

His face and neck turned red. He came closer. The scar on his
cheek looked like the silvery trail of a snail. "My mother left.
She never came back. Ricky's mother left him too. Took off one
day in a cab because she couldn't take the beatings any longer."

"How do you know that?" Ricky had never talked about
his mother with me.

"He told me. He remembers the way she looked from the
back of the cab as it sped off. He tried to chase it but his dad

held on tight," he said. "It's just some work, you know. It doesn't mean anything. It's just about the money. And believe me, he's safer not working in the streets." James went to the bucket of water on top of the hot plate. He reached in with a face cloth, wrung it out, and dragged it slowly over his shoulders. "Ricky knows that."

"Doesn't make it right."

"It's not like that out there. There's no right or wrong. Ricky knows that too. Believe me."

10

I WOKE UP MONDAY to find my mother had rifled through drawers again. I had nothing to hide but I figured it had something to do with smoking. She must have smelled it on my clothes and thought I was stashing smokes in my room. I had booby-trapped my stuff with some thread, crisscrossed it in front of my drawers. I had also put a postcard I had received from some distant relative in Portugal—a close-up of the statue of Senhor Santo Cristo dos Milagres, blood streaming down the statue's face, the crown of thorns digging in—wedged between a pair of socks and a belt. I thought she'd feel guilty for snooping and it would stop her in her tracks. It hadn't.

I left my room and went downstairs to the kitchen to confront her, but she was nowhere to be found. I grabbed my school bag. I was just about to thunder down the basement stairs when I heard the water running from the basement tap. From the top of the stairs I could see my mother bent over the laundry tub. She had dropped her bra in the sink and dipped her head under the tap. Her breasts were large and they swayed with her every movement. I had grown up getting washed in the basement before going to bed. Soaking my feet in a square shallow pail of warm water, I often looked up to see my mother bathing herself over the laundry tubs, her robe flipped over and dropping down from her waist. My mother had called it a sponge bath, even though she used a face cloth. I watched her now, as her drenched hair flowed with the water. She blindly felt for the shampoo bottle on the ledge, her fingers squirming like worms. I was ready to run down and hand her the bottle of shampoo. If she let me, I could run my fingers through her thick hair until it was poufy with suds, the way I used to when I was smaller. I'd swirl my fingers through her hair and dig into her scalp. I would make horns with her hair and she'd purr or groan.

I was twelve now; I wasn't a little kid who helped his mommy wash her hair anymore. I was turning to leave when my father approached her from behind. He must have been in the bathroom and I thought he was going to shave, like he sometimes did, over the laundry tubs. Instead, he began to rub my mother's shoulders and back. He mashed his groin against her bum. He cupped her shoulder and then slid his hands down her arms and under her to grab hold of her breasts.

My mother didn't stop him. I wanted to get out of there. I slowed my breathing and tried to step away from the landing without making it creak. My mother raked her fingers through her hair while my father rubbed his hands farther down her back and around her bum. She kept washing her hair as if he wasn't there. His mouth and chin were pressed to her ear. My father's hand disappeared under my mother's skirt. She jolted a bit, as if she had been pinched, but kept washing her hair.

"Manuel? Não . . ." but her voice drifted off.

He undid his belt. His pants and boxers fell to his ankles. He lifted up her skirt and pressed himself against my mother. She wiggled her bum. I closed my eyes for what seemed forever, and when I opened them again I saw my father rocking on the balls of his feet, bumping up against my mother's behind, his mouth open. His hands traveled up her waist, to her breasts. He held on to her hanging breasts, adjusted his footing a bit before thrusting a little faster. I could feel a sourness traveling up my throat. She continued to work the shampoo into her hair, running it under the faucet. Then she grabbed on to the sides of the laundry tub. My father rocked faster. He made the same sound the men did on *Baby Blue Movies* on channel 79. She turned the taps so the water rushed out stronger, loud enough that I could step away without being heard. I threw on my coat and ran outside. The cold air cut into my lungs. It hurt and it felt good at the same time.

I ran up the stairs to Edite's apartment. "Where were you?" I said.

Edite spun around to face me. Her hair looked matted. She had deep wrinkles around her eyes.

"Hey," she said, in a long, drawn-out voice like she was calling to me from outer space. Her spoon tinkled against the rim of her coffee mug.

"Did you find Johnny? Are you even looking?"

"What's bothering you?" she said. "Did something happen? Sit down and catch your breath. Seems like every time you come over you're in some kind of huff."

"I saw you. In your room."

As she moved from the counter to the table I could hear her slippers sticking to the spot where yesterday I had dropped the can of soda. She sat down and crossed her legs, adjusting her satiny robe to cover her knees. Her foot began to tap against the table's leg.

"Please, Antonio, it hasn't been a good week." Edite's fingers trembled as she tried to light her cigarette. "No riddles today." She went through three matches before she threw the matchbox against the wall, then stretched across the kitchen table to snatch her lighter. I noticed the black gunk under her fingernails.

"You told me my friends and I could count on James," I said. "But I don't think you even know him."

"What do you want to know?" Edite looked pale and she hadn't washed her makeup off properly the night before: you could see it faintly on her face like a mistake that you erase but the smear is still there.

"Everything," I said.

"James and I meet downtown for drinks. You know that? The St. Charles Tavern. It's a gay bar, but I like it there because it's dark and it's filled with a lot of lonely characters. Their stories are so fascinating." She blew smoke through her nose.

"So he's helping you write about queers?"

"Antonio, don't get mean. It doesn't suit you." Edite bit her thumbnail, tried to peel some of it off. "You know, William wants me to leave. He wants me to come home with him." Edite said the words so matter of fact, but her pink toe started twitching.

"Who's William?" I said.

"My husband."

"He's dead." I had overheard my father say that Edite was *uma louca*. Things were worse than I thought.

"That's what your father told you." Her shoulders dropped. "William divorced me. Before Johnny went to Vietnam. Said he needed—what *we* needed—was a change, that things weren't working out for him." Edite mocked the words.

"Where is he?" I asked. I placed my hand on her shoulder and suddenly felt older, more mature. She caught my hand with her cheek, locked it down to her shoulder.

"He's here, visiting." She took a drag, but her cigarette had gone out. "William is black, Antonio. I married a black man."

It was beginning to sink in. Lies had been told all because Edite's husband, Johnny's father, was black. My mother must have known too, but she had kept it a secret.

"William was so good to me—we were good to each other—but they disowned me, my own parents."

Edite had lied to me for a whole year. Did she think I was as Portuguese as my father or my mother? I yanked my hand back.

"I gotta get to school." I wanted to run over the rooftops, soar above the gullies and feel the wind push me forward.

"Antonio."

I stopped at the door but refused to turn back. The steam had frosted the window in the door. I lifted my hand and wrote LIES! in block letters.

"I'm not leaving yet. I'm here for you!" she shouted just before the door slammed behind me.

Things were moving lightning fast. I wasn't able to focus all day at school. I couldn't keep track and I couldn't do anything about it. The secrets and the lies adults told kept tumbling in my head all the way home, walking up Markham and into our laneway. Until I heard the words, "Fire! Fire!"

The call traveled up the laneway, growing louder as I reached my garage. A small crowd had gathered at the top of the laneway and I ran to join them. The yells became screams and soon men and women were emerging from their garages and into our alley. Ants forced out of their ant holes. They ran up the alley, holding kerchiefs to their mouths and hollering for help.

I saw Adam break through the crowd, alone and without his cart, a fish swimming against the current. I thought how strange it was to see him with nothing to hold on to.

"Adam? Adam?" I said, stepping right in front of him. His eyes were glazed over, looking at nothing in particular, no direction. He walked right past me, brushed against my arm, and the hairs on my neck got electric. "Adam!" I shouted. "What's going on?"

He stopped. He looked up into the sky that had turned the color of blue ink. He kept mumbling, "It's time, oh yes, it's time." I reached up and touched the tumor behind his ear. It was hard and felt hot. I don't know why I did it—to heal him, maybe. If I did have any power, this was the time to show it. Adam smiled.

"Don't ever close your eyes, Antonio," he said, his fingers poking out from his cut-off gloves raised to touch his eyes.

"Where are you going?"

Adam strolled down the laneway like it was just another beautiful night and he was going for a walk.

"Adam!"

I left him and ran to the top of the laneway. Adam's garage was being gobbled up by fire. People in heavy coats ran around filling buckets and aiming hoses from neighboring backyards. It was useless. Adam's books had been the perfect fuel. The sirens could be heard coming our way. I looked back, and as he turned the corner out of the laneway I saw the last bit of Adam's red scarf.

A pinprick of light came from the other side of the lane. At first I thought the fire had leapt to other roofs. But when I crept closer, I saw Amilcar. He squatted on the rooftop across from Adam's garage. He looked my way, struck a match, and lifted it to his lips. He blew it out like a birthday candle and smiled down at me. He took another match and did the same thing. Then another.

11

WINTER HAD OFFICIALLY begun when I looked out my bedroom window and saw that a storm had covered our laneway in ice, changing the world into something glittery and beautiful. Trees, telephone lines, awnings, the rooftops and gutters—everything that was black and dirty and broken was sealed in solid glass.

Almost a week had passed since the fire. Despite the winter wonderland outside my window, I couldn't erase the image of Amilcar perched on the rooftop, the flickering flame appearing from his thumb, and the dark shadow of Adam turning the corner of our laneway. Where would he go? Did he have a place to stay? Did he have any friends?

My mother had called to let us know she had taken a Sunday shift and would be going to five o'clock Mass straight from work. My sister was to meet her there. I was allowed to skip it. No one was looking forward to my seeing Padre Costa for the first time since my father shut our garage operation down. For his part, my father had headed off to someone's house to tell them how much it would cost to dig out their basement. Bored and alone, I found myself dressing to go outside, and headed out the back door to the garage.

The minute I stepped into the laneway dusted in snow, I slipped on a patch of ice. Not a smudge or a crack in it. It was perfect. I cleared away the layer of snow with my boots and saw my reflection. I crouched down, and then my heart jumped in my throat. I thought I saw the *lapa*. I jabbed at the ice with my heel, looked closely, and saw only a chunk of bark. Relieved, I made my way up the lane, through the snow untouched by car tires. I snapped an icicle from one of the gutters and sucked on it, quickening my step to pass James's garage, then past Edite's backyard and fire escape, until I had made it to Adam's garage, or what was left of it.

Little of the storm's snow had settled inside, even though there was no roof. The walls were burned down to struts and supports. All the bookshelves had disappeared. A cobweb of black two-by-fours lay scattered like a game of pick-up-sticks. The garage opening was crisscrossed with yellow tape that barely shuddered in the calm. I looked down our long laneway. Everything frozen, caught in time.

On the way back I passed James's garage again, with no intention of stopping. But a high-pitched scream from inside stopped me in my tracks. A quick clang; someone was kicking the garage door. I let the idea of moving on and running home flitter in my mind. It would be so simple to do. Instead, I opened the garage door. My fists were tight, ready to punch. I searched for anything that could be used to hurt him: the shovel leaning against the wall or the coil of wire hanging from a nail. Agnes arched her back in the rocking chair, sliding to the front of the seat, the hem of her skirt slipped up to her knees, pinkish-wet and clingy. Ricky knelt beside her, a bucket in front of him, urging Agnes to hold on. My eyes darted across the room, looking for James. I saw Manny slouched against the blue chest. He had been the one kicking at the door. Agnes threw her head back and yelled. All the veins in her neck popped out.

"James?" Manny said. A spray paint can was next to him and the plastic bag he had filled with it was trapped under the garage door. He was stoned. He sat against the blue chest and puffed on a smoke. "Do something," Manny muttered, his eyes heavy and half-closed.

Agnes's face was red and sweaty, her hair glued to her temples. Ricky's voice was crackly; he kept rubbing her knees, urging her to hold on. She was quiet for a moment before she let out a sound that rose like a wave until it became a high-pitched squeal, the kind that only dogs could hear. As quickly as it came it went away. She let her head fall to her shoulder.

"The baby's coming early," Ricky said to me. "'Hail Mary, full of grace, the Lord is with thee. Blessed are . . .'"

"That you, James?" Manny had managed to stand up. Slitty-eyed, he staggered, before sliding back down into a crouch.

Wind rattled the only window in the garage. The base-board heaters hissed and spat.

"Help, Antonio!" Ricky said, never letting his eyes leave Agnes.

"I think I know where James is," I said.

On Markham Street the street lights shone on the snow banks, the snow drifted down and the salt crystals sparkled on the sidewalk. It made everything look warmer than it was. I had removed the plastic sheet from my bike, unchained it from my garage. I knew this would be the fastest way to get to James. I didn't know how long it would take for a baby to be born, but from the sounds that came out of Agnes I knew I didn't have a lot of time.

I took a couple of wipeouts before I turned the corner onto

College Street and rode up Elizabeth. I thought I was going to explode with relief when I saw James standing near the corner with a few young guys, drinking from a Styrofoam cup, puffing clouds into the falling snow. He saw me and right away knew something wasn't right. He yelled "Move!" and I slid back on my Chopper's seat. He slammed his cup to the sidewalk and hopped on. With his ass in the air he pounded the pedals furiously. I held on tight to his waist.

Drifts had begun to form and it was difficult for James to read the curb. I closed my eyes and turned my face from the wind, wobbling on the back as the bike's tires battled sewer grates and streetcar tracks. There were few cars on the road. The city grader had done its first plow-through and now the salting trucks were coming round, their blue lights flashing. The last traces of street lights had been blotted out. My fingers were frozen. James hopped onto the sidewalk just as a salting truck turned the corner. The salt ripped across my ankles, rattled and clanged across the bike's frame and wheels. It didn't matter. James didn't slow down.

We burst into the garage. Ricky stood off to Agnes's side, cradling the baby. He had wrapped it in the yellow blanket, which hung down to his knees. Agnes wasn't crying. She sat in the chair wearing the same cotton dress, now drenched and pulled up on her thighs. Her naked legs were white against the bloody towel stuck between them. Her sneakers had been kicked off. The stones had become dislodged from underneath the runners and she rocked slowly in her chair, humming the same song my mother had sung to me when I was a child, *põe, põe a galinha põe, põe*. Manny was up now, pacing around the garage, trying to shake it off.

"She won't hold the baby," Ricky whispered, taking a few steps toward us. He held the tiny bundle up to James. "It's not breathing."

The blanket made the baby look bigger than it was. The way Ricky held the baby up so gently made me want to cry. He had done it all by himself. James walked past him, took off his jacket and covered Agnes's lap. He bent over, plunged his hand into her hair, and matched Agnes's slow rocking, to kiss her forehead.

I had caught a glimpse of the baby's gray face, all scrunched up. Its head was bald and pointed, no bigger than an orange. The room swirled. The Christmas lights twinkled colors onto the baby's skin.

"It's dead," Manny said. James turned and looked to the garage door and his painting, squinted against the wind that howled outside.

"Get rid of it," he said, his hair dripping wet, his neck and cheeks red from cold.

Ricky tucked the baby back under his chin. He pinched its nose and breathed soft puffs into its mouth. He nuzzled his lips to the baby's ear and whispered something. I looked past Ricky's shoulder. James had placed a chair next to Agnes's rocker. His lips touched her ear, her eyes half-opened staring at the ceiling, as she hummed and rocked in the garage's heat.

Early the next morning, I stood at my bedroom window looking down on my father's dump truck, filled with clumps of hardened cement mixed with mud and dirt. In the bed of the truck, I could see the slab of concrete we had unearthed. Under it, I knew, was the baby in a tiny dirt hole. Ricky had insisted the baby be wrapped. He had found a dirty apron in the garage. It was one of those touristy ones with the nine islands of the Azores on it. He had swaddled the baby and tied the apron strings around tightly so that it looked like a colorful cocoon. "She won't be cold now," he had said. I wondered if the baby could feel the cold. Manny wouldn't help us; he had slipped away when none of us was looking. Ricky and I did it all by ourselves.

My mother appeared, the wide collar of her fake-fur coat hoisted up to shield the sides of her head. She was off to work her regular shift. I watched her walk down our path. She turned to close the gate, then stopped. She stood motionless as if sniffing the air for danger, like one of those animal mothers on *Mutual of Omaha's Wild Kingdom*. She looked up to the bare chestnut tree. I hid behind the curtain panel. For a moment I thought she might climb into the dumper, dig out the baby, and somehow bring her back to life. She was my mother. She could do that. I held my breath and watched out the window. My mother trudged down Palmerston through the snow, her figure getting smaller with every step.

The flush of the toilet was all it took for me to make my way downstairs. My father was coming out of the bathroom, dressed and freshly shaved.

"Why you up so early?" he said. "You feeling okay?" He raised his hand to my forehead, but I dodged it.

"I can't sleep."

"Go back to bed," he said as he brushed past me toward the front vestibule. He tied his construction boots and tucked the laces into them. He rammed his Thermos under his arm like a football player. "Is too early for school," he said, so quietly I could barely hear him.

"There's no school today."

"Another one?" It was one of his favorite things to do, complain about how many days the teachers took off.

"Can I come with you?" I asked. Before he could answer I added, "I'll be just a minute," and bolted up the stairs, three at a time.

When I went outside the street was quiet, and the world still. I sat in the passenger seat, my hands tucked under my bum. It would take a while before the truck warmed up and the vinyl seats softened.

"Why you want to come with me?" I could tell he really didn't want an answer. After what happened with the *lapa* and the silent treatment I was giving him, he was happy to have me share in his work. I rolled down the window. I liked to drive with the windows open, even in winter.

"You like driving a truck?" I chose a question that I thought he'd take a long time to answer.

"I like being my own bossa. I no take orders from other guys. I decide. I am the captain. You see James? He no come to work yesterday."

I said nothing.

"He call and say he no come to work for the next Saturday. This is a problema."

"You still need him."

"I have lots of business."

"I heard he found another job." It was a good lie because I said it without skipping a beat.

My father didn't say much after that. Maybe he was waiting for me to say what kind of job or that I knew the reason James wasn't telling him flat out.

I was relieved when my father stopped talking. He pointed his chin in the direction of the plaid Thermos. I unscrewed the cup and poured some coffee. I offered it to him, but he motioned for me to drink first. Pursing my lips, I blew over the rim and sipped—double-double. I looked back through the long rectangular window, unable to see inside the bed of the dump truck, only its steel shell. I noticed movement underneath a pile of blankets my father usually kept neatly folded in the sleeper cab behind the front seats. I forced myself to look back, and that's when I saw Ricky, his eyes peeking out from under the wool blanket. My father looked into his rear-view mirror and saw him too.

"Ricardo?" The shock on my father's face quickly transformed to tenderness.

"Sorry, Senhor Manuel," Ricky said as he pulled the blanket off his head.

"What you doing here?"

"I couldn't," Ricky began, but looking at my father, he mustered some sense. "I couldn't get in my house. Must have lost my keys. I kept knocking but my father didn't hear me. Then I stopped because I didn't want to wake him up."

"He no work the night shift, filho?" my father asked, before it all made sense to him. Ricky's father's drinking was the kind of thing adults knew about but never discussed when we were around.

"Why you not come inside our house? You stay all night by yourself? You not cold?"

Ricky shook his head. His soft brown eyes could convince anyone of anything. "I didn't want to make him mad, Senhor Manuel."

"You no worry. I fix things." My father raised his hands off the steering wheel and then slammed them down, hard enough that the truck swerved a bit. He rolled down his window to spit outside. There was a shine in his eyes I hadn't seen in a long time. It made me love him. He lit a cigarette. The cab of the truck filled with smoke. I could see my childhood drifting away from me, those moments when my father hoisted me atop his shoulders so I could look over a crowd.

I turned to Ricky and forced a smile. He smiled back. I was glad Ricky was with me. We would see things to the end together. He jumped up front and sat next to me on the passenger seat, his arm tucked behind my back, and mine over his shoulders.

We rattled east along Lakeshore Boulevard, underneath the Gardiner Expressway.

"We go to Leslie Street," my father said. The city was building a spit out of construction debris that extended out into Lake Ontario. At the foot of Leslie Street, we came to what looked like a toll booth. A man sat in a chair, all bundled up with a coat and fingerless gloves, the kind Adam wore. He slid the glass window open and without looking at my dad shouted, "What ya got?" The man's matted beard and thick neck made his whole head look like it was stuck onto his body like Plasticine.

"Clean fill," my father said. *Please don't check. Please don't check.* Ricky's breath whistled in his nostrils. After a long pause the man simply nodded and slid the glass window shut.

My father drove onto a narrow dirt road that ran down the middle of the man-made peninsula. A light wind riffled across the surface of Lake Ontario. We were the only ones there. This was what the surface of the moon must look like, I

thought, with hills and craters all covered in white dust. Ice
had formed along the lip of the shore. It was peaceful. My
father drove the truck right out to the long finger of land,
then reversed it until it backed onto the shore.

The truck stopped with a grind of metal. Seagulls hovered
above. Some landed around small mounds of garbage, rum-
maging through the heaps. Ricky got all jittery when he saw
this and I thought of the baby too. My father pressed the Lift
button. The dumper slowly inched its way up. Ricky bowed
his head so low it almost touched the heat vent that blasted
from the dash. His hands were woven in prayer.

Just then the truck bounced and the dumper stalled.

"What's that?" I heard myself say the words in fear, even
though I hadn't meant to.

"Is nothing. Something get stuck. I go see. Antonio, when
I say go, you press the button. Okay?"

My father hopped down onto a mound of snow and I slid
over to the driver's side, careful not to knock the stick shift
into another gear. My father's seat was warm.

Ricky remained quiet, his eyes shut tight.

I looked out the driver's mirror. The truck's rear wheels
had cracked a slab of ice on the shore. The rubble would go
directly into the lake. I waited quietly, hoping to hear the cry
of a baby from underneath the dirt. Her last chance.

"What if she floats?" Ricky whispered.

"Okay . . . Okay!" My father had taken some kind of rake
that was tucked under the belly of the truck, and he was pulling things from under the dumper lid, attempting to dislodge
what looked like the large stone we had buried the baby
under. I thought I'd piss my pants.

"Okay!" he shouted. "Stop!"

Instead, I pressed the button and the hydraulic tilted the dumper higher. I grabbed hold of the chain above my head and pulled. The horn sounded, deep and rolling across the water. Again I tugged.

"What are you doing?" Ricky pleaded.

In the mirror I could see my father walking back to the driver's seat, determination in his short stride and anger flashing across his face.

I mumbled an apology as he climbed back into his seat. He looked unimpressed, but the diversion had made him look away from making sure everything tumbled into the frigid lake. It had also sent the seagulls back up into the sky.

I scooched back over to the passenger side and looked in the mirror as the load emptied: red clay and sand mixed with rocks and brick and cut pieces of rebar.

"You see anything?" Ricky barely whispered.

I shook my head, too nervous to even speak.

There were bubbles of air and weeds and sand and cold water. The clouds were drifting and I could see beautiful strips of light hitting the water. I spotted a chunk of concrete steps, partially submerged in the water. On a summer's day, I thought, swimmers could use the stairs to walk into the lake water.

"Pronto! We go home now and I make breakfast."

The truck lurched forward, the slap of the dumper lid sending its metallic clap across the lake. The cold rippled through my body. I couldn't stop shivering until Ricky's small hand slipped into my pocket and he pressed his thumb to mine.

*B*aby Mary—Ricky had given her a name; he felt it was the right thing to do—rolled in the water's current. I could see her curled up, the umbilical cord tugging at her belly, the other end anchored somewhere below, where the lake turned dark. I wanted to reach in and pluck her out of the water, warm the little body in a towel. But every time I tried my fingers rammed into the icy surface of the lake. The baby swayed in the water, kept to the rhythm of the lake's tide. I leaned over. The baby's eyelids flashed open to reveal nothing but black holes. The ice cracked and the cold stabbed me, a million needles covering my skin like a blanket.

"Filho!" My mother held me, crunched my body in her arms and smothered my face in her smell. The swallow charm had been threaded back onto her chain. She rocked me, whispered words into my ears that I didn't quite understand, pecking my cheeks with her lips. My sister stood at my bedroom door, looking worried and sucking on her pajama sleeve. "Filho, this has been going on a few nights now." She brushed my hair away from my forehead. "What is it? You haven't slept in days," she said, her eyes and mouth all squished to her nose. I buried my face in my mother's chest and sobbed.

"We put it in my father's truck, under some dirt, and then we drove it to a landfill and dumped everything into the lake."

Edite let her paper bag of groceries slip a bit. She leaned against the door of a boarded-up store. A streetcar rattled past.

"You saw the baby get buried, then."

I nodded.

"Good." A puff of breath covered her face, fading the red tip of her nose.

"That's it? 'Good'?"

"You did the right thing, Antonio."

"How can you say that?"

"It's not your fault." She placed the bag of groceries at her feet, straddled it so her legs kept it from tipping over. I wanted to kick the bag over and take off. She reached into her pocket for her cigarettes. The pack was empty. She crumpled it into a ball and tossed it on the ground. "James came to get me. He carried Agnes over to her parents' house. We thought she'd rest better in her own bed. She wouldn't let us take her upstairs. I guess there were too many ghosts. I stayed to help clean her—gave her a warm bath. The bleeding had stopped."

"And James did nothing," I said, my voice raised.

"James didn't leave her side. Agnes slept on the basement couch and he lay on the ceramic floor beside her."

"Right, and left Ricky and me to do all the dirty work." I spat on the ground, just missing Edite's boot.

Saturday afternoon I walked by Mr. Serjeant's veranda. I wanted to get to the garage from the front of the house— better not to lift the garage door and expose everyone to the laneway. I hoped James wasn't there. A week had passed since Baby Mary's birth and it was Agnes I wanted to see. I saw a box addressed to Manny. Underneath his name was a large sticker with the words *Baby?* And *Star Santa Claus Fund.* Manny must have written a letter to the newspaper asking for one of the gift boxes they handed out to poor families in the city. I hugged the box and walked along the side of the house into the backyard. I couldn't let Agnes see it. The last thing she needed was to be reminded. In the backyard I found an empty garbage can. I dropped the box inside. It wouldn't make sense to open it now.

Snow melted within five feet of the garage's perimeter. Inside the garage, baseboard heaters had been connected to beat-up extension cords we called the Octopus. They sizzled all night and day to keep Agnes warm.

I found James standing away from the garage door, looking at his painting. He was almost naked, a pair of white briefs, and a cycling cap turned backwards on his head. He looked like he had lost weight. He held the paintbrush in one hand and a roach clip in the other, the tip of his joint burning. It smelled of beer and piss. The heat made the stink worse.

I felt a pinch on my calf. I jumped, thinking it was a rat. A small puppy was trying to climb up my leg. It was tiny, too small to have left its litter. I picked up the ball of black fur, nuzzled the pup under my chin.

"I got it for Agnes," James said, "thought it could snap her out of it." He splashed the canvas with a muddy green paint, short flicks with his brush or with his hand that he scooped paint into from the tin. "It's been a week. She doesn't talk anymore. Think the pup will cheer her when Christmas comes?" He refused to face me. His voice was a bit shaky. "Thought she'd need something to take care of."

James drew the rag he used to dry his paintbrush across his face and around his neck. The sweat glistened over his body. I forced my eyes to look away. The pup licked under my chin.

I placed it in a box James had set up against the wall, between some heaters.

"So she's still there?"

James lifted a beer from the counter and took a swig.

"This is her home," he said. "Manny and I took her rocking chair across the street, set it in front of the TV. I go over there and she just rocks in her chair."

"I'll go see her."

"I sent Ricky over to see if he could get her to eat something."

"She lost her baby."

He took a long drink. His Adam's apple beat like a heart.

"You should have taken care of it yourself," I said.

"Fuck you!"

"It wasn't fair—making me and Ricky get rid of the baby."

James whipped the bottle against the wall, where it smashed. I didn't flinch. The foam trailed down the wall. He raised his joint to his lips, tilted his head up to the ceiling, and blew out.

"You say you're here for us, that you'll protect us. But that's a lie."

"I wanted to be sure she was okay. I needed to stay with her. She was out of it, didn't know what was happening."

"Ricky and I had to watch the baby get dumped like garbage into freezing water while you did nothing."

James looked up to the rafters and opened his mouth into a big O, all the muscles in his neck becoming sharp like knife blades. He was screaming but hardly a sound came out. He closed his eyes, and almost in a whisper said, "Agnes likes to touch my hands, you know."

"You didn't even look at the baby," I said, softly.

James walked past me, reached for a rung, and slowly climbed up to his loft.

I was coming home from the last day of school before Christmas break. Now was my chance to sneak out with the gifts I had for my friends. I had used the forty dollars my father had given me from the collection can after the *lapa* disappeared. I felt too guilty to use it to buy myself something. I had a kite for Ricky, the kind you had to assemble, and a blue hair pick for Manny. I had found the perfect scarf for Agnes, red wool, just like Adam's. I had scored everything from Woolworth's going-out-of-business sale, and Terri had helped with her employee discount. I was tempted to buy James a gift—a leather wallet—but I didn't. The whole time I had the gifts stored under my bed, I thought of Ricky running down the laneway in his bare feet, his hand raised straight in the air as the kite kicked and looped in the wind. I'd be chasing its tail, flying across the rooftops in huge bounds. I thought of the pick I'd bought for Manny and how it would flash against his Afro, Manny plucking away till he looked like one of the kids from the Jackson 5, maybe Michael. The blue against his black hair and dark skin was sure to make him smile.

It was just after five o'clock when I entered the laneway with my gifts tucked under my arms. I hadn't gone far when I heard a whimpering, whistle-like, coming from somewhere in the laneway. I walked toward it, thought it might be an injured cat or dog. I peered around the edge of a garage. Ricky was crumpled up, drowning in his bomber jacket, leaning up in the corner of two garages.

"Ricky?" I rushed to him. His eyes were heavy and dark. He was burning up. "What are you doing here?" His head was heavy and flopped down onto his shoulder. He said something—*bed* or *dead*. He breathed as if through a straw sucking up pop at the bottom of the bottle. I dropped the Christmas gifts in the snow and scooped him under my arms. "You need to get to bed." I lifted him like a forklift. He was light, featherlight. His butt was wet from sitting in the snow. I turned back to make sure he hadn't peed. His spot was blotted like a cherry snow cone. I broke into a sweat. I saw his mukluk footprints trailing from Red's gate. *Red!* With Ricky in my arms, I trudged along the laneway, keeping close to the garages, the untouched snow dotted with what I knew to be specks of Ricky's blood. I stopped in front of James's garage and kicked the aluminum door hard with my boot.

The garage door rolled up and over. James, his red eyes barely open, looked at Ricky's limp body in my arms. "He was at Red's," I said, sidestepping him. "But you knew that." As I went past, James's hand shot out to touch Ricky. I whipped Ricky away from him, wouldn't let him lay a finger on him, and carried Ricky over to a cot James had set up for Agnes. He had positioned it near the blue chest, close to what would have been her baby's crib. I let Ricky roll from my arms onto the mattress, and I carefully unzipped his jacket. I caught James, still in his pajamas, pulling on his jeans. He was a stoned slug, slipping his coat over his bare shoulders. I gingerly took off Ricky's coat. From the corner of my eye I could see James teetering, trying to balance himself as he slipped his long white feet into a pair of rubber boots. I struggled to take Ricky's mukluks off his feet. Ricky wouldn't let me take off his pants, his limp hand trying to push my hands away. Drowsy, he let his head fall back onto the pillow. I let him just lie there, breathing for a while, before pulling his boots off. I tugged the blanket out from under him and drew it over his chest. I unplugged a few of the heaters and threw open the window with its painted panes. In my search for a rag to wet and cool Ricky's head, I realized James had taken off.

I warmed up a can of Campbell's chicken noodle soup over the hot plate, but Ricky continued to sleep. "Ricky," I whispered. It felt weird to speak to him when I knew he couldn't hear me. "You're going to feel better soon and no one's ever gonna hurt you again." I leaned in closer. His breathing still sounded as though he was sucking through a straw. The baseboard heaters were humming full blast. I pulled back the blanket from Ricky's chin. "Ricky. Remember the time we fell into the dumpster at the toy factory? The toys were up to our waist. We could hardly move. It was like being stuck in quicksand. They were all defects but we didn't care. You found that doll with the squashed head, remember? And I found that Smash-Up Derby set? Oh, and the Evel Knievel figure with the missing leg? Then the security guard yelled at us to get out and chased us off the property. I still remember looking back and saw you running with that Evel Knievel doll stuffed down the front of your pants and I couldn't stop laughing." I caught the faintest curl of a smile turning up his lips. I realized I was crying.

James's canvas was a wash of Spackle and paint that had been flung across it or splattered and dripped with turpentine to wash areas out. It was his bad mood on that canvas. The garage door whipped up with a clang. James walked in and slammed the door down behind him. Ricky had not moved; he slept and breathed small puffs between his cracked lips. James carried a large silver box under his arm. It was an eight-track tape recorder trailed by a frayed electrical cord and wires. He slammed the thing on the kitchen table and tossed a whole bunch of bills into the air.

"What happened this afternoon wasn't part of the deal I had with Red." Now sober, he ripped off his jacket and threw it across the room. "Two hundred bucks was all I could pound outta him." He took the backyard hose he had fed through a hole in the window and ran his bloodied knuckles under the stream of water. "You can go now. I'll take care of Ricky."

"Fuck you!" I said. I tried to suck in my lower lip, stop the trembling. James hung his head, and then slowly turned the tap to shut the water. "Fuck you," I said again.

He walked over and reached into the cardboard box where the puppy lay sleeping among some rags. He scooped up the dog in his massive hand. The puppy licked the traces of blood from his knuckles. He sat on the cot and placed the puppy on Ricky's chest. The puppy licked Ricky's face. "Merry Christmas, Hoot," James said.

13

M Y MOTHER HAD BEEN cooking *petiscos* all day long, and only stopped just before we got dressed for Midnight Mass. Street salt crunched under our feet as we walked down Palmerston Avenue toward St. Mary's. My father walked ahead of us. I was behind him with my mother, and Edite—who I still wasn't speaking to—followed behind with Terri, their arms locked as they stepped carefully in their high heels. My father went to church only twice a year—Easter and Christmas—a gift to my mother, instead of the chocolate or flowers the commercials told him to buy. He stopped, turning in frustration at the pace the women had set for themselves. I caught up to him. He placed a hand on my shoulder.

"We're going to be late and I not going to stand up for the whole thing." I didn't care about a seat; I was in a hurry to light a candle for Ricky and Agnes and Baby Mary. I wasn't sure the message would get to God because so many sins had been committed. I let the idea creep into my mind that what happened to Ricky was punishment for what we had done with Agnes's baby. God could be mean. I knew *I* still needed to be punished for my part in everything. I just wanted it to happen soon so I could get it over with. We crossed Queen Street and my father continued to talk about stuff he had read in the newspaper. I was beginning to think he had touched the *música* again. It was an expression my family had about slipping brandy or cognac into one's coffee, *um café com música*. Whatever had loosened his tongue, I didn't care—the sound of his voice made me feel safe.

"This boy, Gretzky, is very good. He's Polish. Those Polish work hard." My father and uncles loved to watch hockey. "Is like *football*," they said, "ice instead of grass, puck and sticks instead of a ball and footwork." My father *was* tipsy. I looked up and saw he was also nervous. I had thought about it—we probably all had. He was going to walk into the church and confront Padre Costa for the first time since he had come to visit at our garage.

We got to church a few minutes early. The smell of wax, spiced with incense and mothballs, wafted up past the traces of lemon oil from the pews. Tiers of candles stood in iron holders. The men wore suits, shiny on the knees. The women were shrouded in black lace veils. And for the first time I could remember, I wasn't angry with my mother for dragging me to Midnight Mass. I wanted to be there, wrapped in the warmth of the place. I wanted to be with my family. So many people don't know what that feels like. It was the *something* my father couldn't fully re-create in our garage.

I wanted to pray. For Ricky, Manny, Agnes, and Baby Mary for sure, and for Adam, that he was warm and had a roof over his head. And even for James, because we were supposed to pray for sinners. Jesus loved them like all the rest, maybe even more. My father huffed and a few people turned. Once recognized, our family was allowed to shuffle onto a bench at the back, everyone sidestepping to make room. They didn't blame us. They were upset to hear the holy limpet had been stolen. We were all victims.

My father pressed his fingers together, forming a steeple. I stared at his strong hands, his white starched shirt cuffs held together by silver cufflinks. Edite nudged her way past my mother and sister to sit beside me, reached for my hand, and snuck it in her coat pocket. The pocket's lining had a gaping hole.

"You always have warm hands, Antonio." She was shivering. "I know you're angry." My father looked at Edite, then looked away, up toward the altar. "Agnes is doing okay. You boys were very brave." I tried to wriggle my hand out of her pocket but she held on. From the corner of my eye I could tell she was forcing a smile. Gazing at the front of the church, she leaned down to my ear. "And your friend Ricky is going to be just fine," she whispered.

James probably went to her again to ask for help with Ricky because he couldn't think for himself. He pulled everyone in to fix the things he screwed up. Even she couldn't forgive James for that. But I doubt she knew James had been pimping Ricky out to Red.

My mother looked tired. She still had to knead the dough one more time before covering it with tea towels and letting it rise a couple more hours. But she would never complain about the length of the service. She'd be up by five o'clock in the morning to bake. There was nothing like the sweet smell of *massa* on Christmas morning, she would say. My mother placed a lace veil over her head and passed an extra one to Edite, who refused it at first, but then took it and buried it in her coat pocket.

Missa cantada meant that high-pitched singing stretched the Mass until almost two in the morning. I had already been pinched by my mother for snapping the bronze purse clips on the backs of the pews. At one point I looked over to see Terri brushing her fingertips on the same clip in front of her. It was something we had done as kids. Her nails had been painted pink, a shade so pale my father wouldn't notice.

"From Mary's womb, He was born to die for our salvation." Padre Costa held the golden chalice. He belted the words out over the heads of the parishioners in the crammed church. The light fell over his head and face, and I had a sudden vision of Baby Mary floating in the lake. "Bread of life, with new life feed us breads from heaven and to heaven lead us." Padre Costa's mouth continued to move, but I could no longer hear. I could only see Ricky, the blood blooming in the snow where he sat; James kneeling at my feet and begging for forgiveness. It was then that I decided I would take Communion and I would follow it up by kissing the statue of Jesus. My father told me I didn't have to—he never did—claiming the thing was a disease sponge with all those people breathing and coughing over it. I noticed the statue was only a little bigger than Baby Mary.

We were all packed into the pews, thousands of candles flickering. The air hung over our heads like in a smoky kitchen. I undid my scarf and loosened my tie, and that's when I saw Manny's head, his hair controlled with globs of Brylcreem. He stood between his mom and dad. Eugene wasn't with them. I used my powers of thought to get him to look at me, to notice that I was standing there, only a few pews behind him. I even stood on the kneeler to look taller. It didn't work.

I was glad when people got up to inch down the aisle for Communion. I was hoping my line would shuffle forward until I could pair up with Manny, but that wasn't going to happen. We would take the host first from some helper priests. Padre Costa stood behind them, about a hundred feet away from me, in front of the altar, holding the baby Jesus up in the air, an offering to the congregation. We got up from the pew when it was our turn. My father poked me in the back and winked, and for a moment I thought about how good it would feel to tell him everything.

We shuffled down the aisle, behind old people with canes and tired mothers carrying miserable children awakened to kiss the baby Jesus. The closer I got, the clearer the statue of the naked Jesus became. It lay on a velvet pillow trimmed with gold cord that reminded me of my own cape. I wanted to believe the priest when he said the spirit's breath would take the baby to a place where there was no weeping. A woman sang "Ave Maria." Her voice warbled up to the vaulted ceiling. *Ave Maria, gratia plena. Maria, gratia plena. Maria, gratia plena. Ave, ave Dominus, Dominus tecum.* There were only about six people in front of me now.

My mother was the first in our family to reach the statue. Not content to give the statue a kiss on one foot, she snapped quickly and kissed the other foot.

"It's not anatomically correct," my sister whispered through the corner of her mouth. "He should have a helmet head for a penis. He was a Jew." I knew she had been influenced by Edite, who had told me Jesus was Jewish and so couldn't have a foreskin, though the statue of Jesus did. My heart pounded as Terri followed my mother and kissed the statue's toes. Padre Costa was about to turn away when Edite faced him. She bent down to kiss the statue. I was standing beside her when I saw her eyes twitch. Padre Costa took in a huge gulp of air. I saw the lipstick stain left on the thigh, dangerously close to the statue's dick. Edite's lipstick was a bit crooked, some pink on her teeth. I looked away, felt like I had at my grandmother's funeral when I found myself on the kneeler in front of her coffin, fighting my giggles. *Just nerves*, my mother had said. Padre Costa brought the statue of baby Jesus up to my lips. The people in line and in the front pews went silent. *In the name of the Father, and of the Son . . .* I placed my lips on the statue's knee. It felt cold. *And of the Holy Spirit*. I hoped I'd feel something, a kind of tingle that warmed my insides, a sign that God had heard my silent prayers. But everything stayed the same. Padre Costa wiped the statue's knee with a cloth just as my father approached. He glared into my father's eyes, dared him.

My father's body coiled, as if ready to strike. He moved close to Padre Costa, who grinned and raised the statue of Jesus to meet with my father's chin. My father's hands were not pressed together in prayer. He held his fedora in front of him and rubbed its brim with his thumb. Instead of kissing the statue, he squinted at the priest before placing the hat on his head and flicking its brim.

I stood at the second-floor back window that overlooked our garage and the laneway. It was almost three o'clock in the morning. I could see the flicker of blue light coming from the TV James now left on day and night.

I heard the bustle of activity downstairs. It had always been our custom to have a shot of Port and open up one gift before going to bed. Our choice. But tonight I just wanted to be far away from them all. I wondered if James was spending Christmas with Agnes, if he was sitting by Ricky's side, patting his forehead with a cool cloth. I assumed James wouldn't be working the streets tonight. I couldn't imagine there'd be anyone out looking.

"Antonio!" Edite called.

Edite leaned against the banister, biting her cuticles. "You can hate me later, but not on Christmas." I decided I'd just have some Port, then go to bed. If I didn't, they'd think something was wrong.

When I went into the living room, my mother was staring at the Christmas tree. She was pale. Her lips trembled, and she seemed on the brink of something.

"You sit there, Antonio, and we'll begin." Edite pointed to the end of the couch. The shot glasses filled with the golden liquid were clustered on a silver tray. My father sat in the armchair, his coat still on, but his boots were off and the toes of his socks were wet. He was drumming his fingers on the armrest. My mother looked at everything in the room except us. My father stared up at the wall, at the picture of his mother standing in a field somewhere in Lomba da Maia with the meanest frown on her whiskered face. Terri was under the tree, a kid again, trying to decide which gift to open.

"*Um calsinho?*" Edite's pronunciation was awful. She lifted the tray and offered us the tiny cups of booze. I threw the liquor back, smacked my lips, then winced at the burning that coated my throat and settled in my stomach.

"Força!" my father said, half-heartedly. "Georgina, why don't you open your letter from Dr. Patterson?" my father said, every word of Portuguese clear and deliberate.

Terri made a big deal of opening her gift from Edite. I knew her well enough to know she was trying to create a diversion. She held up a silver lamé angel top and pressed it across her chest.

My father got up from the couch, his beer in hand. His feet smelled from being trapped in his boots too long. When he reached the tree, he picked up the envelope that sat on top of the television, a large "G" written on the front.

"This came for you today," he said. "Your *friend* came right up to the door and dropped it in our mailbox." My father flicked it on my mother's lap. At first she didn't touch it, but then her hand hovered over the envelope. Shadows of her fingers crossed the letter. She stared at my father. She took the envelope and, without looking, slipped one finger in, tearing it along the crease in a determined rip. She reached in, unfolded the letter. A crisp fifty-dollar bill flittered to the floor. My mother reached down and picked it up. She crumpled it up in her fist. "Is this what you wanted?" she said, her voice firm and in control, and she threw the bill at my father.

My father looked embarrassed, but he held his stare. He took another swig of his beer.

"Antonio, come on, it's your turn," Edite said, trying to tug me off the couch. "Which present do you want to open?"

"What's in the letter?" my father asked. He wasn't going to let it go. "Antonio, read the letter out loud," he demanded.

"Leave it alone, Manuel," Edite said.

He shot up. "This is my house! Don't tell me what to do!" He sprayed Edite with his spit. She wiped her face.

My mother looked up from the letter. "Antonio," she said calmly. "Do as your father says. He's the *captain*."

I hated them all.

"Read it!" my father yelled.

I took the letter from my mother's outstretched hand, unfolded it.

"Read!"

"'Georgina, another year and another letter.'" The paper shook in my hands. "'Thank you for working so closely with me again. I couldn't have done it without you. As you know, it is always at this time of the year that I sit down and take stock of my life, where it is I want to be. I do not have a family of my own, something I have always regretted.'" I looked to my mother for a sign to continue. Her thumbnail was wedged between her two front teeth. Terri shuffled across the room on her knees to sit at my mother's feet. "'I feel a connection to my work in Tanzania and the sisters at St. Michael's have always supported my leaves to work with those less fortunate. I will be returning to them, my family, alone. It is my promise to you that I take with me. You will always be in my thoughts. I wish you'"—I added "and your family"—"'the very best, always.'" The letter ended "Love, Robert," but the words turned to cement in my throat.

"In *my* thoughts. *Promises?*" my father mumbled.

Love, I mouthed so quietly only I heard it as a whisper.

My father wiped his mouth with his sleeve. I looked back down at the letter and made out the shape of a tiny swallow Dr. Patterson had drawn after his name. My mother's fist clenched in front of her throat, the gold chain and the charm hidden in the warmth of her hand.

"Pronto, cama," my father said. "Is going to be a long day tomorrow." My mother did not move. Her face had relaxed.

There were no funny lines on her forehead. I had folded the letter, then rolled it like a cigarette. Terri had taken some strands of her hair and held them taut in her mouth. She stared my father down before wrapping her arms around my mother's legs.

The first move came from my father, who placed a cigarette between his lips. He reached for the crystal lighter on the coffee table and flicked. Nothing. The scratchy sound from the lighter repeated, but there was no flame. My mother didn't look his way. It was one of her rules: no smoking in the living room. My father raised the lighter over his head. "Always empty." He looked squirrelly, not certain of what he'd do next.

Edite jumped up from the couch. She made her way to the corner of the room and cleared her throat. Out of nowhere she began to sing one of Amália Rodrigues's fados. It was about a seagull—*gaivota*. I recognized most of the lyrics right away, but her voice couldn't hit the notes and she made ridiculous gestures with every line. "If a seagull would come . . ." she sang, curling her finger, inviting us to come closer. "A wing that doesn't fly, falters and falls to the sea," she crooned, tucking her hands into her armpits and flapping like a deranged chicken. She twirled a few times, raised her knees and wiggled her hips in round movements. My sister was the first to giggle. "What a perfect heart would beat in my chest." Here Edite grabbed her breast as if she was having a heart attack. My mother covered her smile with the back of her hand. It took a while, but even my father gave in to a thin smile that creased his eyelids. Edite danced in front of the TV, and before long we were all laughing out loud, and for a

moment even my father laughed too. Then he caught himself, twirled the cigarette behind his ear, and lowered the
lighter back onto the coffee table. He stared at Dr. Patterson's
letter in my hand. Then he simply got up and, without looking at any of us, left the room. My mother began to cry and
my sister got up to squeeze into the chair with her. I went to
her side also, took the tightly rolled letter and curled my
mother's fingers around it.

14

WHERE'S RICKY?" Manny sat on the storage chest. I wondered if the tiny blankets and pillow were still inside.

"Why are we meeting here?" I said. Manny whittled a carpenter pencil with his jackknife. "Why couldn't we meet somewhere else?" I hadn't seen James since Ricky had been hurt. He had come to our door on New Year's Eve, asking my father to let him keep his job. My father spoke to him through the screen door, told him he needed someone he could count on. James pleaded, "I need this, man. Give me another chance!" Looking out my bedroom window, I heard my father slam the door. "You owe me!" James shouted, coming into view as he walked backwards to stand on our front lawn. James leaned against the bathtub with Jesus in it, smoking a cigarette. He wouldn't leave. I turned away from the window.

When we woke up New Year's morning, we saw someone had kicked in the Plexiglas that trapped the statue of Jesus in the tub. My father found the statue on the neighbor's lawn, broken in three pieces. He spent New Year's Day gluing it back together, painting over the chips and cracks.

Manny didn't say anything. He sat with a cigarette securely wedged in the corner of his mouth.

"I know what you did," I said.

Manny stopped whittling and began to dredge out the dirt from underneath his nails with the blade. "I don't know what you're talking about," he said.

"I know you wrote in for the baby. I saw the package on the porch just before Christmas."

"What about it?"

"I just wanted you to know that it came. It was a nice thing to do. I was going to give it to you, but then I just thought it would be best to get rid of it. Agnes might have been freaked out if she'd seen it."

Ricky came into the garage with his puppy tucked inside the front of his coat. "Just needed to take him out for a pee." He walked over to the cardboard box padded with rags and slipped the pup inside. He sat down on the floor next to it. The puppy whined and Ricky dropped his arm into the box so the pup could nibble on his fingers and lick his hand. Ricky was so out of it when I found him that day that I wondered if he even remembered anything.

"What did you do with it?" Manny mumbled.

I shrugged and attempted to open my mouth a couple of times, hoping that would trigger a memory of what I had done with the package. "I picked it up off the porch and then—"

"The baby, moron!" Manny blew the cigarette smoke through his nostrils and rolled his eyeballs. "I don't care about the fuckin' present."

Ricky went stiff. The pup yelped.

"You were stoned. You took off." He should have been there too. "We buried it."

"Where?"

"What difference does it make?"

"I baptized her Mary," Ricky said softly.

"What?" I said.

"How?" Manny said.

"With spit," Ricky said. "I licked my thumb and made the cross on her head. Then I prayed really hard." He reached into the box and lifted the pup right under his chin. "God's taking care of her. She's in heaven." He scooped the dog into his arms, kissed its head, then slowly got to his feet.

"Okay then, Padre Hoot, what did you baptize the dog?"

Ricky lifted the garage door, ducked underneath, and was gone.

"What did I do now?" Manny flicked the cigarette across the floor. It landed dangerously close to the turpentine bottle and rags James kept in the corner. "Can't say anything right with that one."

I got up and stomped on the butt. He reached into his back pocket and flicked open his hair pick. I thought of the presents I had bought for my friends, how I had dropped them when I found Ricky in the snow. I went back a day later but they were gone. Manny plumped up his Afro. "It wouldn't have been a good idea anyway," he said.

"What?"

"The baby. Have you ever thought what it would be like if you were never born? Baby Mary was lucky, is the way I see it."

I had never seen Manny so sad.

"They're getting the hell away from here," he said.

"Who?"

"Amilcar and his whole family. My brother's not good enough for their daughter. They think moving to Portugal is going to keep Eugene away. Idiots."

"How do you know that?"

"My brother told me."

"Well, who needs them? My mother says they're snobs anyways and—"

"It won't stop Eugene. No way. He's going to make sure they're together." Manny buried his head in the crook of his arm.

I knew he would hate it if I went up to him or said something to console him. So I just sat there and waited it out.

Manny lifted his head. "What happened to Ricky, anyway?"

"What do you mean?" I said, uncertain how much he knew.

"He was laid up here for two days. Could hardly walk. Had a fever. James kicked me out every time I came near. Like I was going to hurt him or something. Asshole." Manny waited. I said nothing. "You see him with that mutt? Walks around this place with that rope tied around his neck. He's in his own little world."

"Forget it," I said. "You know the trial's going to begin soon. I'm going to go."

"How?" Manny said. "They're not going to let you in the courtroom." He stood up and raised both arms in the air, stretched himself out and yawned.

I had been thinking about, dreaming about Emanuel's killers for almost five months and I wanted to see them, in person. "You wanna come?" I let the invitation just hang there in the air. He'd bite if he wanted to. I wasn't quite sure how I was going to do it—pretend I was sick, I thought—and then when my parents went to work and my sister went to school, I'd make my way downtown.

"I'll think about it," Manny said.

———

I was worried about Agnes. I hadn't seen her since Baby Mary was born. I knew Ricky dropped by and spent time with her, but that's all he'd tell me. After school, I walked up the laneway and found myself in her parents' basement. We used the laneway entrance and entered through the backyard. The door was unlocked. The only light in the whole house came from the TV. Agnes's parents were in Portugal and as far as the neighbors were concerned, the house remained empty.

"I thought you might want something to eat."

She stared blankly at the TV and rocked in her chair over the ceramic-tiled floor. She didn't look at me. In the basement kitchen, I opened the jar my sister had filled with *sopa de estrelinha*, a chicken broth with tiny pasta shaped like stars. Terri continued to keep Agnes's hiding place a secret. Edite hadn't told her about the dead baby, or Terri would have said something. As I stirred the soup over the gas flame, I thought this was all James's fault. He'd told Ricky he'd take care of him, make sure he was safe, made him feel like no one could ever hurt him. And he promised Manny he could be a player—"The world's gonna fuck with you so you better learn to fuck it back." Before he hooked up with Lygia, Eugene used to say stuff like that to Manny all the time. And Agnes thought she had no one until James came along and saved her. Agnes told me she never felt better than when he touched her. Fuck him. I didn't even recognize her now: her skin draped over someone else's body.

I left the soup on the end table to cool off. "What are you watching?" She rocked in her chair. "Padre Costa told us the story of St. Agnes on Sunday." She kept her eyes locked on the television. "She's the patron saint of young girls. They pray to her and do certain things—rituals—so that their future husbands will come to them."

I didn't tell Agnes all the gory details about how her namesake saint suffered martyrdom at the age of twelve or thirteen, or how they dragged her through the streets to a brothel before they killed her.

"St. Agnes prayed, her hair grew and covered her body to protect her. They tied her to a stake, but the bundle of wood would not burn."

It was stupid of me to think that the magic of the story would snap her mind back to reality. We were all doing it, though; trying not to talk, because that made things easier. There was no way that Ricky had told Agnes anything about the baby or what we did to it. He knew she couldn't handle it.

"I still pray, you know. It helps. And you don't have to pray out loud. You can do it in your head." I squatted in front of her and placed my hands on her lap. "Like this." I closed my eyes and said a quick Hail Mary. I opened my eyes. I wanted to see her smile, but everything was coming out wrong.

"I pray for my friends," I continued, "even for James. Adam too. And every day I pray for Baby Mary." Agnes blinked. It gave me the courage to go further. "We took good care of her. We made sure she was warm, and you need to know Ricky baptized her before—" Agnes leaned in and looked at me as if for the first time. Her lip quivered. I felt her finger hooking mine. "Your baby went to heaven."

After dinner, Manny and I were going skating at Alexandra Park on Bathurst Street. Our parents only let us go in groups, and they knew there was a rink guard there keeping an eye on us.

With our skates knotted together and slung over our shoulders, we had just turned the corner when we heard the faint sound of a siren whirring in the distance. The sirens grew louder: the sound was coming in our direction. We slowed down to watch. Police cars, fire trucks, and an ambulance, the three melted into one, and grew louder until they stopped in unison.

We ran through the laneway and out onto Markham Street. I flung my skates into Mr. Serjeant's front yard so I could run faster. The light on top of the ambulance spun against the brick houses. The police cars and fire engines had gathered halfway up Markham Street, blocking traffic close to where Edite and Ricky lived.

Edite stood inside her front-yard fence. She'd pulled a leather maxi-coat over her silk robe. Her slippers sank into the snow. She held a coffee mug, her shoulders scrunched up as she bounced a bit in the cold. Her eyes were dark, and makeup ran down her cheeks. She looked toward Ricky's veranda and didn't even notice me coming. Ricky's front door was open and boot tracks had made their way up his walkway and into his house. My stomach ached as if my insides would spill out onto the snow.

Manny tapped my shoulder. I felt relieved he had followed. I looked back and saw Ricky come outside onto his veranda. He raised his arm to shield his face from the glare of the flashing lights. He was wrapped in a thick blanket and his pup was cradled in his arms. A police officer directed him to the old sofa that was on the porch. Manny scissor-kicked over the fence and ran up the steps, with me close behind. The policeman put out his hands to stop us, but then must have realized we were friends there to comfort Ricky.

We sat down on the couch with a crunch. Ricky shivered. He looked out across the road, his eyes fixed above the roofline. His teeth chattered and his lips had gone blue. With his limp wrist he slowly stroked his puppy, from the base of its ear to the tip of its tail.

"He found out," Ricky said, looking straight ahead above the crowd that had gathered. His words paralyzed me. They had found the dead baby in the lake and were here to arrest Ricky and then me. How could I save myself? What would happen to Agnes? Would they torture me to name names? They wouldn't have to. A bit of pee already warmed the inside of my leg. I'd be more than happy to blame James.

A gurney was pushed out the front doorway and rattled over the porch floor. Ricky didn't look at the figure draped in a white sheet and blanket and cinched down with belts.

"He was so drunk. And angry."

I kept thinking, you never say anything until there's a lawyer.

"He told me he got into a fight. Some man owed him money and wouldn't pay up. Told him he kinda helped him out by throwing his son a few dollars every so often." Clear snot dripped from Ricky's nose.

And then with a swell of relief it all clicked: it wasn't the baby. I sometimes wondered if the men at the billiards hall talked about who was on the other side of the fence. Did they even care? Did my father have any clue?

I stared at the gurney rolling down the walkway. A crowd had gathered, shoulder-to-shoulder to keep warm. Their breath steamed out of their noses and mouths.

"When he got home, I was at the top of the stairs. He began crawling up on his hands and knees. When he got to the top, he fell against the banister and started yelling. He couldn't stand." Ricky looked straight ahead the whole time. "He was soaked. I tried to help him out of his coat and then he swung his arm and pinned me to the wall by the neck. I couldn't breathe. 'You're a little faggot,' he said. 'A good-for-nothing little faggot. They're all laughing at me because you're a good-for-nothing little—'" Ricky licked the snot above his lip. "I thought I had closed my bedroom door, but Snoopy came out of my room and—" He looked at me for the first time.

"It's okay, Ricky. He can't hurt you anymore." Manny rubbed Ricky's back.

"I just wanted to put him to bed so he could sleep it off, but he wouldn't let me. He picked up Snoopy by the neck and held him over the banister."

"I'm sorry, Ricky," I said. Ricky stroked his pup, jiggled his knees every so often to rouse it from sleep.

"Smashed him down onto the ground floor."

"It was an accident," I said. "He was drunk."

"He didn't care. He never cared." Ricky's big eyes looked straight at me as he leaned in. "I pushed him," he whispered. "I pushed him down."

I looked to Manny.

"He fell all the way down . . . down . . . down."

"Son, you're coming with us." A Chinese policeman placed his hand on Ricky's shoulder.

Manny sprang up, pushed himself between the officer and Ricky. "You can't take him. He didn't do anything."

"Relax, son. We're just going to get him cleaned up. We're going to try to get ahold of his mom. We understand she's in Portugal."

"He doesn't have anyone but us," I said.

The police officer lifted Ricky to his feet. "You can't bring the dog with you, son. He's dead."

Ricky began to cry.

"Look, Officer," Manny said, "what if I wrapped his dog . . ." Manny took off his coat, pulled his sweatshirt over his head, static snapping through his hair, draped the sweatshirt over the pup, and tucked the sleeves and sides underneath its limp body. The officer nodded.

They helped Ricky to the cruiser. Before he got in, he looked up at his house, dropped his eyes to meet mine and Manny's, and then he was gone.

✳

Of Monster^s and Men

"It'll be nice, you know. I'll be looking at the stars, too.
All the stars will be wells with a rusty pulley.
All the stars will pour out water for me to drink . . ."

ANTOINE DE SAINT-EXUPÉRY

1

Y OU HAD ANOTHER nightmare last night," Terri said
as she straddled my chest.

"Just hurry!" I lay flat on the living-room carpet.

"What's screwing with your head that you can't sleep?"

"None of your business." I squirmed to adjust the way she
sat on me.

"It is my business when you keep me awake all night."

I tried to get up on my elbows, but her weight held me
down. "We had a deal, so just let me do this." She held her
mascara wand above my eyes.

Saturday Night Fever spun on the turntable and was set to
repeat. Terri dipped the wand in the tube, then brought it to
my eye and rolled it up and through. She bit her tongue at the
corner of her mouth.

"Get off of me!"

"You want me to make that call to school? Telling them
you're not well?"

I had planned to play hooky and head over to Old City
Hall for the beginning of the Emanuel Jaques murder trial.
But everything had changed, and now I was going downtown to find Ricky at the courthouses. I didn't expect Terri
to be home studying for her high school exams. The school
secretary might call home or try to catch my mother at work,
and if she did call my mother at work, my mother would call

me at home and I'd have to lie and tell her I was in bed because I wasn't feeling well. My mother might come home and that's why it was better to let my sister call the school and nip it in the bud.

"Just hurry!" I said, finding it more difficult to breathe from the pressure as she leaned in to swoop at my other eyelashes.

"Such a pretty boy. You need to accentuate your long lashes."

This wasn't the first time she had done this to me, but it had been a while and I was getting too old for it. She had me by the balls, though; I needed her help.

I looked into her face. It was round, like my father's, and you could barely make out her light eyebrows and eyelashes, and no matter what she did to her hair—home perms, washing it with eggs, molasses, or beer—it always looked limp and fine.

"Ricky won't be there," she said, reading my mind. "They don't put kids in the slammer with adults."

"I need to know if he's okay."

"It's called patricide, you know. When a kid kills his father. I'm studying for my English exam. It's what Zeus did to his father, Cronus."

"I don't care what it's called. It's not his fault."

"It's what lots of kids think of doing but you never tell anyone or they'll lock you up in the mental hospital."

"Enough! I gotta go."

Every time she leaned in for another pass at my eyelashes, the pressure on my chest increased.

"Zeus wanted power and control so he killed his father. It's what men do when they have no power. I know, I know, Ricky didn't want power. He's not like you and your pal Manny."

"You're nuts!"

"If I tell you something, you promise not to tell?" She didn't wait for a yes. "I'm going to get away from here. Soon. I wasn't meant to live in a box. Edite says so. I'm going to New York. I'm going to be a dancer." She had a fire in her eyes that made me believe her.

"Dad'll kill you." I squirmed into a better position to throw her off me.

"You ask me, I think Ricky's dad had it coming to him. I saw her, you know," she added. My sister smiled as if the information was delicious.

"Who?"

"Agnes. Late one night, crossing the street from her house and going into the lane."

"So?"

"Where's the baby?"

I tried to look relaxed. I knew the question would come up sooner or later, and I had practised what I would say when it did. But I stammered and then thought it was best just to shut up.

"She had the baby, didn't she?"

I had been holding on to the secret for so long I thought I was going to burst. I puffed out my cheeks to pop my ears.

"Did she give it away for adoption?" I could tell the tears were building.

"Ask Agnes," I blurted.

"I wouldn't blame her if she did."

"Or why don't you ask Edite. She tells you everything."

"Edite's been a bit weird lately."

"What do you mean?"

"For starters she looks like crap," Terri said.

"Once she finds Johnny——"

"There is no Johnny, stupid. Now hold still." Terri gripped my jaw while taking another swipe at my eyelashes. "Long and thick."

"What do you mean about Johnny?" I said.

"You don't know?"

"Get off me!"

"I thought you knew. He's dead. He was killed in Vietnam. I heard Mãe and Edite talking about him ages ago. Around the time Emanuel was murdered."

"That's bullshit." My heart pounded and the blood swooshed between my ears. Another lie. I was so stupid.

"I got to tell you, brother, you may have gotten the eyelashes but thank God I got the brains."

"Are we done?"

"Maycomb had nothing to fear but fear itself."

"What the hell—"

"*To Kill a Mockingbird.*"

Terri took three or four pumps of the tube before she dropped the gooey brush on my eyelashes. They were so heavy with goop, they almost stuck together.

"Edite snooped around, called some of her contacts at 52 Division, and word is they're not going to charge Ricky. It's a sin to kill a mockingbird, you know."

"Where is he, then?" I stopped moving. Why didn't Edite tell me where they were holding him? He was *my* friend.

"They found his mom back in São Miguel. He's going to live with her."

"When?"

Terri sat back, admiring her work.

I scrambled to stand up, knocking Terri onto the carpet.

She twisted to a sitting position, placed the wand back into the tube, and screwed it tight. "I'll call the school," she said. "You'd better go."

Manny wasn't in James's garage. I saw a hash pipe on the kitchen table, next to an ashtray. The sweet odor of tar was in the air. I waved my hand over the stubbed cigarette butts. They were still warm. I knew Manny was doing deliveries for James near Vanauley Walk and the Project area. Diversification, James called it, ever since bike season ended. I didn't know what the hell he meant. All I knew was that Manny didn't deal with any money, only with a list of addresses he would visit and drop little brown bags into mailboxes. James did the collecting.

I found myself at Senhora Gloria's house, crouching outside Agnes's basement window. Before I went to the courthouse, I wanted to be the one to tell Agnes about Ricky. Through the lace curtains I could see her, limp and rubbery in James's arms. He wore an ESSO suit with a sweater that was too small. His roughed-up construction boots poked out from the hem of his pants. He was dancing with her. But he was the only one dancing. They were moving slowly in circles as Agnes's toes dragged across the floor. He kissed her forehead. The strip of fluorescent light bulbs caught the scar that lined his jawbone. He was crying.

I slapped the window, the pain shooting up the heel of my hand. Agnes did not flinch. James turned and looked straight at me.

I took off through the lanes. I thought of going to see Edite first, but she had lied to me about Johnny. I knew I couldn't count on her anymore. No one paid attention to me as I ran. I ran hard and the snot began to freeze on my upper lip. I hopped onto the road because it was salted. Most of the cars swung wide around me but a few came close to sideswiping me, forcing me back onto the sidewalk.

I pushed through the large doors of Old City Hall and ran up the marble steps. I rubbed heat into my thighs.

I wasn't sure where to begin. Who could tell me where Ricky was being held? I needed Manny. I could have used his no-nonsense questions, as if he was owed answers and they better give them to him.

"Could you help me, please?" I grabbed the sleeve of the first cop I saw coming down the stairs.

"You lost, son?" he said.

"I want to see my friend, Ricky Mendonça. Can you bring me to him?" I sounded like a helpless six-year-old.

"You a hustler, kid?" he said.

"No, sir."

He squatted in front of me and raised his thumb to my cheek. I flinched back, wouldn't let him touch me. "You usually wear mascara?" he said. A lump built up in my throat and it hurt when I swallowed. I didn't know what to say or do.

He stood up. "Follow me."

We walked down the wide corridors. There were people everywhere, walking or sitting on benches or being dragged through the hall; a girl being tugged by her mother whose arms were covered in cigarette burns like polka dots; tall men grew taller dressed as women with glitter platform heels and big hair, their skin smooth and nails long and painted; drunks flopped their heads down between their knees; small clubs of what looked like Chinese store owners yelled at men in suits who were trying to explain things to them, their lawyers, I thought. People wearing thick boots slapped down the slush they had trailed in. The wet wasn't allowed to stay on the floor for long—men were at work with their mops, swirling piney disinfectant. The janitors were all Portuguese, I could tell. It was more than their complexion or the way their jaws jutted out slightly. Their hands bore the five-dot tattoo. Those who served in the army in Africa, in Angola or Mozambique—the blood bath, my uncle Clemente called it—all sported the five blue dots tattooed on their hands, near the webbing between their thumbs and pointer fingers. Five dots for the five wounds inflicted upon Jesus during the crucifixion.

The cop led me up to a door with a window of frosted glass. It was like in the movies, the door that reads *Private Investigator*. I expected to see the silhouette of a man in a fedora on the other side, smoking. But the room was simply a lounge painted minty green.

"Sit down, son. I'll get you some water."

I heard the gurgle from the big water jug, and I allowed myself to fall back into the couch and close my eyes.

"Is Ricky Mendonça here? You brought him in yesterday."

"You're burning up, kid." I was too weak to swipe his hand away from my forehead.

"He lives on Markham Street, his father fell down—"

"The Portuguese boy? He's gone, son. They're flying him home."

I got up and reached the door. My chest felt like it was going to collapse. I could feel the tears pinching at my cheeks.

"Hold up there, buddy. I'm giving you a ride home."

I opened the door.

"What school do you go to? Where do you live?"

I don't know how I made my way out of Old City Hall, how I fought past all the people in the hallways, the shouting, large light fixtures that guided me out through the marble halls and past the fancy iron railing onto the front steps, out into the cold. I didn't care about being seen crying; no one knew me. I crossed Bay Street and went over to the subway grates in front of Nathan Phillips Square. The last time I'd stood on the same spot was the afternoon of the rally in August. A blast of warm air filled my jacket, puffed me up like a balloon. If only I could lift off with a gust of wind from the subway vents, strong enough that I could latch on to a plane's belly and fly all the way to the Azores where my mother said it was always warm and green and where I could be with Ricky.

I faced the new City Hall. On the other side of the skating rink, I caught the flash of a red scarf. I used my sleeve to swipe my tears and snot.

"Adam?" I cupped my hands to my mouth. "Adam!" He did not turn. I ran, pushed through all the people putting on skates or lining up for hot chocolate. This is where he once worked, City Hall library. It had to be Adam and he was alive. The speck of red reappeared every so often. It was like the movie they showed us at school, *The Red Balloon*, where the boy makes friends with a red balloon and then follows it on its journey. Adam let me call him by his first name. He'd help me make sense of everything.

I came into a clearing, around the entrance of the new court-house. Police stood guard as reporters and camera crews wrangled thick cables and wires, setting up cameras on tripods. There were trucks parked outside, their antennas twirling in the cold air. They each had chosen a spot somewhere in the square, set themselves up to bring live news into everyone's home. I had almost forgotten this was the first day of the Emanuel Jaques trial. A woman passing by drew her kids close to her legs.

I picked up the trail of Adam's red scarf before it disappeared down a side ramp, around the corner of the building. I stumbled once but dusted myself off quickly, just inside the underground garage. "Adam?" I called out. But there was no Adam. Suddenly, a caravan of police cube vans whizzed by me, then braked. There were four of them, all lined up. A chain rattled as the parking garage door closed slowly. Fluorescent lights flickered as the cops got out. They moved casually to the back of their vans, undid the latches, and then flung open the doors.

Out hopped the prisoners, each from a separate wagon. They barely looked at each other. The police officers handled them roughly, twisted them around by their arms and directed them to a large elevator door. There were two cops for each handcuffed man, one on each side. There were no prison-issue jumpsuits, no paper slippers. These criminals were dressed in suits and thick-knotted ties. Their hair was long.

I stepped forward, right underneath a flickering fluorescent light.

"Hey! How did you get in here?" An officer laid his hand on his holster.

I took another step forward. Everyone stopped.

"Stay back, raccoon boy!" a cop hollered. The other cops laughed, deep man laughs.

"Leave now!" a cop demanded, taking a couple of steps in my direction.

The killers were pushed toward the elevator. One looked back. Saul Betesh's eyes burned into me. His lips cracked open just a bit, enough to see the flash of some teeth. He winked. *Little boy with the pretty hair, would you like to play?* I peed, the warmth spreading down my inner thigh. I caught an image of myself in the window of a parked car. Black mascara lines crawled down my cheeks.

2

I REMEMBER MY MOTHER wiping something cool and soft across my forehead and temples. I wasn't sure how long I had been out, but now she was gone.

"How are you feeling?" Edite whispered as she leaned over to fluff my pillow.

"I saw them," I mumbled, razor blades slashing my throat when I swallowed.

"Shh, it's going to be okay. Nightmares can't hurt you."

"Where's Mãe?"

"She had to go back to work. It's been four days, Antonio." She wrung a cloth over a bowl, draped it on my forehead. "The fever's breaking. You'll be fine in no time. Here, she left you some octopus stew." Edite crinkled her nose as she lifted a spoonful of stew. "She said it was your favorite." I pressed my ear to the pillow and tried to hold back the tears until the lump in my throat hurt. I couldn't hold on. I turned to my side, buried my nose in the pillow in the hope I'd find a trace of her smell. My mother had spent four whole days with me but I couldn't remember any of it. I wanted my mother, her hand on my forehead. I needed to feel her touch.

"I'm not hungry," I said into the pillow. I heard the scratch of Edite's lighter, the faint burning sound of tobacco being lit, and I took in the whiff of her cigarette.

My head felt heavy. I closed my eyes for a little bit, let go just enough so that I slipped away into a dark quiet.

Their hot breath nipped at my neck. They clipped at my heels. I couldn't look back, I was too afraid. They laughed a deep gut laugh, the kind men share around suspended pigs as they hack them to pieces. I breathed in some spit and choked. My heart raced as I ran, arms pumping pistons. I hoped something would come down and pluck me from the concrete, lift me up, away from the men with no faces. A kite—the one I had almost given Ricky for Christmas—whipped into view. It shot across the blue sky, and then dipped from side to side over rooftops. I traced the string down until it met with a tiny fist. Ricky's skin was dark like it got during summer, hair shiny like wet tar. I ran toward him. The men kept chasing me, their fingertips pinched at my shirt, callused hands brushed my neck, my arms. Tiny bolts of electricity ran through me and I wanted to close my eyes. Blood gushed across my temples. "Hey pretty boy with the golden hair," they chanted. But before I could surrender to their rough hands, I glanced at Ricky, who smiled and held his finger to the sky. I stopped, looked up, and found a baby, a tiny gray baby—Mary—flying at the end of the string. The baby danced in the wind, swooped above our heads, her thin arms outstretched. The men could not touch me; a force field held them back. Ricky tugged on the string and the baby seesawed down like a leaf, drifted into Ricky's arms.

I found a newspaper at the foot of my bed. It was Thursday, February 9, 1978. I didn't know time could move like mud. I located a story about Luciano Jaques, Emanuel's older brother, who was fourteen and had testified that his brother was lured from their shoeshine spot by the promise of making thirty-five dollars an hour to help move movie equipment. The hope was that in two days they'd be able to make a total of four hundred dollars. But it didn't make sense, I thought. No one pays that kind of money. He should have known. That's when it hit me. Maybe Emanuel *did* know; maybe he understood that the man wanted something more.

Emanuel's brother went on to describe what Saul Betesh wore that afternoon: long denim overalls, no shirt, just bare skin and light brown boots. James was wearing almost the exact same thing the day I found him whitewashing the inside of his garage. The fine hair on the back of my neck tingled.

From the get-go, one of the accused, Robert Kribs, pleaded guilty. The Crown attorney told jurors, "The treatment received by Emanuel Jaques at the hands of his murderers is nothing short of a horror story."

The phone rang. It rang at least ten times before I figured I had been left home alone. I swung my Jell-O legs out of bed and held on to the banister all the way down the stairs to get to the hallway phone.

"Hello?"

"Meet me at James's," Manny said.

"What for? Manny, I don't—" I was speaking to the dead tone of the phone pulsing back.

I was feeling slightly dizzy but the sensation was slowly coming back to my legs and feet. It didn't matter how I felt, because it wasn't like Manny to hang up the phone. I knew I'd have to hook up with him, figure out what was so urgent.

I pulled a pair of jeans over my flannel pajamas, stuffing the pants down. I stepped out into the laneway through our garage. There was a shine in the alley that looked like wet stones. The quiet of winter would last until the Festa do

Senhor Santo Cristo, five weeks after Easter. Then our garages would be cleaned, scoured, and washed with water and bleach, ready for tables to be set up for the feast, and all the neighborhood would gather to talk about back home. I wondered if Ricky felt like Portugal was his home now, if he ran into his mother's outstretched arms, like it was the place he should have been all along.

My head was still groggy when I arrived, and I could barely lift James's garage door over my head. The electric heaters were on full blast, hot orange glowing off curly coils. It must have been a hundred degrees in there. "Manny?" I wasn't very loud. I waited for a sound. Cups and beer bottles and plates were piled up in a bucket on the floor. When I kicked the bucket, a veil of black lifted; flies were all over the place. "Manny?" I hoisted myself up the ladder to the loft. I stood up in the tallest part of the loft space, where the peaked roof joined. It looked smaller to me, more crammed than I remembered. The sheets on James's mattress were all rumpled and smelled of jeans that had been worn too long. When was the last time Manny had washed them? I had stopped bringing James food weeks ago. Instead, I delivered what I could to Agnes in her basement.

"Antonio?" Manny called, the metal clang of the garage echoing.

I didn't answer right away. I listened to hear if he was alone or if James was with him. There was some rattling around, and then Manny was climbing the ladder. His hair was the first thing that appeared. A great big smile greeted me.

"What are you doing up *here*?" Manny said.

"You alone?"

"Yep."

"Why aren't you at school?"

"I faked a sore gut and got sent home."

Manny climbed up to the top and sat at the lip of the loft entrance. He stuck the corner of his coat collar in his mouth and sucked, dangled and swung his legs into the garage below like a kid on a swing.

"What's up with *you*?" I asked him. I wasn't used to Manny being happy.

Manny's legs kicked wildly. "They've sold their house."

"Who?"

"Amilcar's dad." His grin was eating at his face as he climbed down the ladder.

"Your brother's going to freak."

"She'll be far away in Portugal. She wasn't his first and I'm sure he won't be crying too much before he's banging another one."

"You told me he had made plans. You said after they got married and got a place of their own you'd go over and hang out. You said—" I could tell I was spoiling Manny's moment, so I stopped.

"James said he'd leave me a couple of drop-off addresses around someplace. It's a pigsty in here," Manny said.

I lay on my stomach and watched him scrounging through the piles of old rags and empty paint cans.

"I guess we didn't realize how much Ricky used to do around this place, keeping things tidy," Manny said. "My mom says he'll be happy back in São Miguel, back with his mom."

"You think that's for real?"

He found a cluster of brown paper bags, the kind we would fill with candy at Mr. Jay's, and swiped them up in a fist. "What do you mean?"

"You think they're lying about Ricky?"

"I don't know. They kind of lie about everything." Manny stuffed the paper bags in his pocket. "I gotta go."

"I miss Ricky," I said. I wanted Manny to hear me, but when he didn't respond, I shouted down, "Hey, I need to speak to James."

"What for?"

"He needs to stay away from us."

Manny lifted the garage door. "Agnes was bad news. It'll all work out, you'll see."

"Do you know where he is?"

"Can't help you. He told me he'd be here by early afternoon. Come to think of it, that was yesterday. Hell, doesn't look like he's been here for a couple of days." Manny returned to the table and started shoving a note into his sock. "I almost forgot," he said, taking a deep breath. "You've been stuck in the land of zees the last couple of days. I bet you don't even know that I've been dropping off your homework. It was like you were drugged or something. It was a good time to be knocked out, though. Guys have been going around bashing homos."

"What does that have to do with me?"

"I'm just saying."

"I'm going to check on Agnes."

"I just told you. Agnes is gone," Manny said. He lit a cigarette and squinted his eye from the smoke. "Disappeared right after Ricky got shipped home."

"What do you mean, disappeared?"

"Poof!" Smoke billowed from his mouth as he waved his fingers in the cloud like a magician.

"Something's not right," I said under my breath, hoping the answer would click. I started to climb down the ladder. "Does James know?"

"I thought you didn't give a shit about James."

I pretended I didn't hear him.

"You need to crawl back to bed, buddy. You look like shit. I gotta go." Manny gave me a quick wave before he snuck under the garage door and closed it behind him.

Manny was right, even though it was his phone call that had dragged me out of bed: it was too soon for me to be wandering around the neighborhood. I needed to build up some strength first.

Two blasts from the horn and I recognized Eugene's Trans Am. The car door slammed.

"Manny, you in there?" I jumped back. "Open up!" I hoisted the garage door halfway, up to Eugene's waist, before ducking underneath. "Antonio, hey. Have you seen my brother?" His eyes were all bugged out and red.

"He's at school, no?" I said, trying to sound surprised. I wanted to lean on his car, the energy draining from my body.

"I just checked. He signed out, said he wasn't feeling well." Eugene kept looking over his shoulder, scanning the laneway as if he was expecting someone. Then Lygia came around the corner, running in her Cougar boots and shearling coat.

"If you see him tell him I need to speak to him. It's important," Eugene said. He jumped back into the car and spun out. He skidded to a stop next to Lygia and almost clipped her on her side. She was crying. She fumbled with the handle and got in. The smell of rubber and the buzz of peeling tires was all that remained.

Back in the garage I reached up to the shelf where James kept the crock filled with crumpled five-dollar bills. It was empty, except for a dead moth, powdery white, on its back, its legs pointing up. I tried to beat down the image of Baby Mary in my head. The guilt made the back of my ears ring. I needed to lie down.

I banged my knee against Agnes's cot. I didn't think she had ever slept in it. I lay down. *Not long, just an hour or so.* I fought hard to keep my eyelids from closing. I tried to imagine where Agnes could be hiding—if she was hiding at all or had she taken off. Could she have left with James? I imagined James coming in, the way he always did, strong and handsome. He would ask Agnes for forgiveness. But he wouldn't mean it. It felt like someone was pulling a blanket over me. Ricky was in a better place. James could argue it was part of his plan all along. He'd set Agnes up in a nice apartment somewhere close by, trying to get back on track. Manny would be fine, he always was. Confession. I would tell my mother I had stepped out of the house to go to confession.

"James!" I breathed out. The air was hazy. He sat next to me on the cot. I reached up to touch his sleeve, make sure he was really there and not just a mirage bubbling up from my tired brain. James winced. His lower lip was split open and swollen. I could tell he was having a hard time holding up his head and keeping his eyes open. His head hovered over my face, bobbing like a drunk's. He tried to say something but it just came out as gurgling noise.

"Antonio," he whispered. He rested his face on my shoulder and breathed in deep. His hot breath smelled of booze. "You came back." His words swam in my head like little fishes. I smelled his dirty hair when he curled himself into me. He was warm. His arm moved over me and he drew me closer to him. My mouth went gummy. "Hey, little man," he mumbled, opening up his one eye and looking at me as if for the first time. "I knew you'd be back."

"Antonio!" I could hear the faint call from behind the garage door. At first I thought it was my mother. My fingers inched their way along the sheets until they touched James's arm. I sat up on the cot. The garage door raised and Edite took shape through the veil of snow. "Antonio, we've been worried sick!" I blinked my eyes. I looked down at my lap, too embarrassed to face Edite.

"What time is it?" I could tell it was dark out. They'd all be looking for me.

"You stay the fuck away from him, you hear me!" Edite's face trembled.

James stirred.

"You okay?" she asked, all the while looking at James beside me. She gripped my arm and yanked me away, not enough to get me on my feet. The pillow was blotting the blood from James's lip. I forced a smile, tried to show her that nothing had happened, nothing was wrong, that I was the same guy I was the last time I saw her.

"Nothing happened," I said.

"Did he touch you?" Her voice shook. James began to rouse from his sleep. "Did he do anything?" she said through her clenched teeth. Edite grabbed hold of my shoulders. "Tell me!"

"No!" I said. Edite tried to hug me. I shook her off and swung my legs to the side of the cot. I got up and thought I would fall back again.

"Go home, Antonio."

I staggered to the garage door.

"Go home now!" she yelled.

T HREE DAYS LATER I went over to Edite's. The
ceramic tea animals she had been collecting no longer
lined her windowsill in their neat rows. Edite's mountains of
books had been placed in boxes that were piled up into a high
wobbly tower in the kitchen corner. A few books remained,
pushed up against the kitchen wall in neat smaller towers.

"Where are you going?"

She answered from her bedroom. "Nowhere."

The paper was on the seat of a chair, neatly folded open to
the Jaques trial. According to the story, Gary Keith, a waiter
at a Howard Johnson's restaurant at Yonge and Dundas
Streets, said Saul Betesh came in with a boy that day. The boy
was between eleven and thirteen, he thought. He was very
polite. He said, "Yes, sir." He ordered a dinner from the children's menu but Betesh just had a dessert.

We had to kill him, Saul Betesh allegedly told a police officer.
*We knew we couldn't let him go. We knew that all along . . . no,
that's not right. We never intended to kill him. We had to.*
Valdemira, Emanuel's seventeen-year-old sister, who had been
appointed by the family to attend the trial, was escorted out
of the courtroom. The newspaper described her as "ashen,"
which I thought could only mean white and gray, like ashes.
Betesh was described as blond, long-lashed, and expression-
less. But I didn't need the paper to describe him to me. His

face was etched into my brain. All their faces were. Emanuel wasn't the first kid they had done this stuff to, either. There had been others that had gotten away or that they had let go. Why had things gotten out of control with Emanuel? Why him? I caught myself asking the questions out loud.

"What?" Edite stumbled into the kitchen. It looked like she had cut her own hair with scissors. Her short bangs were uneven and it made her look like she was tilted.

"Do you know where Agnes went?" I asked.

"Agnes is in the garage with James. Poor thing hasn't been the same since she lost that baby." She sat down in a kitchen chair.

"She didn't leave?" Edite shook her head. *So why did Manny say she was gone?*

Edite shrugged. She lifted her foot and her toes clutched at the table's rim. A bottle of red nail polish appeared from her robe pocket. She unscrewed the bottle, then began to paint her toes. The baby toe looked like a pomegranate seed. The smell of nail polish wafted up my nose.

"He'll be gone soon," she said.

"Where's he going?"

"Far away."

"Is Agnes going with him?"

"Probably. She's got nothing left here."

I didn't say anything. I couldn't decide if I was more happy that James was leaving or more jealous that he was taking Agnes with him.

"That's it? Do you want to know how James is doing? You can ask, you know."

"You freaked out when you saw me there. I don't get it. You told me I could trust him."

"I know. I was frightened and worried and I wasn't sure."
Edite fisted her temples. "James will be fine. I got him all
wrapped up in bandages. There isn't much you can do for
broken ribs. I heated up some Campbell's beef barley, not the
homemade stuff he says you guys feed him." Edite lifted her
other foot and continued to work on her toes. Her hands were
shaking. "He told me not to come back. Said he didn't want
any of you around, either. He said he'd manage." She sipped
from her cup. "Antonio, sit down for a sec." She patted the
kitchen chair next to her.

"I've got things to do."

"Okay, I'll just come right out and say it, then. I need you
to know it's okay to have feelings for James."

My head flushed hot. "What did he tell you? He doesn't
know shit!"

"It's normal. I know it's probably confusing and it's hard to
hold on to a secret, but—"

"Stop!" I turned to face the kitchen window. "Nothing
happened!" My voice was hoarse.

"You can't choose who you love, Antonio." Edite got up
from her chair.

"Leave me alone!" I said as she got close. She had lied about
so much. I could see her reflection in her kitchen window, her
face floating above the snow-covered rooftops. She looked
much smaller to me. She reached for her pack of cigarettes
and tapped out a smoke.

"You can talk to me about anything," Edite said. She lit the
cigarette and blew smoke up to the ceiling.

"You want to talk? Let's talk about Johnny. He's dead, isn't
he?" I turned around. My words had punched Edite in the

face, the way I wanted them to. "Why didn't you tell me? Why did you lie?"

Edite staggered to the kitchen counter. She leaned in to face the backsplash of rooster tiles.

"You talk about secrets and I've got some of my own, you know. Stuff you didn't know was going on. Like Ricky and the things he did. James pimped him out. He sent him over to Red's and . . . and that's how Ricky got hurt. Red raped him. I don't know what story James told you but—"

"Stop!" she said, frozen. I waited for her to say something more. I wanted her to say she didn't know, that she was sorry, or that she didn't think things would get so crazy, just something to make me feel like everything was a big mistake. But she said nothing. Edite brushed up against the fridge on her way into the hallway. I heard her bedroom door close. I couldn't take it back and I didn't want to. I needed to hear it for myself—that James was taking off. I needed to be sure.

I stepped outside, onto Edite's fire escape, and breathed out. The vapour was misty white. I ran down, my boots ringing on the metal steps.

The heat in James's garage had made the window sweat. I expected the garage to be empty. Instead, James lay in the same cot I had fallen asleep in a few days before. He must have heard me close the door because he raised his arm and motioned for me to come close. I sat on the edge of the cot and he rolled toward me. The skin around his eye was dirty green and gray. His front tooth was missing and his busted lip had a black line of dried blood through it. If he smiled I was certain it would crack open.

"Does Edite know you're here?" he lisped. His eyes got watery and his Adam's apple bobbed when he swallowed. "You shouldn't be here."

"What happened to you?"

"A bunch of guys thought they'd have a bit of fun bashing the shit out of me."

"Looks like they had a blast."

I turned away from him and caught Agnes's bare feet on the rungs. She looked skinnier than I'd ever seen her, and her eyes bulged out a bit. She wore jeans underneath a spring dress, topped everything off with a sweater.

"Agnes sleeps in the trunk," he said, and smiled. He clutched his chest. It must have hurt for him to laugh. "She lies in there and writes notes," he whispered. "I hear the scratching."

The blue trunk stood where it always had. It was open and its lid was leaning against the garage wall. I could see the hemmed frill of the baby blanket peeking above the rim.

"She's good to me. I don't know what I'd do without her." James fought with his throat to release more words jammed there. "Come with us," he whispered.

"Are you crazy?"

"Why'd you come, then?"

"I came to make sure you're really leaving."

"You should go now, Antonio. You shouldn't be here," Agnes said. She brushed past me. The effect she used to have on me each time she touched me—the ripples running through me, the tingling—had gone.

I had come in from the cold, my cheeks feeling like pin cushions. Senhor Daniel stood in our front hallway. His hair was like Manny's but cut shorter, parted and combed down with grease.

"Antonio, where is Manelinho? He no come home last night."

"I don't know," I replied. My father's gentle tap on my shoulder urged me to go on. "But I'll go look for him."

My father said some encouraging words, the kind fathers share between each other. Eugene and Lygia had taken off and now Manny was missing. My father patted Senhor Daniel's back, led him toward the kitchen for a shot of something strong.

If my mother had been home, she would never have allowed me to go off on my own to look for Manny. I walked through all the laneways until finally, almost home and ready to give up, I saw Manny in the Patch, his hair sticking up behind a refrigerator door and an old box spring topped with a blue tarpaulin. When I peeked inside his little house, I felt my whole body relax. I sat down beside him.

"Your dad's looking for you," I said. "I've been looking for you. Your brother—"

He crawled over me and burst out into the Patch. The cardboard roof came flying off.

"You ever see a plane kick into the sky?" Manny said. His voice sounded funny. "It's like pumping a swing so high before you jump off, or like chasing across rooftops."

"You okay?"

Manny booted at the mounds of flattened yellow grass that poked through the snow. His running shoes were soaked. His twitching fingers managed to light a cigarette. He put it in his mouth and the smoke curled up around his Afro.

"Manny?" I said. He didn't look up. "It's time to go home."
I followed him around the Patch, kicking at the nubs of grass.

"I wanna race," Manny said. "One last time," still not looking at me.

"It's winter, Manny, we can't."

Manny didn't care. He took off up the laneway. I went
after him.

We neared the top of the lane, where Adam's garage had once
stood. Manny tore through the yellow tape and scrambled into
the shell of it. The charred pieces of wood broke through the
snow like the ribs of some prehistoric animal half buried in
snow. Manny stood in the middle of it and looked back at me. He
snorted back his snot. "Race you!" Before I could say anything
he had climbed up the downspout of a neighboring garage and
steadied himself on the rooftop. He bounced on his heels, daring
me to get up on the opposite row of rooftops to race.

"This is crazy," I said, but I found myself climbing up
anyway. I looked along the line of rooftops in front of me.
"There's still snow, Manny. And the ice . . ."

But he was off. I knew I needed to follow. I'd run slowly,
allow him to beat me. Manny wasn't holding back. He ran
across the rooftops, laughing as though he had just stolen a
bike and was getting away with it.

"Manny! Wait up!" A couple of times I slipped on icy shingles. Manny did too, once almost rolling over into a gully
between garages. But he got up and kept running, leaping
from one roof to the next. He was on fire with something I
couldn't feel. I was six or seven garages behind him. He never
looked back. As he got closer to the last garage, he showed no
sign of slowing down.

"Manny!" I shouted.

He sprinted off that last garage. His arms and legs punched at the sky the way a long-jumper's do. It seemed as if he hung in the air for much longer than normal, before he disappeared from my sight.

I hand-dropped to the alley and ran, talking to God as I went. *Please forgive me, I'll never do anything like that again—swear or steal—the* lapa *was a mistake, and Baby Mary . . . I didn't know what else to do. Please, God. Forgive me.*

I knelt down beside Manny on a nest of wet grass and frozen ground. He didn't move and his legs were off at a strange angle. His upper body swayed, his mouth open and silent. His eyelashes flickered, and then closed shut.

— 4 —

M Y FATHER DROPPED me off in front of Toronto
General Hospital at eight at night and told me he'd
pick me up at ten. And I wasn't to talk to any strangers. In the
entrance, a man in a uniform held on to a big buffing machine.
He made slow circular passes down the hall. My mother said
visiting hours would be over, but if I followed the green line
to the West Wing elevators and went up to the sixth floor,
room 603C, that's where I'd find Manny. Manny's father
didn't want me near him, so my mother had called someone
she knew who worked in housekeeping who said I could sneak
in after hours. Her friend also gave us a report: Manny's
broken legs had been set, one surgically with a plate. His
spinal cord was okay, and he had a severely bruised coccyx,
which normally would have made me laugh because of the
way my mother said it. It was going to take a long time for
him to get better.

The night before I had watched Senhor Daniel climb into
the ambulance with him. He worked in construction and
could piece together a few English phrases. Manny's mother
had been a teacher in the Azores, but here she cleaned houses
and didn't know much English. She stayed behind and fell to
her knees in the slush. The women encircled her. They tried
to lift her to her feet. The men smoked and huddled together
in a corner of the laneway.

I stepped out on the sixth floor. The lights were dimmed. I was afraid to see Manny—I wasn't sure what he'd look like, if he'd be hooked up to machines. I managed to sneak by the nurses' desk and worked my way around the corner until I saw 603C above a door. A strange blue light flickered over the bed. Manny's head was wrapped in a turban of gauze. His legs and one arm were in casts. He was strung like a puppet, his thick white casts up in the air, suspended by pulleys. A tiny television glowed just above his night table, mounted on a big metal arm that was anchored in the corner. He was awake, but didn't look at me.

I hated the smell of hospitals. They always reeked of the glop of hot food that melted the plastic trays it was served on. St. Mike's smelled exactly the same. Every hospital did, I bet. I sat on a chair beside a partitioned tray with food barely touched, a noodle dish with green beans stuck together.

"You need anything?" I whispered. He didn't answer. I figured he was super-drugged. Walking past the foot of his bed, I tried to figure out the cat's cradle they had him in. I waited for a few minutes. His eyes blinked slowly, watching the opening to *The Six Million Dollar Man* on the small TV set high above. *We can rebuild him. We have the technology. We have the capability to make the world's first bionic man. Steve Austin will be that man. Better than he was before.* I sat quietly, watching along with him, thinking about Manny and how screwed in the head he was. I worried he'd never get better. I watched the whole show with him, and both of us never moved, never said anything. I got up to go, even though my father wouldn't come to pick me up for another hour or so. I figured Manny didn't want me there and I was beginning to feel I was making things worse by sticking around.

"Okay. I'm going now. You need anything?"

"Don't go," he said, and I could tell it hurt him to talk. I nodded and sat back down. The room was so quiet I could hear him swallow.

"You sure you don't want anything?"

His pillow was wet. He had been crying.

"Tell me how it's going to be," Manny said, choking on some spit.

"Okay."

"Use your big words."

"I don't know what you want." I heard the desperation in my voice.

"I want Ricky back, and I want my brother home," Manny said.

I slumped back in the chair and told him how our lives were different now, everything had changed—shooting the shit, he liked to say, using the biggest words I knew. I didn't know if his brother had found Manny before leaving, or if they had spoken. It didn't matter. I told him that the minute his brother found out Manny was in the hospital, he'd drop everything, no matter where he was, and he'd come and visit him. I sat there and talked until he fell asleep.

I decided to wait outside the hospital for my father on University Avenue. Every so often, a car would drive by and slow down. I knew what that meant. I'd turn my back to them and start bouncing up and down to make it look like I was just a kid on the street trying to warm up, anything so I didn't have to see their faces. Finally, I saw my father's truck pulling up. I climbed in.

"You okay?" he said.

"Yeah, I'm fine now."

———

Not much was said on the way home. My father let me out, told me to tell my mother he'd likely be a while; he had to scour the neighborhood to find a parking spot big enough for the truck. I went into the living room, flicking the snow from my hair. Edite held a folded newspaper in her hand and was reading aloud.

"'Robert Kribs left the University Avenue courtroom yesterday convicted of first-degree murder. Known as Stretcher, the thin man who left his Windsor home at the age of sixteen smiled as he sat down in the prisoner's dock after hearing the verdict.'" She held on to the couch's armrest with one hand, slurring. "'*I'm not trying to be maudlin*,' Goldman had said, nodding at his bearded client, '*but there's still a human being in there, and I think he should get whatever help he can before going to a penitentiary*.'" Edite flapped the newspaper in the air with her other hand. "Hold on! Here's the best part. 'Those attending the trial had all looked at Robert Kribs, who had burst into giggles.'"

"That's awful," my mother said.

"It's sad, really, that the paper prints that small detail." Edite motioned my sister over. Terri had just turned away from the liquor cabinet carrying a tray full of shot glasses. "There's a human being in there, somewhere."

My mother looked puzzled. "I meant the fact he giggled."

My father came in and went straight to the kitchen, came back with a bottle of wine and some glasses. He poured himself a large glass. His coat and boots were still on. He poured Edite a glass and slid it across the table from where he was about to sit. "Go ahead," he said. "You no drink too much."

"You should talk."

Even though spider veins crawled across my father's nose and cheeks as he grinned, I could tell he wasn't drunk.

"It's time to go to bed!" my mother said. "Come on."

"Antonio had a nice visit with Manelinho," my father said. "Why you no tell us how he is doing."

"Manuel, they have school tomorrow. I want them to go to bed."

Terri didn't move and I stood close to her.

"Georgina, why don't you relax?" Edite said, then downed the wine in three gulps. She had left her job with the newspaper over a month ago, shortly before the case started. It had something to do with her having access to files she shouldn't have had. I overheard my parents discussing it one night, my father suggesting she got herself fired for doing things she shouldn't, always sticking her nose in the wrong places. My mother defended her, insisting that sometimes things needed to be done to get the truth out.

"I made some piggies in a blanket," Edite announced, "and while the oven was hot I thought I'd throw in some Pillsbury apple turnovers. They're on top of the stove." Terri and I would plead with our mother to buy the stuff we saw advertised in commercials, but she never did. Now Edite had made them for us, or for me. Maybe it was her way of saying sorry. I went into the kitchen to fetch the tray and brought it back to the coffee table in the living room. I folded back the plastic wrap and grabbed a sausage roll.

"The killers are going to get life, Pai," I said.

"Now families can have some peace around here," my mother said.

Edite said, "Do you really think the problem is going to go away and you can all go back to living your safe little lives?" She tilted the *garrafa* of wine, let it gurgle into her glass.

"You talking stupid things," my father snapped. He got up and walked into the hallway. Edite followed, and we all shuffled into the kitchen.

Terri went straight to the stove and began to make squiggly lines with the icing over the turnovers. She knew if we had any chance of staying up we had to make ourselves look busy.

"What they did was wrong but it doesn't change—" Edite began, almost pleading.

"They kill a boy! They do things with him and they throw him away like garbage." My father banged on the kitchen table with his knuckles.

"Your lives will never be the same, is all I'm saying," Edite said quietly.

"You think I no know this? You think you are smarter than everyone here?"

"It will happen again!" Edite shouted.

My mother busied herself opening the fridge, reaching for a carton of eggs and placing them on the counter.

Edite and my father sat there, their faces leaning into each other over the kitchen table. My mother cracked eggs on the side of a Pyrex bowl.

"Are you making a cake?" I asked. My mother did not turn around.

Edite finally broke the spell. She stood up slowly, then raised her cup in the air. "To you, Manuel, the man of the house," she said calmly. "I'm sorry. This is your home and this is not the time."

"Why you do this?" my father said. He looked crooked at Edite and lowered his voice. "Why you think you know everything?"

"I don't, Manuel." Her voice had slowed down and it was clear she was very drunk. "Listen, let's just—"

"You listen," my father interrupted. "You live here for a year now. I can see, you know. I see the way you work your way into our vida, the way you make friends with my family. You is not a judge under my roof!"

My mother turned from the counter. "Manuel, Edite apologized. Leave it alone."

"That is not apology!"

"Apology? For what?" Edite spun around to confront my mother. "For speaking the truth?"

"Terezinha, Antonio, go to your rooms." My mother straightened her arm in the direction of the hallway. "Now!"

"No!" my father said. "We *all* want to hear the truth. Edite is coming from America to tell us the truth because we is too stupid to know."

"You're just being an ass now." She slurred the word *ass*, made it bigger than it needed to be.

"An ass? I think you is right. If a man has to live in his own house and you speak about me to my wife, and you give ideas to my kids so they listen to you and everyone spit in my face, then I am ass."

"Manuel, please," my mother urged. "Calma."

"Is that it?" Edite's voice got high. "Does that frighten you? Does it frighten you that when you're not around she tells me things?"

My father knocked the chair over and moved around the table. He tried to make his way past Edite, but he bumped her and she teetered a bit before finding her footing.

"She tells me things she could never tell you."

"Stop it, Edite!" my mother said.

My father reached the doorway but stopped mid-step. He leaned against the archway that led into the hall. "*You* want to talk about secrets?"

"No more games." Edite grabbed her purse from the back of the chair. She slung it over her shoulder and almost fell over. "You're a waste," she said, the look of disgust pulling at her face.

My mother opened the sliding door that led to our backyard. Edite made her way toward the door. My father scrambled to block her.

"No! You come into my house and say things that you want to say and then you leave so you can go for quiet. But my head is like a machine." My father knocked his head twice, hard. "It no stop so easy. You think I'm garbage in this country, you no respect me and my family and—"

"That's not what I said!"

"Go! Go ahead and tell me what I should know about my family because I no know what the hell you is talking about. All I know is—"

"Your wife, Manuel!" she yelled, taking a couple of steps back and steadying herself on the back of a kitchen chair. "She doesn't love you."

My mother took in a big breath.

Terri's hand tugged at my sleeve. "Let's go," she whispered.

"I'm not stupid." My father's voice had softened.

"She's in love with someone else. And Antonio, he . . ."

"Antonio, Terezinha, go to bed now."

"You should leave," I said. I wanted to rush at Edite, to stop her from telling my parents what she thought she knew about me. "Go home, now!"

"Antonio, there's nothing to be afraid of."

"What you want to say about Antonio?"

"Get out!" my mother said, stepping in front of me.

Edite took a couple of steps to the patio door. "I've got to go."

My father sprang at Edite, and spun her around to face him.

"Your kids are ashamed of you," she sputtered. My father let go. My mother stood between him and Edite. Edite seemed immune to the world. "All these years in this country and you still can't manage to string a proper sentence together. They're all embarrassed by you!" she shouted. My father's eyes blinked as if he'd been sucker-punched.

It was so quiet I could hear my own breathing. My mother steered Edite through the patio doors, out onto the back porch. My father had quietly moved back to the table. His face was streaky red and white, crabmeat. He stared down at his hand, which he opened and closed, slowly. I thought I could hear the air seeping out of him, getting sucked out the open door.

"Edite," my mother said, just as Edite took a few more steps. Edite wobbled a bit before turning to look at my mother. Terri stood beside me and took my hand.

From her profile I could see my mother's lips quivering. "It's time to go home—to America." Her voice was soothing. "Your Johnny is dead."

Edite turned away and started walking to our garage. Terri squeezed my hand. Edite walked along the narrow path, the same one I walked almost every day for two months—protector of the limpet, *Jesus Boy*.

Edite reached for the door of our garage just as my mother flicked on the outdoor lights. She tried to grab the door handle twice before her fingers touched it and she held on.

She wasn't wearing a coat and it was cold. She tilted her head to the night sky and into the light that hung above the garage door. I could see the tears streaking down her cheeks.

My mother stepped back inside, closed the door behind her. I heard the lock click. I let go of my sister's hand and she ran up the stairs and slammed her bedroom door.

I went to the window, looked out into the cold. Edite had slipped into our garage and was gone.

5

O N SATURDAY, March 4, 1978, the newspaper reported
how Saul Betesh had dismissed the twelve-year-old boy
he raped, strangled, and drowned with a shrug and a rhetori-
cal question: "What was Emanuel Jaques? I wasn't thinking
of Emanuel Jaques, except possibly before and possibly after.
I suppose he was part of my fantasies." He had smiled.

I sat atop Senhor Coelho's rooftop. My chin nestled in the
valley between my knees. I focused on the spot where Manny
had landed. He had fallen far, and it was no wonder he had
been hurt so badly. Spring was coming. I could smell it. For
what must have been the millionth time, I scanned the horizon, skimmed across the surface of worn shingles and the
madness of poles and lines and antennas like steeples reaching up to nothing.

"Antonio! Get down from there!" my mother yelled. My
head snapped. I saw her coming through the laneway. I scrambled down from the roof, hand-dropped from the edge. I was
dusting myself off when she got to me.

"I told you I don't want you on top of those roofs anymore."

"But—"

"But nothing. You're not a kid anymore."

She reached for me and tried to draw me to her. I took a
step back. My mother turned to look at James's garage with
disgust.

"You stay away from that man, you hear me? I just came from Edite's." She let her words float a bit, and something in me knew that Edite had told her everything about James and Agnes and Ricky and how it was that James had wiggled his way into our world. I had been avoiding James. There had been no sign of him for five days. I assumed he had packed up his things and had taken off with Agnes. "Edite wants to say goodbye to you," my mother said. "She's leaving, today."

Edite's convertible turned into the laneway from the top, near Adam's burned garage. The white ragtop moved down the laneway and turned into her parking space, where she kept it covered all winter. My first thought was that James might be driving it; maybe he hadn't left yet and he got it tuned up for her before she left on her long drive back to the States. I walked sheepishly along the car's side. The driver's window was half-opened and smoke was coming out.

A large black man sat in the driver's seat, the white of his eyes like bone against his chocolate skin. He sat all bundled up in his coat and scarf, smoking a cigarette, one of those stinky American ones Edite smoked when she first got here. I managed to catch a whiff of his aftershave. The back seat was stuffed right up to the roof with garbage bags.

"You must be Antonio," he said, his voice deep and strong like wood. He reached out his hand to take mine. I took it and shook. His huge hand engulfed mine and made me feel safe.

"Mr. William?" I felt stupid the moment it came out of my mouth.

"That's right," he said, nodding. "Edite told me you were a bright boy."

"Is everything okay?" I asked, nervously.

"Fine, fine," he assured me. "Edite's just collecting a few things before we head off home." I nodded at him, then drew my hand back. I had to say goodbye to Edite.

She sat at the kitchen table, side-saddling a chair. A single plume of smoke curled up toward the ceiling. It hit me that it would be the image of her I'd always remember. Her hair was tucked inside a knit hat with a pompom on top. There was swelling under her eyes, which were fixed on one of the kitchen cabinets.

"It's time to go," she said, and took a long drag on her cigarette.

"I'm not mad." It was only when I said it again in my head that I noticed how selfish that sounded, as if everything that had happened was all about me. "I mean—"

"There were so many things I should have been more honest about," she said, turning to look straight at me.

"Where are you going?"

"Home," she said.

I wanted to go up to her and hug her. Instead, I backed up to the door and the landing. "Why didn't you tell me about Johnny?"

"Sometimes, the things we want most in this world we guard preciously. Saying the words may make it disappear."

"I don't have anyone to talk to."

She exhaled her smoke. "Antonio, before I go I want you to understand something. Your father is a good man. He lost his bearings at one point in his life, that's all. It can happen to any of us. I think we're a lot alike that way."

"My mother told you to say that."

"No, I mean it. I did this to myself, Antonio." Edite smiled a bit and it calmed me. "It was easy to do. The other day you stood here and called me a liar."

"I didn't mean——"

"No, you were right. And deep down it feels good to tell the truth because that's the only way you can move on. So let me tell you the truth, or at least let me tell you what I remember because things aren't so crystal clear in my head anymore, they've changed around a lot over the last couple of years. I lied so often that I convinced myself the lies *were* the truth. It just made everything easier. Johnny is dead. I don't know if he was killed by a bomb or a rifle or by an enemy soldier. He was found dead near his air force base in Da Nang. The government swept the details under the rug. That's what they do." She rubbed her eyes. "It's what I did."

I moved to the chair next to her and sat down. Her lit cigarette was in the ashtray. She lit another one.

"They came to the door, two of them, all dressed in the standard military uniforms. I had just washed my hair and had set it in curlers." Edite said the words as if it was happening all over again a few feet away from her in her kitchen. "I didn't want to open the door for anyone, but I did. I shouldn't have. I sat in the living room in my robe and I heard their words and things that didn't make sense, that didn't seem possible. The war would be over soon; he only had a couple of weeks to go before troops were going to be pulled." She allowed herself a chuckle. "And all I could look at was the American flag, all folded and tucked in a triangle, carried like a pillow by one of the men. I wouldn't touch it. When it was offered, I didn't reach for it. They left it on the coffee table. I remember hearing

'We're sorry, ma'am,' and wondering why they would use the word 'ma'am.' I wasn't from the South. How many more flags did they have in the back of that car they drove up in?" A tear rolled down her face. She wiped her nose with the side of her cigarette hand, her eyes squinting with the smoke. A honk came from out back.

"That same day, I knew I had to leave before the neighbors came in with their casseroles all covered in plastic wrap. I drove around all over and went to places I had never seen before. The farther away from home I got, the less real things seemed to be. And the news that my Johnny was dead became just another story—it didn't hurt so much. Took me a long time until I finally made my way here. I'm not sure why, but I figured it was all so fresh in my mind that I could reverse it somehow, turn back the clock and pretend nothing ever happened. It was easier." Edite stubbed her cigarette out in the hill of ash. "I don't like casseroles."

After a moment's silence she reached for me and swiped the hair from my eyes. "'Christ robs the nest—robin after robin. Smuggled to rest!'" she whispered. "I'm so sorry." Edite cupped my ears and pushed my head back. "You're a good boy, Antonio." She got up and pulled her leather coat over her shoulders like a cape. "Actually, you're not a boy any longer, are you?" she said, opening the kitchen door. I stepped out onto the landing with her, our breath making clouds in the chilly air. She locked the door and placed the keys under the mat.

The beginning of March break brought flurries, even though a few warm days had fooled us into thinking spring was around the corner. I walked through the laneway alone. I stopped at James's garage, where tarpaper was flapping. The winds had picked up, and the tarpaper curled itself like a finger asking me to come in. It was a sign, I thought.

I willed myself to be the Six Million Dollar Man, with his bionic eye. I wanted to see far and through things. Better, stronger, faster. I stood in front of James's garage, fought hard to have my sight penetrate the aluminum door. Finally, I grabbed on to the chrome handle, hesitated for only a moment, then twisted it and lifted, the door rattling over my head. The strips of electric orange were the first things that seared my eyes. The baseboard heaters lit up the space. I unplugged the octopus. I stood there, waiting for something. I wasn't quite sure what. Much of what was once there was gone. The rug had been rolled up and pushed to the side, its fringe dangerously close to the heaters. The disco ball hung still. The blue trunk remained, its brass hinges and locks catching the light. I was stunned when I saw a familiar tray on top of the trunk. On it was a chunk of cornbread and some cheese, a large bowl and spoon. Beside it was the old tin my father had kept in the garage, the one that people dropped money into when they left; the same tin my father would set on the kitchen table every night before counting the takings.

I climbed the ladder up to the loft. The mattress had taken on the form of James's body, and I lay down on it. I stared up to the peak in the roof, swirling dust—garage glitter, Ricky had called it once. I wondered what it was James thought of when he lay down here. I thought I heard movement below. "Agnes? James?"

"I'm feeling well enough to get out." James was talking fast. He was short of breath as he lifted the garage door.

"I no want you here!" my father's voice boomed. "You still no understand. I want you out. You get away from my son, from my family."

There was nowhere to hide. I rolled off the bed and lay on my belly.

"Calm down. I would never hurt Antonio."

"You no tell me to calm down."

"All I'm asking is for my job back. I know—"

"I no need you!"

I was afraid to move. Looking down through a knothole in the floorboard, I was uncomfortably close and could see everything clearly. James had one arm bent and tucked close to his side. My father wore his best suit, a scarlet tie below his starched collar. He wore his felt fedora with the special feather and satin ribbon.

I tried to breathe slow. I still had my winter coat on and the loft was hot and stuffy.

"You need to leave," my father said, his voice shaky. My father looked over his shoulder and saw the tray and tin on top of the trunk. He went over and opened the tin.

"My wife come already," he said.

"You can take it with you," James said. "It's dirty money, made off the back of your own son. You're the one who hurt him."

"I make mistake. But I tell you I get rid of the lapa when I see Antonio hurt. You know that. And I live with my mistake. That's why I here. You no going to make a mistake with my son. Stay away from Antonio, you understand me?"

I'd given James credit for destroying the *lapa*, but it had been my father all along.

"Antonio is a good boy. I won't hurt him."

"My wife tell me everything. She tell me what you do for money. You take this money and you go far away." My father turned around as if that would be it; he had spoken and James would now leave. He stood in front of James's painting.

"Is that it? You got all dressed up for that?" James's voice had turned, become stronger. He took a few steps toward my father. James took off his jacket, let it fall off his shoulders and drop to the floor. My father appeared taller, face to face with James. That was when James's voice became a whisper. He leaned in to my father's ear and said something. My father's eyes twitched as James squatted down in front of him. James reached for my father's belt buckle. I felt cold and dirty. My father tilted his head up to the rafters. A sick feeling crashed in my stomach. I shouldn't have been there. I had no right to be in his garage. I started to heave. What was my father waiting for? I tucked my knees up to my chest, tried hard to hold in the stream of drool that tasted like acid.

"I kill you!" My father drew back his elbow. Surprised, James lost his balance and teetered back. My father's shadow crept over James. He held his cocked arm in the air, ready to let it drop and jab James in the face. I wanted to close my eyes but couldn't. James lifted his chin to my father, invited him to punch. For a few seconds my father held his stance, but then his arm relaxed. He unclenched his fist and shook out his arm. Stepping over James, my father spat on the floor before staggering to the garage door. "You are garbage!" my father said, almost out of breath. "Take the money and go away." My father's voice grew distant as he walked into the laneway. James struggled to get up, then stumbled out after him.

I could hear them but couldn't see them. I crept over to the tiny window that looked out from the loft onto our laneway. It was dusk but it was still bright. A dusting of snow had fallen like icing sugar. I craned my neck and peeked out. My father had just opened our garage and stepped inside. James remained in the laneway, standing crumpled and alone, soaked in the yellow light fanning out from inside our garage.

6

I RETURNED THREE DAYS LATER. There was even less left in James's garage: the hot plate, a couple of pro-pane canisters underneath the counter, the old kitchen table, and the blue trunk.

"You came," James said.

I jumped. He had entered through the door from the backyard. "I thought you had left."

"Not yet, but when I do I don't want you to see me go." He ambled toward the shelf near the hot plate. The crock, once filled with colorful bills, was gone. In its place was the tin my mother had offered.

"My father would kill me if he knew I was here."

"So why did you come?"

"To make sure you'd gone," I said, wondering if Agnes still fit into his plans somehow. "You going alone?"

"Agnes is tagging along. Sit down," James said. I looked around for a chair. James patted the lid of the trunk. He went and leaned against the table. "I've done some bad things. I didn't mean to—" He dropped his face into his hands and exhaled deeply. "You were here, weren't you? When your father came to see me?" He wiped his eyes, swiped at the snot above his lip, and shook his head in disbelief. "You saw everything."

I couldn't look at him.

"I get lonely," James said, collecting himself before walking over to me. He took in a deep breath and straightened himself up. He cupped my cheek and with his rough thumb he stroked my bottom lip. "It's the only life I know." I could feel the nervousness between my legs.

"You understand?"

"Don't touch me."

James let go. I thought of Adam, what he said about not letting fear get in the way.

"I gotta go before—" I shifted, about to get up.

"Everything is kind of safe for you, isn't it?" He said *safe* as if it was a bad word. "You don't want your life to be about that, do you?" He lit a cigarette, pinching it between his fingers so that his hand curled. "Come with us, Antonio."

I didn't say anything at first. All the words I had expected to use were jammed in my head.

"I came to say goodbye." I got up and took a few steps toward the garage door. He strode across the garage to block me.

"I'll leave when I'm ready," James said. The goose pimples crawled up my arms and back. I shuddered. He hugged me tight, his chest next to mine.

"I know your secret," James whispered, squeezing tighter. I couldn't breathe. "We're the same, Antonio."

"Let go!" I pushed him—hard enough that he fell against the metal door. He looked much older just then. "I'm *nothing* like you," I said.

I woke up to the sound of my mother buffing the kitchen floor and the smell of lemon paste in the air. There were times Terri and I would come down wearing fresh tube socks and we would slip and slide with the radio on full blast. That would never happen now, I thought, as I grabbed the paper from the veranda, my bare feet stinging on cold concrete. I ran upstairs, dove into the pocket of my still-warm bed.

The front page of the *Toronto Star* ran a story on the verdicts in the trial, but the headline had already been dwarfed by other news, about how fast the Concorde was, Prime Minister Trudeau's defense of a fifty-thousand-dollar campaign blitz with public money, how the little guy was facing insurance hikes, and how seal hunt protestors from the U.S. had turned violent. All we got was a little paragraph buried in the middle of the paper, no bigger than a stamp.

Saturday, March 11, 1978

Werner Gruener walked out of the courtroom a free man last night, leaving two of the only friends he has in the world behind. Werner Gruener was acquitted of first-degree murder in the slaying of Emanuel Jaques. His co-defendant Joseph Woods, a man he describes as a good friend, was found guilty of second-degree murder, while Saul Betesh was found guilty of first-degree murder. The 11-member jury took two hours to reach its verdict in the Supreme Court. Werner Gruener, as he was being led away from the courtroom, read the Bible continuously and murmured, "God bless. God bless."

I heard a light rapping on my bedroom door. "Can I come in?" My mother's muffled voice sounded uncertain.

"Okay," I said, a little confused by her need for permission.

My mother stepped into the room wearing her hospital uniform and her Dr. Scholl's shoes. She wore the same outfit every Saturday when cleaning the house. But something was different about her. At first I thought she had her hair tied back, but when she got closer I realized she had chopped off her long hair.

"Mãe!"

"Do you like?" She cupped her hand behind her head and raised it a couple of times. She was playing it up but I could tell she wasn't too sure it had been a good choice.

"You look nice," I said. "But isn't Dad going to freak out?" My father had always loved my mother's long, wavy hair. He had said once it was the thing that made him fall in love with her. I tried to bury the image of her washing her hair in the basement, my father behind her.

"It's my hair," she said, a bit shakily. "If your father doesn't like it he can find himself another wife." She began to giggle and plopped herself onto my bed like a schoolgirl. "I heard you talking in your sleep this morning. You were calling out names. Some of them I didn't know. Adam? Baby Mary? Who are these people, Antonio? Are you in danger?"

"No." I shook my head. "I'm okay." I turned the newspaper over, hoping she'd change the topic.

But she flipped it back to the page I had been reading, and a look of satisfaction washed over her. "God bless!" she said. She repeated the words, then turned quiet and distant.

"Are you okay?" I asked.

"Funny," she said, hugging herself as if a gust of wind had blown into the room. "It's what I came to ask you."

"I'm fine."

"Because so many things have happened."

"I'm fine."

"I need to ask you something, Antonio. It's about Agnes's baby."

I dug my face into my pillow, but soon the sobs came. Her hand made small circles on my back.

"Look at me," she said, calmly. "Is that who Baby Mary is?"

I nodded, breathed deeply into the pillow, let it soak up my tears and snot.

"Filho, it happened and you can't change that. I just want to make sure you're okay. It's not fair you were put in that position. You need to know it's not your fault."

"I didn't know what else to do."

"You're a strong boy, I know. I'm proud of you. I trust you. There was so much I didn't want to say because not saying it made things easier. I know that's not right now."

I lifted my head from my pillow.

"He's gone, Mãe."

She had shifted herself on my bed and now sat on the corner, looking up to the ceiling as if in prayer.

"Did he hurt you?" she said.

"Never, Mãe," I said, and the color returned to her face.

My mother's body softened. "Antonio, I don't want you to be afraid of life." Her lips trembled, even after she said the words.

I sauntered to my window and looked down onto Palmerston Avenue. Some of the neighbors were outside scrubbing down their front walkways and sidewalks. A few people had begun to chase the suds and chemicals with a hose, washing the dirt onto the road where it all would collect and then pour down the sewer.

7

Rays of sunshine streamed in through the kitchen
window. A small patch appeared on the floor. I walked
into it, closed my eyes, and let my body melt into the warm-
ness. I figured nothing and no one would be able to hurt me in
the force field I had stepped into. *The Little Prince* was tucked in
my back pocket. I had been reading a section from it every day.
I thought of Adam and his gift. I liked the words and the way
the Little Prince just dropped out of nowhere; how he lived on
a planet hardly any bigger than he was and how his only real
pleasure was to sit and watch the sun set. My body tingled the
way I thought it would if I was getting beamed up, like on *Star
Trek*, my entire being dissolving into confetti.

I climbed up onto the roof of my garage to look out over the
backyards and laneway, all the rooftops. I stood tall, letting
the spring sun warm my face. My father had knotted the hose
through the chain-link fence that separated our yard from the
neighbors'. The hose had been turned on to a fine mist that
dusted the vegetable garden, away from where the fat robins
dipped their heads into our lawn, throwing wriggling worms
down their gullets. Not even a year since I had last pressed
my head into the bulge in the screen-window mesh to see
my mother climb onto the worm-picker. My mother saw me
up on the roof and forced a smile. "Get down from there,
Antonio," she said, gathering sheets from the clotheslines

like she was squishing clouds. I could trace the worry in her face. Her whole body gave off a low-level hum of danger and only I could hear it. I heard the harmony of Abba's "Dancing Queen" coming from an upstairs room. Through her open window I could see my sister twirling in her tube top, a towel draped over the windowsill. She practised every day. When she saw me on the rooftop she leaned out her window and yelled "Mãe, he's going to break his neck." She smiled as she said it. Through everything, especially when Edite returned home, Terri continued to be tough and strong and I knew she'd always be there for me. We never talked about all the people we had lost; that's just not the way my family was.

"Antonio!" my father yelled from two backyards over. He stood beside my uncles, who were in the middle of lifting the fig tree from out of its sleeping hole. "Ajuda! We need one more man."

The sun was strong, made me feel like God was everywhere, watching everything. I skipped over the rooftops, my feet feeling confident and assured.

I returned to the ground and stood next to my father. I was almost as tall as he was. The hair on his arms was speckled with dirt. My father placed his hand on the nape of my neck, guided me into position. My uncles—Clemente, David, and Luis—coiled rope around their wrists and handed me my own rope. With a collective tug—*um, dois, três*—the fig tree, its branches stuffed with pink insulation and newspaper, rose from its sleep. The root ball descended deeper into the soil and the crown rose, floating like cotton candy amidst a cloud of dust and dirt. Their dirty hands pounded my back and the small tumblers of wine passed among us to be shared. I looked at my father, his face thin and tired but his eyes beaming.

The air was warm. I dusted off the handlebars and wiped the seat of my Chopper with my palm. I thought of Ricky's letter tucked in my tube sock—I had read it over a hundred times. *When I wake up in the morning my mother makes my bed, and the best part is she makes breakfast. For me.* I mounted my bike and rode out into the laneway. My kneecaps hit the handlebars. I got off. I stood next to my bike and stared up to the top of the lane. I noticed some old men sitting in their lawn chairs in the laneway—smoking, spitting, and talking. It was when I saw James's garage door wide open and a man stirring inside that the wind was kicked out of me. I waited for my breathing to return before walking my bike up the laneway.

"A bloody mess, this is."

"Mr. Serjeant. You're back," I said.

"Call me Paul," he said. "Came back early, seems running a pub on a beach isn't as easy as it looks."

The walls of the once whitewashed garage were spattered with paint—blue, green, yellow, the kinds of colors people in my neighborhood painted their houses. James had thrown cans of it against the walls; in some spots it had run down to pool and dry on the floor. He'd smeared the paint with his hands and fingers. In places I could see his handprints. Daubs and splashes of pure color made the room feel alive. I couldn't help but smile.

"Why would anyone do this? I'm going to have to clean up this bloody mess. Paint over it." He took off his cap and scratched the red band on his forehead. "You didn't know the bloke who rented my garage, did you?"

"Not really," I said. I hopped on my bike and pedaled up the laneway.

TELL THE WORLD THIS BOOK WAS		
GOOD	BAD	SO-SO

ACKNOWLEDGMENTS

I would like to thank the Canada Council, the Ontario Arts Council, and Diaspora Dialogues for their support with my research and with this manuscript. To the Toronto Public Library and all the librarians who supported my research, particularly, the *Toronto Star*'s database, *Pages from the Past*, which allowed me to travel back in time—thank you. I am deeply grateful to everyone I interviewed—too many to be named here—who lent their insights into their respective communities during that fateful summer in 1977.

This book is a work of fiction, inspired by the real-life event surrounding the 1977 murder of Emanuel Jaques. Research, relationships, and family histories have collectively inspired this story. I have taken liberties with places and people depicted in this book to frame a narrative. Also, I have simplified the reproduction of Azorean dialect that was part of my childhood—of my world. My gratitude to José Abreu Ferreira and Onésimo T. Almeida for helping me re-create the orality of speech. If there are any inaccuracies, they are my own. Thanks to Jane Rosenman, who had faith in me. Thank you to Andra Miller at Algonquin, for taking ownership of this book and for her precise editing.

I also would like to thank my trusted early readers for their presence, friendship, and support during the writing of this book: Susan Mockler, Bernie Grzyb, James Papoutsis, Rekha Lakra, Susan Shuter, Sheila Murray, and Jann Stefoff. I'm grateful to my friends and colleagues for feedback and advice as this story evolved. I owe special thanks to my agent, Denise Bukowski, who read the manuscript through its various stages and who never wavered in offering valuable criticism.

A thank you to my publishing family—Doubleday Canada—for being there during the most difficult times in writing this book. Thanks to Maya Mavjee, for giving this book a home early on, and to Kristin Cochrane, who championed it to the end. To Scott Richardson, thank you for turning my words into beautiful images. To Scott Sellers, who believed in and understood this story from the very beginning, thank you. To the rest of the Doubleday team—Lynn Henry, Susan Burns, Martha Leonard, Zoë Maslow, Nicola Makoway, Shaun Oakey, I appreciate all that you've done through the journey. I'd like to offer a special thanks to Martha Kanya-Forstner—for her tender insights, fine editing, and unfailing calm amidst the storm. This novel is the product of our work.

As always, I thank my wife, Stephanie, for her patience, encouragement, and wonderful understanding of my story. To my sons, Julian, Oliver, Simon, you will one day understand how much you inspire me.

NATHAN RIDDELL

Anthony De Sa grew up in Toronto's Portuguese community. His short fiction has been published in several North American literary magazines. *Barnacle Love*, De Sa's first book, was critically acclaimed and became a finalist for the 2008 Scotiabank Giller Prize and the 2009 Toronto Book Award. He graduated from University of Toronto and did his post-graduate work at Queen's University. He attended the Humber School for Writers and Ryerson University. He teaches creative writing and is currently a teacher-librarian at Michael Power/St. Joseph High School. He lives in Toronto with his wife and three sons.

A NOTE ABOUT THE TYPE

Kicking the Sky is set in Monotype Van Dijck, a face originally designed by Christoffel van Dijck, a Dutch typefounder (and sometime goldsmith) of the seventeenth century. While the roman font may not have been cut by van Dijck himself, the italic, for which original punches survive, is almost certainly his work. The face first made its appearance circa 1606. It was recut for modern use in 1937.

BOOK DESIGN BY CS RICHARDSON